CONFESSIONS WITH KEITH

Confessions with Keith

Extracts from the Journals of Vita Glass

Pauline Holdstock

A JOHN METCALF BOOK

BIBLIOASIS
Windsor, Ontario

FIRST EDITION
10 9 8 7 6 5 4 3 2 1

Library and Archives Canada Cataloguing in Publication

Title: Confessions with Keith / Pauline Holdstock.
Names: Holdstock, Pauline, author.
Identifiers: Canadiana (print) 2022025687X | Canadiana (ebook) 20220256888 | ISBN 9781771964975
  (softcover) | ISBN 9781771964982 (ebook)
Classification: LCC PS8565.O622 C66 2022 | DDC C813/.54 — dc23

Edited by John Metcalf
Copyedited by Chandra Wohleber
Cover designed by Natalie Olsen
Typeset by Vanessa Stauffer

Published with the generous assistance of the Canada Council for the Arts, which last year invested $153 million to bring the arts to Canadians throughout the country, and the financial support of the Government of Canada. Biblioasis also acknowledges the support of the Ontario Arts Council (OAC), an agency of the Government of Ontario, which last year funded 1,709 individual artists and 1,078 organizations in 204 communities across Ontario, for a total of $52.1 million, and the contribution of the Government of Ontario through the Ontario Book Publishing Tax Credit and Ontario Creates.

PRINTED AND BOUND IN CANADA

CONFESSIONS WITH KEITH

ONE

May 10

Mother's Day. You'd think you wouldn't be able to forget. You'd think, after four good reasons to remember, it would be etched in acid on the frontal lobes. Apparently not. Nothing farther from my thoughts in the shower this morning, dragging a Master of the Universe out of the drain. It had engaged with something resembling a dead mouse. Feeling feted would have been a stretch.

Gagged a bit but got over it. Dried and dressed and went downstairs. Rummaged through the recycling to find something to read with my coffee. Found the *NYRB* and that piece about eschatological vision in apocalyptic literature. Perfect. A dose of eschatological vision before the day begins.

Was still reading on the kitchen floor when Felix made a surprise appearance.

He said, 'It's Mother's day.'

'Well happy Mother's Day to you, too,' I said.

'Yup,' said Felix. He too rummaged in the blue box, and dragged an old *Monday Magazine* from beneath the mess of papers.

Nice, I thought, that he was up so early for once. Like Kate, who is a year older, Felix took to his bed at the beginning of his fourteenth year and has made it a point of honour not to rise before noon unless compelled by the Education

Act. He shambled over to the counter like a bear up too early in the spring, cleared a small island the size of a placemat in the sea of jetsam, and hunched over his dog bowl of Cheerios to begin reading. Cleared my own small island and joined him there. Could be we help alleviate the garbage crisis by keeping it all at home like this.

'*And...*,' Felix said. In the crop of syndicated news items about the attempts of the mentally unhinged to rob corner stores and the sleazy revenge tactics of American celebrities, he had found a nugget. '*And*, in the States two weeks ago they had a National No Housekeeping Day.'

'They are a backward nation,' I told him. 'Some of us have No Housekeeping Day every day.'

Challenged self to reach the second paragraph before Miles and Hettie came down. I could hear them in their room. Miles and Hettie. All sweetness and light and mostly love but, God, not at seven in the morning please. I had about a dozen more lines to go—but too late. I could hear them coming. Loud for such small persons. Like several heavy suitcases being thrown downstairs at once. Shoved the paper behind the toaster and drank some more coffee.

'Sweethearts!' I said. Decided it would be my word of the day even for those with yesterday's ketchup dried onto their pajamas and teeth a bit on the furry side.

'Put your coffee down.' Hettie's dimpled fingers were pushing the mug to one side even as she spoke. 'Close your eyes.'

She took my hands and placed them round some other receptacle. Hoped she wasn't going to ask me to drink its contents.

'Happy Mother's Day!'

I opened my eyes. Between my cupped hands, a parade of tiny pea-green web caterpillars were crawling nose to tail round the rim of their jam jar.

'Sweetheart!' I said again.

'I trained them.'

'Oh, the clever things!' I said, and wondered if the little bleeders had crawled their way out of the incinerator where I dumped them yesterday.

'Open mine,' said Miles, who had been busy wrapping his gift in a half page of the personals. I unfolded the newspaper and gazed fondly at Miles's familiar photograph taken off the door of the fridge and now nestled on the buxom charms of escorts Tawny Rose and Nikki, Mistress of Night.

'Sweetheart!' I said. 'This is lovely. Shall I put it on the fridge?'

'Uh-huh,' said Miles absently. He is a precocious and ferocious reader. '*Well-hung BGM*. What's that?'

'New kind of BMX,' I said. The mind works fastest under pressure and it's true: sometimes lying is the wisest choice. Years ago, before Miles or Hettie were born and when Kate was just four—Hettie's age now—promised self I would never lie to my children. Silly thing to do. If I weren't so conscientious—or as Kate, now fifteen, puts it, anal—I would have broken that vow long ago. Would have broken it when Kate asked that first devastating question. 'Do everybody get to die?' Have never forgiven myself for telling the truth. Nor has Kate.

Cleared up the recycling and got started on breakfast. Proceedings interrupted by smoke alarm. Had forgotten about the paper behind the toaster. Cabinet doors above toaster now sport fashionable marbled grey effect. Thank God they didn't ignite. Stupid alarm, however, had woken Jack, who rushed in in his boxers ready to save hearth and home. Most unfortunate. Before we had alarm, could set fire to toast, put it out and clear the smoke all before Jack had woken up.

The row we have about responsibility shows up with dreary regularity. Couldn't we have a wholly new and absorbing row?

Decided to paint the stairs. Martyrdom? Self-flagellation? Who knows? Better never to examine one's conscience. It only leads to trouble. Better to work and forget, and not to probe the vast mystery of the universe. An Italian said that.

Sunday morning devolved into a trial of wits and nerves as the treadable passage on the stairs narrowed. Interior decorating on a Sunday is a mistake. 'Why don't you all go out?' I said. And because it was Mother's Day no one suggested that I might take a walk, a hike, preferably a leap off a tall cliff, myself.

12:10 p.m. Kate surfaced. Like a dazed but beautiful inmate from a nineteenth-century asylum, she trailed white-faced down through the wet paint and shoved an exquisitely wrapped box towards me. I had a jar of white paint in one hand and a wet brush in the other. 'Oh, sorry,' she said, and took the brush just as I opened my mouth to protest. Before I knew it she had stuck the handle in my mouth and I had involuntarily closed my teeth around it.

'Kake!' I said. 'Treetart!'

'Can't stop,' said Kate, and trailed on her way.

Disencumbered self and went to kitchen to open present. A box of truffles.

Miles said, 'Handmade. You can see the thumbprints.'

Kate said, 'Don't you dare give him any, the jerk. If you give him any I'll kill him.' Kate's role model used to be the Wicked Queen. Now it's Lady Macbeth. Her behaviour is always dramatic but, I fear, involves very little acting.

Felix and Jack were in the kitchen, too. Felix had finished making his present and handed it to me. A drawing? It was tied with a ribbon. I unrolled it. He was looking at me hopefully. It was a scroll of illuminated lettering spelling the words *Can I go to Lollapalooza?* I said, 'No. Sorry.'

Jack looked up from his coffee and asked me what I wanted to do for the day. Jack has never really caught on. He is a beleaguered man who only rarely puts his head over the barricades. For this reason he knows little of the customs of the happy households of North America. He is always relieved when we let him hunker down again.

Miles and Hettie made pancakes. It rained. By three o'clock you could see no more than halfway across the inlet. Spent the rest of the day on the stairs. Opened soup for dinner. A very long day. At eleven thirty, while I was cleaning my teeth, the shower drain gurgled twice with convincing special effects then gulped and belched a random sample from the septic tank—like a final offering revisiting the bathroom.

Took to my bed feeling as if I'd received some important but not yet decoded message from the universe. Snapped awake just on the brink of sleep. A vision of pea-green caterpillars. Caterpillars are us! The mystery of the universe *and* the answer. Thought, That's okay then. It's all okay. It's all really okay. Jack got into bed. He said, 'You're smiling. Are you awake? Did you have a nice day?'

May 11

Do not understand it. My own children—raised to regard dirt as a harmless familiar—now dismayed by the loss of a little sanitation. Seems they view this symbol of Western luxury as their birthright and civilization's greatest achievement to boot. When told that three-quarters of the world live in total innocence of the experience of relieving themselves in porcelain, they were not at all consoled. Kate indulged in a spate of haughty head-tossing and made a flamboyant departure for the Rec. Centre there to deplete the municipal water supply with one of her showers. Felix and Miles came round to the situation as soon as I directed them to the big cedar tree to rediscover the joys of the open air. Hettie, however, wouldn't have any part in it. She said she'd already been—one and two. 'But I know it's broken,' she said, 'so I didn't flush.'

Fished it out with a yogurt carton and put it in the compost. Voilà! Sent them all off to school early.

Phoned Bangs and cancelled my appointment with Keith. Phoned Brown's (is that their real name?), the septic tank people. Man with a dark, lustful voice answered. It occurred to me that he should be in another business altogether. 'Okay,' he soothed, 'just relax. Now go to your bathroom. Okay. You in your bathroom? . . .' Well Poopsy Brown and I together, courtesy of BC Tel, determined that yup indeed there was a blockage and yup she was backing up and yes, ma'am, they would be right around to pump me out. 'You know where your tank cover is located, don't you, ma'am?'

He said it with such smooth assurance, such confidence. Only a fool, an inept fool, who felt herself superior to the material world, wouldn't know the exact location of her septic tank cover.

Sense of inadequacy lingered but spirit soon lifted at sight of the truck with a skunk on the side pulling into the drive, heralding the arrival of Ted and Frank.

Ted and Frank were full of reassurance. No, they say. No problem. No way that's a problem, is it, Frank? No way, Ted. They'll just start digging, they say. It's what they always do. They just start digging. They'll find it. Easy-peasy.

I had no doubt. Teds and Franks always get where they're going, find what they're seeking. Noticing obstacles, though, is my duty. I never neglect it. I surveyed the area they were about to dig.

It's bricks, I say.

Yup, say Ted and Frank.

Duty is like that. Not too many rewards for the conscientious.

Decided to take my mind off it all and drive into town to buy a cake for Jack's birthday. Thought it might make amends for my lack of responsibility in the sanitation department and provide a welcome change from the collapsed home-baked disappointment I offer every year, believing the effort and tears involved will mean so much more to him than the high-end chocolate confection he purchases for our birth-days—with a flash of plastic and barely a wince—from Chez Pierre. Decided against chocolate since we are having such a brown time. Settled on vanilla almond torte. Ever since the French bakery opened, have hoped in vain that Jack might buy me a vanilla almond torte. Car was filled with its subtle, sweet aroma on the drive home, as if a bouquet of early blossom lay on the back seat. Might this be the secret of happiness, I wondered? To please only oneself, to stop trying to provide chocolate when what you really want is almond? It had such beautiful clarity and simplicity, that thought. You have to wonder if most practising philosophers have been less than sharp all these years.

Arrived home in good spirits, put cake in fridge, and went outside to find striking replica of the pyramids at Giza where patio used to be.

'Lot of bricks,' Frank says, pausing in his work and looking up.

I say, 'Yup.' Nothing more suitable sprang to mind. It was starting to rain again and they were digging out sand. Wondered who would say 'Lot of sand,' first. Probably me.

An hour or so later, I am at my desk doing my best to detach myself from what is going down on the patio when I hear Frank's cheerful voice.

'Found it!' Such a triumphant call. I go outside. He is standing in his rain gear in the bottom of a metre-deep hole and banging on a metal cover at his feet to prove it.

'That's buried very deep,' I say.

Ted says, 'Deepest we've ever seen, eh, Frank?'

Frank says, 'Yup. Deepest *we've* seen.' They both have rain pouring in rivulets down their coats, dripping from their earlobes and they don't seem to mind.

'I'll leave you to it, then,' I say. The rain is running down my neck.

Ted says he'll bring the hose round.

'Funny thing,' he says, about fifty minutes later. He's leaning round my kitchen door, rain dripping off his nose. 'We've pumped her out and she's still blocked.'

'Funny?' I say.

'I'll have to go down,' he says. 'Get right in there.'

He looked thrilled. He said he'd never seen a tank as deep as that. Must be nine, ten feet deep.

It was time to get an umbrella.

I went back out to the excavation site. Little streams were coursing through the sandy, gritty bed that underlay the bricks. The hole in the middle, its rusty iron cover leaning against a pile of sand, was exhaling noisome vapours of the kind Macbeth's witches might enjoy.

Stood a little distance off as Ted positioned himself on the edge and watched with the sort of riveted attention I usually reserve for Harrison Ford. Here was a man with no visible life-support system carefully lowering himself into the hole and about to drop voluntarily into my septic tank.

It seemed cruel at this moment to point out that the depth of the tank was greater than Ted's reach so I settled for: 'How will he get back up?' It is necessary sometimes to temper duty with kindness.

May 15

Wrote last entry with a kind of mad gaiety but read it over today with decided gloom. All too easy to imbue the whole episode with heavy symbolism: the destruction of our marriage, the advent of foul weather, the unearthing of the putrid waste that underlies the domestic arbour.... So that's exactly what I'm doing. I see it all now, how our lives are signalling to us constantly, indicating themselves, describing themselves for us in the pattern of the daily havoc. Like God sending messages to earthlings in code. Jack doesn't see it, didn't ever. He can't see past the Master of the Universe headfirst in the outlet pipe and it's all just another clear-cut case of poor household management and the wife being more trouble than she's werfe.

Personally I think that is a pity, for while it's desirable to be in the moment, it's even more desirable most of the time, especially *during* the time, to be out of it, to be lifted up and away by the powers of metaphysical speculation. The weather's a lot more settled up there. I often wish Jack could join me. Would join me.

His birthday did not go well. A general air of savagery prevailed as the children vied for almost everything—

attention, plates, second helpings, naming the baby gerbils, order of gift opening, and avoidance of the bendy fork that stabs you in the lip. They gobbled up the cake like gannets so there were no leftovers and Jack pointedly went and made himself a cheese sandwich. Kate said it didn't matter, he told her he didn't like vanilla almond anyway. And then she reminded me she had told me to get chocolate. Tried to refocus my attention and since Kate's life promises the most immediate diversion offered to drive her to the dockyard tomorrow, where she and some intrepid friends have volunteered as crew on one of the tall ships that are to be relocated. She answered, 'Like, how else will I get there at four in the morning?'

To bed early, then. Jack said he is staying up late to do some work. God code for 'watch a violent movie.'

May 16

Four a.m. drove into town with eyes like pinholes in white sheet. Orange cones lined every curb so parked a great way off and walked with Kate in the dark to find the right gate. She spotted it first and said, 'You can go back now,' in a tone that strongly suggested my compliance. Felt inexplicably lonely as I headed back. Something about delivering her to another, brighter world? A rehearsal for leaving home? The birds were engaged in a demented dawn chorus in the park across the street so I walked around the block—twice—for their cheer. Got back to my car only to find it gone. Towed. Young man in a traffic vest gave me the number to call. Said it was free. Then gave me a quarter to call a cab.

To Bangs eventually for my appointment.

Keith said, 'You look tired.' Have been going to Keith for years because he does not adopt the usual affectations of the salon. He cuts my hair absently as if its length is of no consequence whatsoever while he chats about what other customers have told him. He pauses often, scissors aloft, while he marvels at the infinite wonder of the world, forgetting completely about his professional role. The forgetting part is his only drawback. When we begin to spin down the conversational drain I have to remind him of the task at hand by looking at my watch and feigning surprise, *Oh no! Look at that. My parking will run out soon.*

This morning he didn't believe me when I told him what I had been doing between the hours of four and eight. He sat me down with genuine sympathy and told his assistant, Biloxi (of the blue hair), to bring me a coffee.

Biloxi said, 'Cream or morphine, sweetie?'

Biloxi himself is a sweetheart but I worry for him, pierced and decorated as he is and sending very particular signals. If I were his mum I'd want to know when he got safely back to his apartment at night.

I say, 'Morphine, please, dear.' Bless him.

It's bliss at Keith's. Bliss. That's why I go. Of course. Admitted that to self years ago. It's not really for the henna or the haircut at all, though that part is a bonus. No, it's to forget about the septic tank and the towed car. I'm the next generation of those middle-aged ladies I used to see as a child, all lined up under their great prosthesis-pink and chrome domes. They weren't there to get their hair permed at all. They weren't even there to read the magazines, flipping the pages of tea-bread recipes and bedroom etiquette the way they did, with disdain. Nothing there for them, no. It wasn't permanent waves they were after. It was alpha waves. They were meditating—long before it became a thing. They were having their moments of pure being, of

Oneness. They were probably having glimpses of Other. Or if they weren't, they were writing their diaries in their heads or having a steamy time with Omar Sharif.

'It's bliss here,' I said to Keith.

Keith said, 'Yes, but the plumbing needs work.'

May 17

Hettie has a nice new friend, Meghan, with a kayaking mother called Sue. We met at the school when I went to pick up Miles. They have just moved here and could be a breath of fresh air. Meghan is a sweet girl who loves earthworms. Sue is tall and rides a bike. She is just one of the many other mothers I'd like to be. She is tanned and lean and dusty-looking and has a terrific pair of rugged-looking hiking boots. Clearly does not spend her time palely poring over syntax. She told me about a kayakers' convention and I immediately thought, Jack, and made a note to tell him.

Called Marlene to say I'd be late for lunch. Marlene said, 'You are always late.' She is a very forthright friend.

I said, 'No, listen. I have found a pet shop that will take the baby gerbils. I absolutely have to stop there first.' Was actually too good to be true. Had feared the gerbil market might already be flooded with the prolific output from Miles and Felix's fecund little friends. They are sweet creatures but not without drawbacks: charming but smelly, cheap but randy. Something one would not want said of self. Bought as two males last December, one for each of the boys, they have already produced seven litters. Thought this time I was going to have to stage a mass gerbil extinction, but they won a last-minute reprieve when Miles's friend Ryan told me about the new store. 'There's a wicked snake in the window,' he said. Miles, reared on a diet of *Wild Kingdom* to protect him from the violence of *Ninja Turtles*, was not impressed. He knows exactly where gerbils fit on the food chain in relation to snakes. Found him in tears before school this morning. Please, he said, would I make the pet store owner promise not to feed them to the snake?

Drive into town set my nerves on edge. The gerbils scrabbled all the way. The store was no comfort. It was dark and its tanks contained no apparent occupants but dry twigs. It smelled the way I imagine intestines smell. Waited in line behind a blond lady buying nail clippers for her iguana. Owner seemed pleased with his sale and licked his twig-dry lips while counting her change. Disliked him so much by the time he looked inside my cardboard box that I began to feel psychotic urges rising.

'Sure,' he said. No problem. He could take them off my hands...

'To sell?' I said. 'For pets, I mean?'

He said he couldn't make any promises. But not to worry, Monty the python didn't like them much with fur on anyway. Ha ha ha.

Arrived late at Puccini's. 'I'll have to be quick today,' I said. 'I've got six gerbils in the car.'

Marlene said, 'For God's sake, Vita. I thought you were dropping them off.'

'I tried,' I said, 'but the circumstances were too distressing.' I said there was something about newborns of any species. All the future in store. You know. Maybe literally. It was almost as bad as a visit to a maternity ward. 'You remember maternity wards,' I said. 'All those pink and blue terry-wrapped sausage rolls. Into the jaws of life.'

'Or in this case the jaws of Monty the Python,' Marlene replied. 'Drink up. You'll feel better.' Marlene used to be a journalist. Her finer feelings have been abraded.

We had a long conversation about newborns and pain. I told her I believe all pain stems from the first wrenching from the breast.

Marlene said she thought I fed them small rodent mix and laughed immoderately. Then she said, 'No, listen. Don't complicate things. Go back to the store and give them the bloody things. Say you've changed your mind. Then when you get home you lie. That's it. Simple.'

'Lying is never simple,' I said.

'But necessary,' said Marlene, 'and nearly always kinder than the truth.' I wondered aloud how she could reconcile this philosophy with her profession, although George Orwell did it. He saw lying as the necessary lubricant for political life. I think Marlene sees it as the lubricant for Life. She said, 'Don't pretend to be naive. There's a place for everything,' she said. 'Knives and forks. Truth and lies.'

Told her I had had this conversation before. It started with Disneyland. I'd once confessed to Keith at Bangs that I would never, ever, either in their lives or mine, take my children to Disneyland and had told them so. I said I had made a point with each of them of establishing in their minds as early as possible the certain knowledge that they would never see Mickey. Not ever. Keith had been deeply, deeply shocked. He said this was the equivalent of telling children that there is no heaven.

Marlene said, 'Well at least you show good sense *some* of the time.'

'And talking of lies,' she said, had I heard the rumour about Mitzi at the Galeria Toxicana?

I'm always ready to hear news of Mitzi. Mitzi is the owner of the gallery and attracts a string of admirers and hopefuls wherever she goes. She wears her black and cement-coloured hair in a state of fixed alarm, standing straight out from her head like the recipient of a massive electric shock. A breath of charged air in this tired city of tourists and retirees from Alberta. Mitzi apparently had decided unilaterally that it was time for a child but her boyfriend, the music director Daz, had refused to cooperate. *However* (one always knows when the good bit is coming), however, Daz it seems had been more than cooperative with a local potter, who was also getting broody, though singularly so, not having a current partner, and he had donated his sperm to her. Mitzi, of course, did not believe for a moment that a turkey baster was involved. She tossed out the idea at once and was now plotting a terrible revenge. Marlene said unfortunately she didn't know any more but promised to keep me basted.

May 21
To Bangs again to top up the henna and afterwards to opticians. My new contact lenses have failed to guarantee my satisfaction. Only one stays in place so have developed embarrassing tic, as if have been looking through a telescope for too long. I know it's clearly noticeable because when I drove into town the driver in the truck next to me at the lights winked back at me.

Keith told me about the latest report on laser technology for myopia. Keith always knows about 'latest reports' and 'extensive surveys.' And 'recent studies.' I think he hears about them on the *Morning Show*. Keith and I disagree about studies. He says they are important indicators. Violence is on the increase, for instance. Studies show. I say they are merely describing the world for insensate vegetables who cannot see for themselves. But that, of course, is not how I put it to Keith.

'Paying attention to studies,' I say to Keith, 'is like calling the weather report in a downpour. They detract from one's sense of immediacy in one's contact with the world. It's as if you'd just discovered E=MC^2 and I said to you, "Oh, studies show that's the Theory of Relativity."'

'Well it is,' said Keith.

Sometimes I get the feeling our conversations do not forge ahead as they should. I said, 'Tell me about this report, then.'

'Well,' he said, 'according to this report the discomfort has been halved and the accuracy doubled.' It seemed to me that if the accuracy had room to double, the first wave of clients must be walking round bumping into lampposts. 'Apparently,' Keith said, 'it's supposed to be *beyond* now. Just beyond,' and he proceeded to tell me about Biloxi's auntie who was almost legally blind when she had the surgery and has just taken up computer programming.

'Then she's probably legal by now,' I said.

'No, seriously,' said Keith. 'She could hardly see a thing before and now she's twenty-twenty. Her life has changed ... .' And suddenly, as Keith continued to talk, I could feel my life changing, no, evolving. Could feel myself falling away from the ranks of the Luddites. Here was high tech that lived up to its name, technology with the power to raise us to new heights. This was not technology to drag us down and snare us in its sticky world wide web of message pads and PalmPilots and VCRs. No need for any of that. I could leapfrog over all of it and land in the arms of true, life-enhancing progress. With perfect vision I could be Out There with the rest of the world, not stuck behind blurry windows contemplating possible meanings for the weirdness of the shapes outside. I would be *part* of the weirdness.

I did not say any of this to Keith. Kept the dream to myself and told him instead my sorry history of fraught relationships with optometrists. The first, I said, asked if I had had a blow on the head and sent me for a complete physical. I could see Keith was paying close attention, processing what I was saying for recycling to the next client—he does this—so I told him next about the doctor who gave me the physical, making me sit naked under a paper sheet while he rapped me on the kneecap with his hammer and upbraided me for not getting my eyes seen to sooner. 'But unless I had already *had* a vision test,' I argued, 'how would I know if my vision was deficient?'

Keith put down the pot of henna and shook his head in amazement. 'Well that's *it*,' he said, 'isn't it? That's exactly it. It's like that thing with red. You know,' he said, 'I think about that all the time: how do you know what *red* is? How do you know *your* red is the same as my red? How do you know it's not *blue*?'

It is not the first time Keith has plumbed the depths of this conundrum. I can tell.

Jack came late home from work. Again. Is it by design? Probably. Studies show most women prefer to go to work than to stay home. Keith told me. And why would it be different for men? No one *wants* to do the dishes.

Announced to Jack after dinner that I am thinking of having my eyes zapped.

He said, 'What with.'

I said, 'Laser treatment. *You* know.'

He said, 'I *know*. What *with*?' And he made that nasty little money gesture with his thumb and the side of his forefinger.

'Well,' I said. I had to think for a while. 'We have too many possessions as it is.'

'Meaning?' said Jack.

'Well these material things. Look at us, we're drowning in them. All these consumer goods. They're consuming our lives.'

'I haven't noticed it making any of you miserable,' said Jack. He was buttering his bread so hard it was beginning to tear.

I said it wasn't fair to say that. I said he knew I objected to lots of this stuff.

'Well don't use it,' he said, and threw the bread at the dog.

'I was just thinking,' I said.

'What?'

'I was just thinking we could sell some of it.'

He gave me a rather Jack Nicholson stare with his top lip sort of pulled up and said, 'Like?' And if he hadn't looked like that I probably wouldn't have said the next thing.

'Well look at your car...,' I said.

I knew it was not prudent as soon as the words were out of my mouth.

'Look at my car,' said Jack, 'and I'll fix your eyes myself.'

'Good God!' I said. It wasn't as if I wanted him to walk to work or anything. I just thought he could use the truck.

I got up with what I hoped was a great deal of dignity and was just removing myself from the scene when he turned and said, 'Did you get rid of those blasted babies?' For a horrible moment I thought he was referring to our children and then I remembered the gerbils.

'Yes,' I lied. And then, stoutly, just for good measure, 'I did.'

Marlene would have been proud of me.

May 24

A long weekend. Jack is away at the kayaking convention. His late birthday present from me. Marlene unkindly suggested I was pushing him out to sea. The thought. He has a paddle. We haven't actually spoken much since our little exchange. It is just as well he is away. In fact it is probably for the best. The children have reached the age when they feel so much more comfortable if he is away while they are defying him. Better for Jack, too. This way he need never know that Felix has defied me and taken himself off to Lollapalooza—unless of course Felix is careless enough to get moshed to death.

Took Hettie and Miles to the Children's Festival. Was going to take Ryan, Miles's friend, but Ryan's mum is seriously religious and never seen staggering around in highheeled shoes or dropping her kid off late for school. She drew a sharp breath and said, 'Street performers,' the way you or I would say, 'Nuclear waste.' 'Yes,' I said. 'Street performers. So much fun.' 'Oh,' she said, 'oh,' and shook her head for such depravity. 'No I can't allow it.' She is bent on stamping out all attempts at enjoyable distraction from the senselessness of human existence. Then, visited by a sudden thought, she said Ryan had to go to his grandparents. So Hettie and Miles and I went and risked our eternal souls for Major Conrad Flapps the clown and three gumboot dancers from Quebec while Ryan was saved by his gran.

We did indeed have fun. Nothing more life affirming than a gumboot dance. The sun shone and up on the stage a small piece of art was being created just for us. It wasn't there before and it would cease to be as soon as they stopped and no one who hadn't actually been present would know that it had ever existed. It was a shared experience of human life, a little bit of eternity together. Was led to reflect on how the mums of Ryans prefer to equate Disneyland with heaven and how impoverished our imaginations have become if the best heaven we can think of for our children is a land of fake heads and artificial glamour when what really exists—and we know it does because of these little glimpses, these leaks—is an experience of pure, simple being. Was sure Kate would relate to the value of performance art and told her all about it when we got back but she said the only simple being around here was me because I'd left Miles's favourite sweatshirt behind on the seat and it happens to be the one that *his* grandma sent and she's coming to stay in two days time—in case I had *forgotten*.

May 25

3 a.m. Haven't slept. Wish Felix hadn't snuck away like that. Too bad his buddies drive. *Do* people get moshed to death? I can't ask Kate, she's away, too. Camping. What if at this very moment she is being raped by a drunk dude or eaten by a cougar? Wish I hadn't let her go even if it is with seven of her friends. I wish she were here. Can't ask Jack either. Wish *he* were here.

Oh *God* I wish he were here. Wish we were both in bed. Wish he would roll over and throw a heavy arm over me and say *For God's sake, Vita stop worrying* and then I wish I'd answer *Okay* and turn to him and put my leg over his thigh because that's his favourite. Oh. I am so done with kid stuff. I am so done.

5 a.m.

Chamomile tea doesn't work. Am still awake. Wish it were Tuesday. I shall drink some of Jack's scotch.

May 27

Slept most of yesterday. Jack came back late last night. He didn't wake me so he must have slept downstairs and left early. Sticky on the mirror said, *Out of toothpaste out of toilet paper*. Good job he didn't do a head count. Anyway, Kate's here. She got back after he left. Felix still not home but he phoned so at least he's alive, and with friends, which I suppose is a good thing. Though he may regret it later.

Spent the entire morning making phone calls and have finally booked our annual vacation accommodation. Family of six, though the number seems variable at the moment. We are going to Hornby Island. Again. Kate regards the decision as grounds for cruelty. 'But you've just been camping,' I say. 'It's not that different.' She says, 'But we didn't *go* anywhere. We camped in Asta's yard and her dad projected four movies on a sheet. Her dad is really cool.' She cannot reconcile herself to the prospect of a week on Hornby without telephone, stereo, or TV. I say, 'Think of it as a kind of Indoor Survival program.'

'We are always sick on Hornby Island,' she says. I point out that Miles doesn't have a problem with it. He's managed to be sick on more holiday locations than all of us put together but he still enjoys himself.

To Vancouver this afternoon to meet Mother off the plane from London. Took Miles and Hettie with me on the ferry. Truck inexplicably leaked all its water on the car deck and would not start on arrival. Traffic crew very accommodating and pushed us off the boat. Sorted it out on dry land, refilled radiator and limped off to airport. There was only just time before the flight arrived to find some more water for the radiator. Went to the Launch Pad restaurant and explained my plight. Said I needed enough water to get us back to the ferry and to refill, should we break down on the way. Manager took an assistant off salads to help us. She cheerfully washed out two large plastic pails and filled them for us. There was no time to take them to the car so we took them to Arrivals with us. People do stare.

Mother on time but last off. Could scarcely walk for the weight of the bottle of vermouth she was carrying, a special size perhaps for passengers of jumbo jets. Nice to see she still has the good sense to provide for her own survival while she is staying with us.

We found a cart to manage the two heavy pails and the luggage and the vermouth and on hearing the purpose of the pails Mother at once volunteered to help me pour, if necessary. I could see she was getting into the spirit of her holiday already. She has a knack—which she has not passed on—of immersing herself in the moment and practising full engagement with others. In the back of the car, she played I spy, handed out the yield of half a cocoa plantation, and sang 'Ten Green Bottles' all through—twice. After ten hours in the air? I am the daughter of a deranged woman or a saint.

Reached the ferry without incident and Miles was sick on it. He does not give much notice. Luckily we were just passing a recycling bin. He almost got it in. Mother, well equipped with tissues and travel wipes, helped to clean up, all the while murmuring grandmotherly endearments. Decided not to risk offence by mentioning excessive ingestion of Cadbury's chocolate and possibility of milk drawn from mad English cows. No, I kept quiet. I know a godsend when I have one.

Jack was waiting at the front door as we pulled up. He was looking particularly thunderous.

'Where's Felix,' he hissed as we got the bags out of the truck. 'He's not here and my single malt is missing.'

'Tell you later,' I said. Always play for time.

Turned round to see Mother reeling and clutching her face. Overcome by emotion on arrival, I wondered? But no. 'Someone help Grandma!' Hettie was calling. 'Blackguard jumped up and hit her in the eye with his nose.'

'Bloody dog!' said Jack.

I said, 'Calm down, Jack. It's only natural. It's excitement.'

He said, 'For God's sake go and help your bloody mother.' His language is so inappropriate these days.

Mother as it happened did have the tiniest trickle of blood running from her nostril. Asked her if she'd like her vermouth now.

May 28

Day began at 3 a.m. Heard noises in the kitchen and found Mother and Felix making grilled cheese sandwiches. Felix, forgetting all about her visit and the fact that she had been assigned his bedroom, had climbed in through the window and found her, still on British time, sitting up in his bed wide awake and waiting for the day to begin. He had offered her a grilled cheese sandwich and she had said yes, it was about time for elevenses. So there they were, in amiable collusion in the kitchen, Mother at the table flicking through Miles's *Lords of Death* and Felix at the grill with the slightly over-focused look of one in the throes of the munchies. It was a refreshing change to witness such harmony. Postponed Felix's own grilling until later.

Miles asked at breakfast if we could cancel our cabin at Hornby. He said Ryan wanted him to go to Disneyland with them instead. Just as I thought. Ryan's mum, street performer phobic, is a pushover for the powers of corporate evil. Then he asked if we could save the next batch of babies for Ryan's pet snake. Please, he said. Miles the animal lover! Oh the fickle hearts of the young! He said they produce every three weeks and another litter would be due tomorrow. He began explaining how to flash freeze a litter in the most humane way possible. He said it's okay, they just fall asleep when the temperature drops. Oh fickle and gullible, too!

Took the truck in for repair and cycled back.

Dinner not a flawless affair. Miles brought up the question of Hornby again and made Hettie cry by reminding her of the hornets' nest she stepped in last year, which in turn triggered a joint offensive by Felix and Kate on Why Hornby Sucks. Mother was just demanding to know the exact meaning of 'suck' in this context and how the word had come to acquire it when Jack remembered that Felix had been AWOL since Saturday and promptly grounded him for two weeks without a hearing.

Marlene called later with the kiss of death for the day. Said she has solved her vacation problems. She is taking her two to a blues concert in Washington. I said I did not have time to explain but she should know that this was a decision which could put a severe strain on our friendship. There was something about it that smacked of vote-garnering among the young. Marlene said, 'Nonsense. Come over for a drink, bring your mother.' Mother declined. Said her eye was still too black and she didn't mind dark glasses in the day but it would look funny at night. She said it would be good to take advantage of her babysitting services while she is here.

Marlene and Danny were suave and sophisticated as they greeted us. Music on, house clean and orderly. Jack and I not. We looked like a couple caught in the act and forced to make a semi-public appearance, our clothes only just thrown on, our hair awry. We should be so lucky.

We did not stay long. Drinks poured, Marlene and Danny were keen to interrogate the current madness of the world and tackle the problem of capitalism. But Jack and I had become one of those pitiful couples who wait for an appropriate pause in the proceedings to take another stab at one another, on constant watch for an opportunity to resume hostilities: '*Free market economy?* That's what Vita thinks we live in: a giant market where everything is free.' Once we had begun there was no stopping us: 'Oh, *controlling our lives*. You should ask Jack about controlling our lives. He's the expert.' It was good to have the excuse of Mother to fall back on. We all knew what was happening and it is a mercy we left before we got drunk on our own punches. Marlene and Danny displayed wonderful cool reserve and made no comment on our tiresome behaviour. Wonderful cool reserve is the last thing you want from your friends.

So to bed early.

Very difficult to cry in a houseful of seven.

June 2

Dashed in this afternoon for a quick trim while Mother went shopping. Mother surprised I could obtain an appointment so readily but looked at my hair and added that she didn't suppose my hairdresser could be in very great demand.

Keith said he's off in August for Toronto. 'Advanced Hair-Tech for Professionals.' Shall keep that to myself. Told him about my trouble finding the time to arrange a vacation, especially one which would please everybody. Keith said it sounded as if I need a pause button for the family the same as for a computer game. Then they could all pause, he said, while I got something done. Keith has flashes of brilliance. I thought about the possibilities.

'The difference is,' I said, 'one always wants to resume a game.'

'Not always,' he said. 'Sometimes you quit.'

Thought this idea more wonderful than the first.

Arrived home to find the gerbils had had more naked babies. Total head count now fifteen. Miles was showing them to Mother, who was making all the right noises but whose left hand kept rising to cover her mouth as if she was holding something back.

June 3

Truck repairs have cost a total of sixteen hundred dollars. Am receiving looks full of loathing and mistrust every time I mention transport to Jack. Does he think I took a hammer to the engine block myself?

Kate chose this inopportune moment to say she'd lost her new jacket and has nothing to wear when it rains.

Felix said, '*Sold* it.'

Kate said, 'Excuse me. *I* don't sell my clothes for drugs.'

'Cheer up, Jack,' Mother said when things had calmed down. 'At least you haven't got fifteen to worry about.'

'Fifteen?' Jack said warily. 'What do you mean?'

I glared at Mother who for once did not follow her instinct for merry mischief-making.

'Just that things could always be worse,' she said.

Jack said 'Hrmpf,' and then announced he is going to Denver for two days.

Felt bad later that not one of us had asked why. But you can't manage every little detail.

June 10

Yesterday Mother made a remark to Jack about not seeing very much of him these days and alluded to the kayak. 'I suppose you must like it,' she said. 'Out there on the open sea. Away from it all.' And then she said, 'All by yourself.'

In retaliation and with lightning response time, Jack arranged a biking trip to the lake along the Galloping Goose Trail with Felix and Felix's friend Dunk. His own version of the family outing. The rest of us were to take the newly repaired truck and meet them at the lake for breakfast. Mother said, 'We are the medic and road crew, aren't we?' She seemed not to mind, though it was hardly the same as a stroll around the Butchart Gardens.

Everyone asks me if I have taken my mother to see the Butchart Gardens. We haven't actually been in but on Tuesday we did drive by three times at high speed. We were trying to find the school board meeting. It is too boring to explain why we had to attend. It seems to me that the school year is itself something like a runaway truck loosely filled with people and events; in June the truck hits a brick wall and we all hurtle to the front. We cannot get out until we have attended all events, none of which involves smelling roses. And, to be fair, it is not only school events; we ourselves have not yet arrived at the Time of Smelling Roses. This explains why we fill vacant spaces with activities, not all of them leisurely. As yesterday.

The boys appeared pale and shocked when we met them at the lake. Their bodies are attuned to being horizontal until midday on weekends and Dunk is not accustomed to riding farther than the corner store. Blisters were beginning to develop on his palms and fingers. He is lucky Felix has a grandmother who wears socks. Resourceful as well as game, she took them off and modified them with a pair of nail scissors so that he could protect his hands with them on the way back. Sometimes I think the experience of the war must be responsible for her attitude. Or perhaps she displays qualities that develop with age. This is a new and encouraging thought for me: there may be a day when I too will be able to cope with the vicissitudes of life—if there are any. In the rose garden.

June 15

The weather has not been good. We are trying to make Mother's visit enjoyable but it is difficult to go on living. By this I do not mean to be melodramatic only to say that Life, and especially Laundry, is a hindrance to our goal. Mother was spotted last night at ten thirty dragging the folded ironing board across the hall. Jack said something about Calvary. Kate said no, the cross would be on her shoulder not under her arm. I said for God's sake won't somebody put it away for her?

The fact that people will not stop eating or dirtying clothes or falling sick makes it very difficult to pursue leisure. It is an interesting paradox, this need to put life on hold in order to enjoy it. Mother does not seem to suffer from it; she claims to be enjoying herself regardless. That is because she is what is known as a good sport or, sometimes, a brick. I shall have to ask Keith what he thinks about this Leisure/Life dichotomy.

June 17

Went this afternoon to buy a lily for Marlene in atonement for what we did to her bed. She invited us all over for dinner last night. Danny had kindly rented a movie for the children. With hindsight it is easy to see that it was foolhardy to announce its commencement so abruptly, the TV being situated, as it was, in their bedroom, so far from the yard. As one animal the young people tore in and jumped on the conjugal bed. Jack and I enjoyed our dinner immensely, being the only ones present who had not heard the crack and therefore remaining ignorant of the extent of the damage until Marlene called this morning to let us know that everything was all right: she had put Janson's *History of Art* and the last six years of *Architectural Digest* underneath and it was as good as new. She said she understood: Jack and I were likely deaf to the sound of breaking furniture.

June 25

Mother leaves tomorrow. Helped her buy gifts to take back to her English grandsons. She passed up baseball hats emblazoned with Blue Jays and Maple Leafs in favour of T-shirts with Jimi Hendrix, Kurt Cobain, and NOFX. I was so proud of her. We shall have a last supper tonight and play T-shirt music.

Saw Keith in the supermarket buying two dozen watermelons for his window display. Hope they don't crash through. He asked Mother if she had enjoyed her stay. Mother said she had had a wonderful time and would be back next year. When she was out of earshot in the frozen foods, Keith watched her pushing the loaded cart and said, 'Is she serious?' I said, 'Perfectly. She enjoys being with us even though it is such hard work.' Keith looked surprised.

'You'd have to really think life was worth it, wouldn't you?' he said.

I don't think Keith always knows how close he comes.

'That's why she'll live longer than most,' I said. Though perhaps not in our house.

June 26

Mitzi called to invite us to a special event at the gallery. It is to be called Monóclinate Conception and will feature three curtained booths and a stage lit only by candles. Behind the curtains and to music, three anonymous artists will perform self-insemination while an overhead video installation shows what Mitzi called 'provocative images to redefine our concept of ourselves.'

'Ooh,' I said in what I hoped was not a transparent manner. 'I think we'll be away then.'

June 27

Ruby called from England. She's coming to stay in August. Only a sister can get away with that. Bringing Harry, too. Kids were delighted when I told them. As children of immigrants they are short on relatives. They like their cousin Harry and regard their aunt Ruby wistfully as the sort of mum they could have had if fortune had favoured them. I said, 'More family. If you tell your father before I get a chance to prepare him I'll never speak to you again.' Felix said, 'Promise?'

The Canada Day weekend is approaching and we are planning a party. It too is proving difficult. It is not easy to make joint decisions when one's marital relations have been reduced to brief encounters by the sock drawer. I said to Jack, 'We have to do something. The day will be upon us before we have even started phoning.'

'Okay,' he said. 'What day?' We could not agree on a day.

In desperation have resorted to telling everyone I meet that there will be a party, maybe Friday, maybe Saturday. We will let them know in a couple of days. People I have not seen in several years are surprised by this sudden attack of hospitality. I am hoping to have my new contact lenses in time for the day so that I can tell at a glance who has arrived. It is a faint hope. My visits to the optician are not welcome. I have made five visits in pursuit of satisfaction. Now, when I approach his department on the fifth floor, he pretends not to see me coming. A strange trick for someone so committed to the promotion of visual acuity. Like a heart surgeon who cannot stand the sight of blood.

Looked over the guest list Jack left on top of the dresser tonight. It is not the same as mine.

July 1

In bed and it's only twelve thirty. What happened? It was a pleasant evening. Not too hot, not too cold. A bit like the party. Altogether too orderly for my taste. And too sparse. A great many did not show up. Should we have given people more notice? Or are we dull? Even the children disappeared, seeing no chink in the armour of adult civility. We were like an advertisement for a gas-fired barbecue. There was chit-chat where I had hoped for entertaining banter and lethal wit, polite revisitings in place of searing engagement. *So are you going away this year?* is a very useful phrase but no substitute at all for *So! Can we ever prove the continuity of soul except by way of the body? Well?*, which is the sort of opening gambit my friend Dmitri favours. But Dmitri didn't come. Nor did Annie who always used to make the trip from Pender and would have stories to tell about her latest pharmaceutical experiments and sometimes even have samples, like the Avon lady, for the more open-minded among her listeners, only she is said to have renounced all that in preparation for a month-long acoustic bath. Ryan's mum came but only because Miles had invited Ryan. She was chaperoning her son. No one flung their arms around me, or anyone else, crying, *It's been an age!* and no one let their concentration waver for a moment from the task of keeping an orderly traffic flow between the dip and the salmon. They were not even really eating. They were nibbling. No one danced. They did not seem to like Prince. Someone even turned him down. Jack would have put it right but he somehow vanished for about two hours while I was left to wander, lonely as a leper, carrying trays of rejected nibbles among the chipmunks and saying 'excuse me' a lot. Only the unpredictable could have saved such a party from sliding into the realm of the profoundly staid.

Everyone said politely that they had had a good time and no one hung on late to see if they could have a better time, probably because Ryan's mum put on an apron and started doing the dishes.

July 2

Saturday. There was a great deal of food left. Asked Marlene and Danny over to do a post-mortem on the party. Marlene said the leftovers were the reward for hosting; the conversation and the food were always tastier. We were just sitting down to leftover salmon, leftover rice, a platter of eggplant salad that had been left in the hall, stale pita bread, and several already-opened bottles of wine when Peter, who works at the airport, and Carol arrived with their teenage sons. Peter said, 'Well we're not late for once.' I said, 'Wrong, darling. You are a day late. Ha ha.' There was a moment of confusion but it was quickly dispelled by the arrival of Annie and a new friend called Hawthorn. Annie had baked a number of tarts. Fifty-four. She said she knew the party was going to be a fifty-four-tarter so why piddle about with a dozen. They were aroma tarts and would enhance our auras. Jack's reply was more of an acid reflux but fortunately muffled by the sound of more guests arriving. Peter and Carol were clearly heartened by the sound of vehicles drawing up. Daz came in on a gust of air kisses, and then Martin, the bad-mannered Englishman, and then dusty Sue in another neat pair of boots and with her little daughter, Meg.

'So!' I knew it was Dmitri even before I turned round. He had his arms wide open for a bear hug. 'So! Is there a central core or only a dark abyss! We will crack this nut, tonight, yes?' The man I had been waiting for. He will dance to anything when he has sorted out the world. A second party was just the thing to dispel the first—though Jack did not look thrilled. It is a strange thing about friends and their lack of diplomacy. Several of them seemed to enjoy repeating the phrase *But I'm sure you said Saturday* well within earshot of Jack and for all the world as if it were as harmless as *Where's the corkscrew?* Jack has a good line in killer body language and sent me a whole document.

By the time Mitzi blew in with seven visiting writers from Newfoundland in her wake, the leftovers were all gone and we sent out for pizzas. Sent Jack and Sue out, that is, so that they could talk kayaks. Began to enjoy the second party a great deal more than the first. The freak wave from Newfoundland had a tonic effect on conversation and voices rose considerably, much as they do in salty water that threatens to overwhelm. Spent a convivial half hour with one of the writers, a poet who had a wicked line in deadpan and rather nice eyes. Very nice eyes. We discussed Walker Percy's fine dissection of the writer's need to drink in order to return to earth. Felt myself going into orbit so said I should look after the guests. He said, 'They're all grown-ups.'

I found Mitzi, who had set a place for herself at my desk and was demolishing what looked like a four-course dinner with several tarts for dessert. I said, 'Mitzi, where were you all yesterday, when we needed you?' She said, chewing, 'You told me Saturday, I have it in my calendar.' I explained how polite yesterday's party was and complained that I had failed to connect with anyone at all. She said it was Host's Syndrome. You cannot enjoy your own party unless you abdicate all responsibility.

We were just discussing the phenomenon when Jack rang from the station. Yes he said, Sue was fine. No he wasn't hurt, either. No, just the car. Yes, his car. Yes it was really unfortunate the way the stop sign was placed. And right outside the police station, too. You'd think they would have noticed that. He said four of them came out and stood on the top step when they heard the sound of breaking glass. In fact one of them was waiting for him right now.

Danny said, 'Tell him to have the pizzas sent over.'

July 9

This weekend very flat after last. Am greatly outnumbered by children. Marlene is away. Sent by her new publisher on a tour. Sounds like a holiday to me. Annie has gone south to New Mexico with her friend Hawthorn to sell BC soapstone stress relievers. Jack had to go back to Denver so he is away, too. Dusty Sue is also away, kayaking again, so I have Meg here to stay with Hettie. Even Ryan's mum has gone away—to Bible camp—leaving her pestilential offspring and all his bad influences with his gran.

July 15

To Bangs to get my hair cut short for swimming on Hornby. If we go. Jack has hurt his back. Keith said studies show 98 percent of back injuries are self-inflicted. An odd descriptor, I thought. Making it sound as if self-flagellation were our national pastime. Thought 'self-induced' a better choice but it was too early for semantics. Keith said back injuries happen to people when they find life a burden. I objected to that on personal grounds. To a faithfully married man, life equates with family, so as the spouse of a back-pain victim I might easily take exception to his theory. Couldn't a bad back be the result of wild sex? And anyway my spouse was taking out the empties when it came on and there were an awful lot of them. Keith said, 'No, you know what I mean. You're a writer. It's all sort of symbolic.'

'Well exactly,' I said. 'Disease is the symptom of our dis-ease. The medium is the message is the metaphor. And the lump on Felix's gerbil's tummy probably means it wants more babies.'

'What?' said Keith. So I told him how, being overrun with babies, we had instigated divorce proceedings on the couple's behalf, how the adult pair now lived a life of celibacy in separate apartments and how the father since then had developed a suspicious lump on the belly.

'Interesting that it wasn't the mother,' Keith said, 'wanting the babies.' He clearly recognizes that gerbils may not only carry metaphors but may in themselves be one. He asked what had become of the babies and I told him that they were in cold storage. How I had finally conceded defeat in a glutted market. How, unable to drown them, I had put them in a nest in a yoghurt container and placed it in the freezer where, I was told, they would quickly fall asleep from cold.

'Then you buried them?' said Keith.

'No,' I said. 'Miles wants us to keep them for his friend Ryan's snake.' I said it was a terrible thing to see one's child betray his most tender feelings and become a mere marionette under peer pressure. Keith said he sure hoped I had labelled them.

Left Bangs for the opticians. Prepared to fight to the death for consumer rights. Stepped out of the elevator on a surge of adrenaline to find the enemy had decamped. Across the hall, a wall of grey-painted plywood sealed off the area where the office had been. There was a notice hastily tacked up: CLOSED FOR INVENTORY.

'Yes,' said the kindly photographer in her office next door. 'They've gone into receivership.'

'A coward's strategy,' I said.

'No,' she said, 'I think it was a surprise to everyone. The manager's just down the hall if you'd like to see him.'

'If I could see him,' I said.

'Pardon me?' she said.

Arrived home to find Jack flat on floor. Suffered a momentary wave of panic with regard to frosted gerbils and their resemblance to leftover gnocchi.

'It's my bloody back,' said Jack.

'Oh,' I said, 'thank goodness.' It was out of my mouth before I could stop it. Even before I had finished enunciating I could see the row approaching—a pugnacious street fighter, the great menacing brawler we know so well, with a thunderous brow and lugging dull Stone Age weapons for bludgeoning. We covered a lot tricky moves and unyielding holds before we finally limped away into our own stony silence for the night.

July 19

Hornby. Finally. We think ourselves lucky to be here at all, Jack having been forced to undertake the whole journey in a horizontal position. It was difficult, given his length, but somehow, and in flagrant violation of the seat-belt laws as Hettie repeatedly pointed out, he contrived to lie flat with his knees poking up like a pair of bald babies looking out of the window. It is a five-and-a-half-hour drive. I made sure to stop at a self-serve gas station to avoid tiresome exchanges with attendants but there was no escaping notice at the ferry. The ticket seller seemed to be trying to protect himself from the likes us. Wary and sullen, he did not respond at all to Felix's lighthearted remark about dangerous cargo. An embittered man, I thought, who clearly is not enjoying the prospect of the rest of the summer.

Conditions in the car were extremely cramped but Miles was very good about climbing over the luggage to throw up. Kate covered herself in Body Shop vanilla lotion, which helped her (but possibly not Miles), Felix plugged in a Walkman, and Hettie ate her way through three packets of KeRRRunch potato chips. On arrival everyone promptly lay down, exhausted by the gruelling journey. Except Jack, who gingerly went for a short walk to stretch his legs.

July 20

We are not camping as we usually do. Jack's back is too bad. We are installed instead in what seems to be a self-sufficient toadstool. It is a charming residence built from coloured plywood and hippie vision in the style of a Kurdish hut. Everything is circular. The wood stove and the beautiful claw-footed tub for taking hot baths are sensibly in the same room as the dining table and the conjugal bed. Sensibly, that is, for the beyond intimate or for the celibate. It is of course nowhere near big enough for all of us and the dog but, thankfully, we do not have goats.

July 22

It is a strange holiday. We are being sick by turns. Miles's travel sickness turned out to be something viral and each of us has been visited. By night we tramp a steady path through the long grass to and from the privy—the gaily painted composting privy which Miles had mistaken for an abandoned circus wagon. By day we put out mattresses for the sick on the deck and lie on them in the manner of plague victims while the recovered go down shakily to the beach. In this sanatorium Jack's back is slowly getting better. He has borrowed a home acupuncture kit which is effective but time-consuming. We spend forty-five minutes night and morning puncturing his body, an exercise which requires him to remain motionless for long periods on his hands and knees in his boxers while the children lie round like pagans before a golden idol—or in this case 'idle'—waiting for a miracle, which by their definition would be a sales representative from Future Shop coming by with a thirty-six-inch TV and built-in VCR. To alleviate the boredom, Jack read aloud to us this morning from *Life After God* while the others made friendship bracelets which they fondly hope to sell at the entrance to the beach, an idea to which I was at first opposed. 'It is a desecration of the spirit of friendship,' I said. 'You are supposed to give them away.'

'Don't listen,' said Jack. 'At least you will be contributing.' He then delivered a lowish blow to do with *some* people being under the impression that it was against the law of nature to have more than *one* gainfully employed worker in the house, and how these *same* people did not know how lucky they were not to have to sell their children, never mind their children's handiwork, to pay for expensive holidays. But it was lost on us all because Kate at that moment had found a Spanish guitar and was beginning to strum loudly asking us if it didn't sound a lot like Bryan Adams's 'Everything I Do.' In the interests of harmonious living we all said yes, except Felix who threw himself writhing on the floor.

August 3
The success of the holiday is a source of astonishment to everyone. Marlene said it sounded like material for a Peter Greenaway film, perhaps something where the family members decide to perform back surgery on the fully conscious patriarch. She gets carried away.

Made Felix take his gerbil to the vet as soon as we got back. He was not happy. He does not like to go out unless he is in the company of other six-foot youths with unusual hair. He carried the gerbil in a McDonald's orange plastic pumpkin with a handle. At the vet's he put it down on the stainless-steel counter and went to lurk under his hair in the opposite corner of the room. Gerbil, however, was not so reclusive. Managed to propel its pumpkin at some speed along the stainless-steel counter by scrabbling from the inside. Receptionist, busy rubbing out appointments, understandably startled as it went by but vet visibly impressed to see one of his patients coming to meet him in this fashion. Wanted to know the name of this energetic specimen. Felix now had the attention of the entire waiting room and I felt that justice had finally been served. I had never thought that naming the father Alice after Alice in Chains was particularly appropriate. Safely in the surgery, Felix shrugged and said he didn't really have one. The vet insisted on a name for such a fine little chap, and, catching sight of the tumour as he picked him up, suggested Lumpy. Felix brightened at once.

'On second thought,' said the vet, 'that isn't very nice. But we should find a name that suits him.' He suggested Ben since the gerbil seemed to be a sprinter. More interested in a prognosis, I interrupted his musings. He was suddenly very forthright. 'Sixty dollars for a lumpectomy.' The pumpkin was now scooting across table. 'Roger Bannister?' he said. 'The man who first ran the mile in less than four minutes?'

'I think we'll choose someone from *The Great Escape*,' I said, thinking of the wide-open field at the end of the road. 'Steve McQueen?'

Went to Bangs this morning. Keith thought my hair had suffered from too much sun and surf. Had he not read his postcard?

'Got any gerbil stories?' he said. Seems our relationship is growing stale.

I said, 'Yes but it depresses me.' I was thinking of Felix and how lonely he looked carrying Lumpy up the drive to freedom and thinking too what strange power the animals have. 'He'll like it,' Felix had said, 'being able to run around at last.'

'Let us instead discuss the liberation of animals,' I said to Keith.

'Animal rights?' he said. 'I got my shop fire-bombed in '88 because of them. For using products tested on animals. He said a recent report showed that 96.5 percent of all products we consume have at some stage been tested on animals—even pencils, he added cruelly. 'That's terrible,' I said, 'but guilt is always aggravated by information. "Ignorance is bliss" is a favourite maxim of the prospective transgressor. Like my grandfather who gambled away the money for his children's shoes. The more we know, the more we find ourselves implicated in the Chain of Guilt. It's what we create from the Web of Life through our unremitting greed.'

Keith yawned and said, 'Do you want it a bit darker at the back, then?'

I said, 'I want it all dark. The darker the better.'

August 8

Only three days to go to Ruby's visit and I have two manuscripts whose deadlines coincide. It is not easy working under pressure. Everyone is at home, even Jack who is repairing his kayak in readiness for a trip up island. Stroking its sleek sides he is oblivious of the children and their friends but I cannot ignore them. They operate a tightly coordinated program of interruptions and synchronize their activities so that the kitchen is never without at least one of them opening cupboard doors with gusto and smacking them closed again with curses, crying through to the office that there's nothing to eat or drink, we're out of bread, we're out of salt, we'll need a rock benefit just to get us going again, and where are the Band-Aids for God's sake, and did I know the cat's left a hairball behind the TV again? It is this running commentary on life outside the office that makes creative work so difficult within it. The presence of children makes it impossible to get into orbit. They take it in turns to appear at fifteen-minute intervals for a spot of verbal provocation, goading me to a negative with, 'Can I have a ride to Nanaimo?' or 'Can Mara, Tara, and Lara McNamara sleep over?' and quickly following up with, 'Why not?' It is a code of honour among them never to be satisfied with 'Because.' Jack has no sympathy. He says it is learned behaviour and I am a naturally argumentative person. I'm not.

August 9

Work on the manuscripts is more and more pressured.

It is Felix's birthday. He has a second-hand electric guitar. He is in heaven. Two of his friends came to try it out.

And then Matthew S. came by. He had his daughters with him. Matthew is a pig farmer though he doesn't look like one. He doesn't, for instance, wear great big manure-caked boots, and he's tall and elegant. Anyway he thought it very funny that we were barbecuing falafel. Matthew is an old and dear friend but a busy man raising his family, not to mention his pigs, single-handedly. We rarely see him except when he drops by, as he did today, unannounced. They stayed for a while.

Kids played basketball while we sat outside and drank wine until the sun went down. I tried not to think about getting back to my desk.

August 10

The last day to finish the manuscripts. Jack is away. Children are mostly occupied, except Hettie. Gave her one of Kate's tapes to listen to and banished her to her room while I finished. Defending mental space is a struggle. It demands a certain ruthlessness of heart. Became a vile old harridan barking at phone intruders and snapping at all enquiries, innocent or not. Defences cracked when I heard the sound of sobbing. Not the petulant sobs of the spoiled child, but great heavings of mortal anguish, profoundly stricken sobs rising from a wellspring of grief to rack her body head to toe, as if the dreadful truth of the human condition had just come home to her—as indeed it most inexpediently had.

'I can't stop thinking of Lumpy,' she said. 'I've been listening to the tape and I can't help it.'

'There, there. Lumpy's happy now,' I said. 'He's free. Put the music back on. Think of something happy.'

'I ca-an't,' she wailed. 'It's the mu-usic that m-makes me cry.' Hettie is afflicted by a feverish imagination. I can't think where she gets it from. I looked at the cassette box. '*Cats*!' I looked at Hettie. What sickening exhibition of feline carnage was playing on the screen of her mind's eye? The newly free Lumpy meeting a sticky end in the bloody maw of Wilson the cat next door? But I have learned that you can never tell what children are thinking and that the most ill-advised policy of all is to put words into their mouths. I was careful. 'What is it…exactly?'

'It's that l-lady at the end,' said Hettie. 'Aooooh! She's s-so sad. Oaaah!'

And there it was again, the loneliness of the minor key, the twilight of the solitary soul with all its bitter-sweet nostalgia for life's loveliness slipping forever out of reach. Oh, thank you very much, Mr Lloyd Webber. Well done! That's just what we need.

So what to say to Hettie? What do you say when this moment comes, this sudden awareness of loss and the certain knowledge of mortality? What do you say when you've promised yourself that you will never lie?

'Music is like that,' I said. And I left the manuscripts. What else could I do? Sometimes words are nowhere near enough. We sat together for a long time. In a little while Hettie felt better. I changed the tape and the frenetic jollity of *The Bare Necessities* worked its dubious magic. Oh, Disney, I know. But just till I finish the final read.

Set out to post the manuscripts without the feeling of satisfaction I should have had. Confidence severely undermined by Hettie's performance. Questioned the validity of jerking other people's emotional strings in the name of Art. Plato said Art only waters these passions which should be allowed to wither away. He said, sounding a lot like my father, who couldn't bear a scene, that the goodness and happiness of our lives depend on the passions being held in subjection. Abandoning oneself to emotional excess is the way of spiritual calamity. And anyway, Plato said the Artist is at three removes from reality. A conclusion certain members of my family have reached without his help.

I got the manuscripts to the post office on time but saw before I sealed them that one was missing its last page so returned for that. Found it under the empty bread bin and had to wipe a bit of jam off.

August 13

Ruby and Harry arrived yesterday from London. The boys were clearly appalled that their respective mothers appear to be identical copies. Mother clones. The stuff of horror movies. It does not help matters that we communicate largely in sentence fragments and a steady stream of meaningful looks so that our laughter can only be construed as the outpouring of idiots. This is why we prefer to be alone.

August 17

Just returned from Whistler. Ruby wanted to see a mountain, a big one. 'Mount Jasper,' she said. 'Whistler,' I countered, thinking: one mountain is surely as good as another and some are a lot closer. 'As long as it's big,' she said.

We drove up. Harry watched for wildlife all the way but the only bear he spotted had been hit by a truck. Ruby unimpressed when we arrived at the Village. 'But it's a shopping plaza up a mountain,' she said. She started knotting her bandana testily as if she were going somewhere. I said, 'Mm,'—it seemed safest—and looked wistfully at the hotel balconies where high-end guests were taking the sun and quaffing elaborate coffees. 'Good thing we're not staying there.'

Our youth hostel had considerably more character, hand-hewn logs and Nirvana posters behind the front desk. The boys went for a hike while Ruby and I watched the light change on the lake. As we sat on the deck with a bottle of far-from-detestable wine purchased at the detestable plaza we were both invaded by a sense of déjà vu, but could not place it.

While a fiercely independent young woman tried to seduce Felix and Harry together over a game of dice, Ruby and I had a long conversation about marriage and the possibility of its ever working. I said I didn't really think about it. I was too busy doing it. 'And it's hard work,' I said.

'That's why I've given up,' Ruby said. 'Life is for living and I mean to.'

Was a bit put out at this flagrant resort to cliché. I said, 'But Jack and I are all bound up together. After twenty-odd years it is the Gordian knot.'

'Too literary,' she said. 'Have fun. Live. Go hostelling.'

'What I mean,' I said, 'is that I don't think it can ever be undone. We've sort of bonded, clumped together like nylon rope over a flame.'

'Become one?' she said. 'Ugh!' She said, 'That's ghastly. Don't tell me Jack likes it. You can feel the loathing from across the room.' Then she said, 'What? I'm your sister, for God's sake. I'm supposed to tell you the truth.'

Went to bed and dreamt there was a giant spider as big as a coffee table on the wall and Jack wouldn't do anything about it.

Queued for the gondola next day with hordes of others wearing hiking boots that like mine had previously only walked the dog. Gondola jammed on the way up. Sea of mountains extending all the way to the horizon and over it in a breath-taking corrugation of rock and snow grand enough to awe even the most jaded tourist. 'It's as if we've come to our true home,' I said. Ruby said, 'I don't know about that but it's a sense of returning.'

Boys found a patch of ice and an old garbage bag at the peak. Amused themselves sliding down. Ruby and I joined them. She is in a foreign country and feels she can take liberties. 'Sled till you're dead,' she said. I pretended to be British, too, and hoped that if any of Jack's smart clients were sipping iced latte in the roundhouse they would not see me through their Ray-Bans. Fell off to the side once and had the luck to find a second garbage bag. Twice the fun. Possibly more fun than a day's skiing could afford. Laughed till our sides hurt and then the source of déjà vu came back.

'I've been here before,' Ruby said suddenly. 'With you.'

And it was true. More than twenty years ago. Ruby's first visit. We stared at each other and enjoyed what you might call a joint flashback to a party in a ski cabin by the lake. 'So you have!' I said. 'January 1976.' We had all decided to go skating on the lake and some of us had got lost and I went back to the wrong cabin with a painter from Norway and for some reason Jack wasn't even cross.

'What?' said Harry in disbelief. 'You've been here *before*?'

'Yes, but I thought it was Jasper,' Ruby said. 'It was the night Jack got lost. And some woman with a man haircut brought him back.'

'That's right,' I said. 'Liz. With a kind of buzz cut. Who always had exotic stuff to share. Who probably felt responsible. Fancy forgetting.'

'*Mum!*' said Felix. Neither he nor Harry had words to express their scorn for our mental debility. We chose not to tell them the whole story of the ski cabin by the lake and the party and the joints the size of Cuban cigars, although there is a salutary lesson in our example, living evidence of the correlation between drug use and brain damage.

August 18

Ruby told me today that what I need is a lover. Says she has been observing Jack. 'Seriously,' she said, 'he is not a happy man.'

'Then it is Jack who should have one,' I said, but Ruby didn't respond. She just looked at me. It was a long steady look with eyebrows climbing. It was how Miss Hardcastle used to look when I'd say I'd left my English homework on the bus. 'Anyway,' I said, 'Jack's perfectly happy. He's just busy. Like me. We have a lot on our minds.'

Ruby said, 'I've noticed.'

I said, 'Ruby, you can't sit around telling people their lives suck.'

'I didn't say that,' she said. 'It's a revolting expression.'

Felt very grumpy and couldn't think of a reply. 'I just think,' she said, 'that you two look like people who could use a good enema.'

'Thank you,' I said. 'I'll take the lover.'

August 19

A bit rough around the edges on waking. Spent too much of the night obsessing over my glib remark to Ruby yesterday. All very well in a movie but how to produce a lover from thin air in real life? And if one appeared, would I ever really follow through? Upset the domestic apple cart? Send the kids flying face down onto the dusty track? Run off and leave the patriarch to pick up the pieces? It's not in me. I am not known for my balls.

Ruby cheered me up. 'Chinese village women,' Ruby said, 'visit each other every morning to laugh.' 'Then they would feel right at home with us,' I said. We were sitting on the veranda in the lemony light, drinking green tea and applying Ruby's face cream which she insisted would make us both feel normal. A good time to talk, when the teens are comatose and the littles are eating their Cheerios. I offered up one of Keith's nuggets: Laughter reduces the incidence of unwellness. 'But that's not why the village women do it,' Ruby said. She said they laugh for beauty. 'It tones the facial muscles wonderfully,' she said. 'It's why we both look so good . . . ' And we laughed like hyenas.

It was an oasis of calm and I was enjoying it, but Ruby wanted to make plans. Whistler having proved altogether too tame, she was after something more rugged. 'Okay,' I said, catching her mood. 'We'll do something rugged.' But not *very*, I thought. Best not to mention the West Coast Trail. Rugged is what I try to avoid.

August 20

Went to bed last night feeling wistful. Jack is avoiding me. Or perhaps us. Would have liked to lie down with Jack, face to face on our pillows. I remember that. The gaze. The gazing without searching. We didn't need anything, anyone, else. Why would I want a lover?

Asked Ruby on the veranda this morning if she had had many lovers. She said I must be joking, she was far too busy.

'Doing what?' I said.

She said, 'Searching.' She was searching for the Real Thing. She had tried the church, she said, and then the dog pound and that was nearly it and the ukulele and two years ago she thought she had found it in the soil but then she had joined the a cappella group that met after tai chi.

'And...?' I said.

She said she was still looking. She said she had an inkling it was in the wilderness.

I said, 'You mean, like the movie? We go backpacking and we find the Coke bottle.' She will have to be cured.

August 21

Have planned a camping trip to French Beach. Hope Ruby will not notice its proximity to Victoria. Have stipulated too that everyone has to come. Safety in numbers I always say. Find it extraordinary that my fellow nationals routinely leave their homes, their safe havens, and drive out to sleep on the home turf of cougars and bears. In a tent! The only tents I like to be in are large white ones at weddings. Meanwhile, toast and coffee and 'normal cream' on the verandah again this morning. A moment of sanity before we recklessly cast off the bonds of civilized society.

August 25

Our camping trip, thank God, is over. An experience of the utmost privation for Kate, but not nearly rugged enough for Ruby, it was marred from the start by a serious lack of almost everything, including Jack who declined to come at the last moment. He said he could do with a break from dreadful women's laughter. Dreadful women or dreadful laughter? Both? Said he was going kayaking instead. Ruby said later, 'He does a lot of that, doesn't he?'

She was at first disappointed to learn that we were going to a provincial campsite. I said, 'Ah, but better than the wilderness. They have all the prime spots. You will be bowled over.'

We had spent every waking hour of the previous day packing for one night under the stars—a logistical conundrum that, like many aspects of camping, troubles me. Nevertheless, when we arrived and Ruby had finished being bowled over by the towering firs, we found the lexicon of what we did not have extended all the way from Aces, inexplicably missing from our deck of cards, through Butter, Coals, Dish soap, Egg flipper, Green pan, Hettie's jacket and Kerosene almost all the way through to the small but essential X-shaped piece of aluminum that holds up the canvas roof of the aging jousting tent Ruby and I were to sleep in. We improvised with two coffee spoons. 'You remembered those,' Ruby observed. She suggested that the shortfall in certain key areas was owing largely to my lack of vision. 'Because you didn't want to come,' she said, 'you had trouble envisioning.' I agreed. Proper planning requires an act of the imagination, a projection of the self into the future situation or event.

'And, this trip,' Ruby said, 'is more like a drive off the edge of the map.'

It was beginning to get dark when she said this, and that certain gloom peculiar to the forest was descending like damp. Miles said we had only two candles and we should probably burn them one at a time so they would last longer. Felix said, 'Shut it, why don't you. You'll scare your sister.' Hettie said, 'Why? What? What did he say?' I said, 'Thank you very much, Felix. Now listen, we have to get on with this because I expect we'll all want an early night.' Hettie said, 'And I have to sleep in your sleeping bag because you're scared without Daddy, right?' Mouths of babes. We had some unsalted spaghetti not so much simmering as suspirating, and possibly even suppurating, on the stove. It was beginning to spot with rain. We nevertheless put a brave face on the situation like wartime evacuees, drew our logs in a circle round the hissing fire and even resorted to singing. Thought the sound particularly forlorn, especially when the children struck up the one about the prune. When the spaghetti had sufficiently coagulated we served it in wedges. Harry said it was a pity about the sauce tipping in the fire, wasn't it. Felix said he felt weak from lack of protein and Kate said he would come out in zits from eating too much starch and why didn't we bring the parmesan? Ruby said we were all feeble spoiled wimps and this was nothing like the camping she had imagined where morsels of succulent meat would be roasted on a spit over an open fire—a fire, she said, kindled from deadfall we had gathered in the woods. She said she couldn't believe that someone had actually felled half a forest and split it for us. She said, Numbered campsites! Number fifty-seven! It didn't seem, well, kosher. And all this business with washing up and plastic bowls and a tap. She said what she had had in mind was more along the lines of mountain becks and foaming rills. 'Look at that,' she said. The trailer on the site across from ours was glowing bluely from within where the occupants were evidently watching TV and eating one of its dinners.

'Hey, that's *Friends*,' said Kate. 'I can hear it.'

Miles said, 'If you've got two mirrors you can watch it, too. You crouch outside...'

I said, 'Never mind. We make our own entertainment, remember,' and Harry started up with the filthiest verse of 'The Foggy, Foggy Dew.' For a while he kept the children amused with a small store of cheerfully rude versions of traditional songs.

'The British are more open-minded about these things,' I assured Miles. 'They have a long history of being rude.'

Harry said, 'That's right,' and began 'The Hairs on Her Dicky Dido.' Ruby said, 'That's enough.'

Made the best of our limited all-ages repertoire and went to bed.

Lay awake most of the night listening for bears. It is one of my most firmly held beliefs that, if asked to list the ten things that scare me most, I could find them all in a provincial park. Find it particularly distressing that the fresh air causes the rest of the party to fall soundly asleep leaving me alone to keep stark-eyed watch on the untrustworthy night. Hettie snored a little from the depths of my sleeping bag. Ruby on the other side muttered 'Make her stop,' and then started up a soft purr of her own. Gradually the noises of the campsite wound down in a long decrescendo from shouts and laughter in the dark to footsteps and car doors and finally to whispers and zippers. Even the rain stopped. At first there was only the occasional hum of traffic on the distant highway to break the quiet but after that came the thing that provokes all other fears: NOTHING. It is called the dead of night and for good reason. It is the silence that occurs when all the good in the world are asleep, all small birds with their heads beneath their wings, all tousle-haired infants suckled and at peace, all lovers sated and blissed. Only the shriek in the night breaks this silence, only the marauder is at large. And, if you have the misfortune to be in the woods at the time, a nameless dread will descend and you will be filled with a sense of the inexorable. Blind, anonymous unswerving Nature about to swallow you. And utter, utter loneliness.

So that is why you lie awake listening for bears.

Twelve fifteen: heard dogs barking somewhere distant, then nothing.

Twelve fifty: a suspicious snuffling at the children's tent. The moment of truth. Get up and face it armed with six-dollar flashlight from Kmart? Do not have to get up because at twelve fifty-one it is at ours. Heart stops beating.

Silence. Heart resumes, double time.

Twelve fifty-four: unzip the tent and bring the axe inside. Not a sound anywhere. Check watch every two hours and each time find that only five minutes has elapsed. One twenty-seven: revellers return from beach making hostile noises. They chop wood. Please God don't let them use a chainsaw. I nudge Ruby. She says, 'Sorry,' in her sleep and stops snoring.

One thirty-seven: a car door slams. Someone starts to shout. He is not a happy man. Another unhappy man shouts back. Obscenities bounce off the tree trunks and the unhappy men bounce lawn chairs off each other.

One forty-eight: two loud reports.

Murmurs then silence. I remember all the words of the Hail Mary and add a few of my own. *Please, please, please both of them or neither.* Let's not have one left with no one to pick on. Ruby turns over. The dogs start up again, closer surely.

Two fifteen: something shrieks. Ruby turns back again. At last I hear something for which my heart gives thanks. Rain! Hard, steel-belted rain coming down with the force of buckshot. The kind of rain to keep bears and drunks in their holes. I thank God and fall asleep lightly, happily, until the tent takes on a greenish hue and the crows begin screaming abuse about the state of the campsite. Crawl out of tent and light a fire. Number fifty-seven looks like a gypsy encampment. Mr and Mrs Winnebago opposite have a check cloth on their picnic table and it is held there by blue plastic clips. There is a bottle of pancake syrup in the middle of the table. Along the way at the next site the crows have begun clearing up the mess and arguing over the empties and the chip bags. Ruby and children still sleeping, as are, presumably, the drunks. The young in one another's arms.

Get so cold I get up and pull on more clothes and go for a run along the beach. There is a bank of fog out to sea, glistening kelp on the surface of the water near the shore. Meet Mr and Mrs Winnebago on a companionable walk back for their pancakes. It's quiet. So quiet. The breakers must be out there under the fog, regrouping. The sun is making the fog look as if it is filled with light.

Finish the run at a gnarled tree stump hurled onto the beach by Titans, convoluted roots clawing at sky.

Jog back along the beach to be met by consternation in the camp. Mr and Mrs Winnebago have had their TV and their microwave stolen. Kate is calling, 'Where's the pancake mix? Where's the ice chest? Who moved the ice chest?' We need a minute to come to terms with this loss.

Returned home, late, cold, tired, and dirty to find the laundry room flooded. Irony of Jack's kayaking is not lost on me. He needn't have bothered. He could have stayed home. Spent a long and sodden evening unpacking gear and mopping up the basement. Difficult to say now which is worse: camping or coming back from camping.

Ruby, however, seemed to have forgotten the shortfalls and the disappointments. 'That Winnebago breakfast,' she said, 'was the best meal I've had in my entire life. Weren't those people great!'

August 28

Took Ruby and Harry to the airport, stopping first at Save-On-Everything to buy a tote for last-minute purchases. A plastic construction with yellow, pink, and turquoise flowers on a white ground, a fine anti-Gucci statement. It had long handles for the shoulder, which incommoded everyone at the checkout. Ruby tied them together on top. They looked like rabbit ears. We all watched it go off on the conveyor belt. 'You won't lose that,' said Harry. 'In a hurry.'

Something in the colours perhaps struck a chord and made our eyes sting. Possibly Ruby like me was remembering our matching childhood beach towels and there it was, a bagful of memories, childhood disappearing. Perhaps a bagful of our youth. Anyway, she was crying too and we had to give the boys money to go away. When it was time to go through, we were helpless with loss. It was too dismal. Wondered if Ruby from her side of the glass could see what I was seeing: all the imprints of lips where lovers, like prisoners, had pressed their mouths one last time. Ruby is great, yes. And I love her. But yes. I wish I had a lover.

August 29

A day to myself. The spider on the wall loomed very large.

Attended to my mail. First found my desk. Excavated it from beneath layers of kid stuff. Byron's desk in contrast was probably covered in kid. I am quite certain he did not sit down to write in the company of leaking Magic Markers and mauled copies of *MegaSlash* and, if he'd had a computer, it would not have said 'Freak you, man, freak me!' when he turned it on. There was a great deal of mail. Among it was a response from Pentboy. Had only written to them—'him'?—as a kind of joke: *I am sending you this short piece about a man who makes a clay cast of his lover's penis* ...But here was the reply: *Dear Mr Glass* (Well? Mr George Eliot, after all ...) *Dear Mr Glass, Thank you for your submission, 'Makin It, Bakin It.' It nicely meets our needs—raunch without rancid. We enclose a cheque for five hundred dollars* ...Raunch without rancid? Five hundred dollars? *Five hundred dollars!*

About eight o'clock thought I heard a rat in the attic. They come back each year. After their summer holidays, I suppose.

Oh, and there was a note from the Newfoundland poet. How could I forget? The one with the soft shoes. And the eyes.

August 31
Not sure how I'm going to write this. Not even sure what happened, the day so fraught with mishap and muddle from the start, a sorry saga of missed appointments, appliance malfunctions, and a kind of globalized aggravation brought on by back-to-school meltdowns and a deficit of pizzas. Returned home exhausted and cross with a trunk full of overpriced, unnecessary, name-brand purchases from four different lists. Miles went to bed with anxiety. Hettie got up because she could not sleep.

Then Jack came home.

Unlike Jack Nicholson who came home in a psychotic rage, wielding an axe and a door-splintering grin, Jack simply walked into the kitchen in silence and took a seat at the table next to a pile of wet washing where he started on some cold macaroni left over from last Thursday. He didn't answer when I said he should look at the overdraft. I said it twice.

Then perhaps just to get his attention I said, 'I don't think our lives are worth living like this.'

And Jack said, 'You're right. I think we should split up.'

Still can't believe I'm writing this.

It's 2 a.m. now. I'm alone and in the kitchen but this time it's me next to the wet washing. Can't bring myself to move.

It was the only time he's ever told me I'm right.

TWO

September 1

Yesterday was a thunderbolt. The full meaning of the word is suddenly, blindingly, clear. My father, a gentle man, was the only person I knew who ever used the word, applying it for the most part to unusually high electricity bills, as in: 'Well! This is a bit of a thunderbolt!' The mortgage payment presumably would have been a whole thunderbolt.

This was different. Jack's thunderbolt came hurtling from the sky, an unforeseen flying object, a thing of black power and the speed of light, a thing of mighty impact. Like one of the greasy, inert lumps of metal I imagined Zeus picked up, like wrenches off the celestial garage floor, and lobbed at those who crossed him. Yes it is safe to say I was thunderstruck.

In response I did not have a thunderbolt or lightning bolt to my name. 'You're kidding?' I said. But no. Jack was not kidding.

Called him a variety of unseemly and unoriginal names, some of them repeated many times, and was only just beginning to get creative when he heaved himself from the table in one gigantic move and went out, putting the leftovers of the cold macaroni in the dog's bowl on the way.

Left the children to the attractions of *Star Wars* and retreated to the bedroom where I could sit on the floor with my hand over my mouth and nobody would ask *What's the matter?*

Returned eventually to resume role of Capable Mum seeing youngsters to bed and then took Jack's place at the kitchen table. Blackguard lay at my feet, perhaps unwilling to grasp that all the macaroni was gone. The phone did not ring. Went to bed reluctantly about 1:30 a.m.

Woke around two when I heard him come in. Awake again at six. He must have slept on the couch. God. The *couch*! We are a soap opera, a living cartoon strip! How could he do that? The cliché! If this marriage is over I want a fucking blaze of gory glory not an ailing cliché expiring on the couch. Went in to the living room at once to tell him so.

He was getting dressed. He said, 'For God's sake, Vita. Can't we talk tonight? I've got a breakfast meeting.'

11 p.m. now. I'm still waiting.

September 2
Marlene called to invite us over. Told her we all have a terrible case of strep throat. She said, 'All of you?'

I said, 'Well Jack has boils as well.' Childish, I know, but slander helps you feel better. 'As well as flatulence,' I added.

He did not come back last night to talk.

September 8
Everything is in pieces and I don't know where to start. He did not come back at all until the third and we are now living with a new family member called The Situation. Talking as most people understand it is not a thing we do. Instead we glide past each other, eyes downcast, postulants in a new religious order under a vow of silence. All bodily proximity, all eye contact forbidden. This morning we stood at opposite

ends of the counter to butter our toast. It is embarrassing. The Situation is an amorphous, gelid blob that is growing in the middle of the living room. Neither of us can address it but we both inadvertently feed it and watch it get daily bigger. At night it wobbles into the bedroom and settles in the middle of the bed, leaving Jack and I clinging to the outer edges of the mattress like survivors about to slip off a raft.

Discussion is not an option. Twenty years of 'Where are the car keys?' and 'We're out of Syrah again,' is no preparation for this. This is big. Something from our very own *X-Files.* Our very own blob, still growing and not about to go back to its own planet without some serious psychosexual analysis. But we are no special agents. We are only Mum and Daddo—and Mum and Daddo have already abandoned attempts to disarm the blob, knowing the exercise is doomed from the outset by my unfortunate tendency to write the script for a disaster movie, littering explosive cues every turn—*This isn't going to work, is it?* and *Why don't we just call it a day right now?*—while Jack settles into the role he loves best, the smouldering building from *Towering Inferno.*

But I could manage anything, even the blob, if only life did not have to be lived. How can a person go about daily tasks with her heart disintegrating like offal in an acid bath? How to meet the teacher and make peanut butter sandwiches with the self slowly coming apart, cell by bloody cell? And—here is the really spooky part—NO ONE ELSE CAN SEE IT.

September 12

Have no heart for writing. Have no heart. The children are back at school. All of them—except Felix—seemed thrilled to escape. So. An empty house, but not much use to me. I cannot concentrate, cannot focus. One paragraph a week will not produce another *Moby Dick* by Christmas. Only output for entire week is letter to government railing against pharmaceuticals in our food supply—and only managed that because Felix was threatening to leave school and join a radical protest group to save the world from megacorporate evil. I said, 'There are other ways to fight it, dear,' and he said, 'Prove it.'

Marlene came over. Could not bring myself to tell her what has happened. I told her instead about all the interruptions: the hydro man on Monday and then BC Tel crawling about in the ceiling; the dentist and the blood test on Tuesday, the doctor and the gynecologist on Wednesday followed by a pulmonary function test for Hettie at the hospital, then shots for Miles, then on Thursday the dog tore his leg open. Marlene gasped. I said, 'His own, silly.'

It was then that the rat dropped to the table. We were sitting out on the veranda, trying for a certain restrained elegance with our mint tea, when it plopped onto the table between us. All three of us were stunned. It was a long drop from the rafters above. The rat shook its head once and then froze, the hairs on its back electrified with fright. We stood up and I said, 'Quick, quick, quick!' Marlene, who is always more focused, said, 'Hammer!' I said, 'Shovel!' We exchanged common nouns for a while—'baseball bat,' 'hose,' 'box,'—until Marlene spotted the compost bucket. She flung the potato peelings over the lawn and upended the bucket over the rat, a solution which impressed us both but only for a second or two. Sat down again to consider how to get bucket and rat off table at same time.

Marlene said, 'I didn't know you had rats.' I said, 'Yes. In the ceiling just above our bed. And they mate on a considerably more regular basis than those below them.'

We were still sitting there when Felix came home. His friend Dunk was glad to help.

While he was drowning the rat, I said, 'I suppose I'll have to go up into the attic again to set some traps.' Marlene was shocked.

'Get Jack to do it,' she said. Duties in her house are strictly delegated and one of her mottoes is 'Never deviate—ever.'

Was suddenly overwhelmed with the gravity of my circumstances. 'Jack is away. Kayaking,' I said. 'Or Denver. I've forgotten. He's not back until after the weekend.' I didn't say any more.

Marlene was waiting, but she is not a patient person. She would never mislay her husband like that. She rose to go and the subtext of her parting words was *Okay. Have it your way*.

'His pectorals must be pretty impressive by now,' she said.

September 15

Jack is home again but The Situation only gets worse. It continues to grow and is now behaving like a big, pushy teenager, grabbing the chair one is about to sit in, sullen and ill-behaved, trampling on all the clean feelings. And consuming, consuming, consuming. And we are helpless, hopeless. We feed it at every opportunity, rummaging in dark cupboards, scraping out the back of the fridge for any old mouldy items we can find and it gobbles them all and is not satisfied.

Must talk to someone other than Jack but am paralyzed.

It took him twenty years to decide he can't live with me?

September 25

The Slough of Despond. Perhaps I shall rename the house.

Days and days have gone by and still I am paralyzed. Can't write, can't speak. Can't think. Can do nothing. Feel as if I am slipping into the company of the living dead, a grey zombie with festering wounds and trailing bandages. Can't anyone see them? Are they not apparent when I go to the PTA ? *Good God, Vita! Have a seat! You look most unwell.* But no. There is only the customary stage whisper, 'Here's the agenda. We're at number three.' You'd think at home the children at least would notice but there they are, all hale and rosy-cheeked in a robust Victorian sort of way, plunging into life—well lolling on the couch, actually—but unaware. Is this innocence? Is it a good thing, preserving the illusion that they are safe in their garden? Dissembling? What about truth and lies? They will have to know soon.

September 26
Have thirty-seven unanswered messages on my machine. Will have to talk about it sooner or later.

Later.

October 1
Keith said, 'Good God. What happened?'

I said, 'Keith, I don't think many hairdressers in this city, perhaps even in Canada, greet their clients in that fashion.'

Keith said, 'But you have to admit—'and pulled at a hank of hair as if he were cleaning something out of the vacuum head.

'I've been busy,' I said. 'Is the coffee hot?'

Keith left to find out while Biloxi led me to the sink but he was back the very instant I was done, hovering behind me like Edward Scissorhands. I know he enjoys my visits. I am the *je-ne-sais-quoi* in his career, like the asafetida in the curry. But today I did not feel spicy. Sitting in front of the mirror, swathed in black nylon, I thought it might be more appropriate to my mood if he shaved my hair off completely. I could go into retreat from the world. Perhaps he had a white-walled room back there where wan-faced women practised stark asceticism, purging themselves of the torments of the world with rigorous meditation techniques.

'Pardon?' I said.

'I said, "So what's been happening?"'

'You could ask,' I said, 'what has not. It would take less time.' Keith raised his eyebrows in anticipation.

'We haven't, for instance, had a nuclear war or an outbreak of pellagra—'

His face morphed into one large all-receiving ear but suddenly I didn't have the heart to go on. 'But maybe I'll tell you next time,' I said. 'Why don't you tell me instead what you've been up to.' So he told me with some delight how he and his partner had bumped themselves all the way to Acapulco.

'It was great,' he said. 'We were bumped from every flight. We had one night in Vancouver, one in Seattle, and two in San Francisco. The best hotels and first class all the way.'

This story did little to cheer me.

'Last time we flew,' I said, 'We were bumped, too. We were stuck in a holding pattern and bumped for half an hour by the turbulence above Heathrow. Both the littles threw up—simultaneously—each time we went down a level. I had one on either side of me and it was very difficult to attend to both at the same time. Sometimes they missed the bag. When we landed, the steward handed us a six-pack of soda to clean up. "There you go," he said. I think he was concerned about the seats.'

'Well you were on the wrong airline,' said Keith, some-what petulantly, I thought. Sometimes people do not like it if others are not having fun like themselves.

'I was certainly in the wrong seat,' I said. 'But I'm sorry. My stories are all full of woe today.'

Keith said Biloxi had used that very word just today. He said his new boyfriend told him, 'Woe is a constant.'

'That's a very sad outlook,' I said. 'He should tell him to get over it. Everything's a matter of outlook. What's yours?'

Keith said, 'What's my what?'

I said, 'Never mind. Just tell me more of your stories. They're always good.'

Spent the rest of the appointment listening to tales of unannounced good fortune and sudden boon. There were relatives who won lotteries, faulty appliances that won their owners huge insurance claims, and friends who were awarded a year's supply of groceries just for finding a cockroach. Together the stories had a dispiriting effect.

Pulled into the parking lot by the lake on the way home and stared glumly at the Canada geese shitting on the beach. Thought over what I hadn't told Keith. Telling people is going to be the hardest part. There should be a place for it in the Announcements section of the paper. Births, Deaths, Marriages, Divorces, Bankruptcies, Arrests of Firstborns on Drug Charges, perhaps just Woes. In their own column.

October 4

An alarming dream. Something to do with a slug in a cage and a wicked metal crab dancing on the outside. Jack and me? Who is the slug, who the crab? Who is in and wants out? Who's out and wants in?

October 5

Still haven't told anyone. Keep the phone off the hook most of day and stay in where I can cry without being seen. Drive up to the school when it's time to pick up Hettie and park a little way down the road. Lurk inside my car like a potential child molester so I don't find myself trapped in some cheerful conversation on the endearing shortcomings of partners. Hands shake a bit on the steering wheel. Dizzy a bit too, but that's lack of sleep. Wear dark glasses a lot.

October 7

Spent most of the night lying awake practising what to say when I talk about it. Jack and I are through. We are through, out the other side. No longer one. No longer two. Jack is leaving me. I am left by Jack. Jack and I are splitting up. Jack has split. Up. I am splitting up with Jack. We are going our separate ways. Jack and I no longer see eye to eye. Sleep face to face. Oh God. Toe to toe. Oh. Oh. No. All right. We, Jack and I, cannot see our way clear, cannot see any way, any point, any sense, any future, any farther than the ends of our noses. No. Jack and I have seen the light. Yes. Jack and I have seen the light, come to an understanding. Jack and I have come to an amicable arrangement, an agreement, a consensual disagreement, a bump in the road, a bit of a roadblock, something of a pothole, a rock slide, the end of the road, the great big black hole.

Finally got up at six. Made coffee. Sat and watched the sky lighten and the bay turn that inexpressible colour between pink and blue. A blush of pale mist above the water and the hills turning that soft Toni Onley blue. The kitchen filled with pink light. Blackguard began to bang his tail on the floor though he was too lazy to get up. They were all asleep. Pets, children, all, the house their coiled shell, their safe haven. And Jack quiet as an unexploded bomb beneath the duvet. Resolved there and then to take control, to tackle

The Situation in a calm and rational manner, protecting the sensibilities of all involved. But in a little while Jack came in already dressed for work and clearly not stopping for breakfast and the sight of him all clean and pressed and shaven had an unexpected effect. Was suddenly filled with wrath of biblical dimensions and asked him where the bloody hell he thought he was going. An unfortunate opening, leaving me, as it did, wide open to justifiable contempt.

'TO WORK,' Jack said slowly, gently, but in capital letters big enough for the terminally stupid.

Pretended he hadn't spoken. It was the only way. Press on. Take the ridge. 'And another thing,' I said, 'I've had enough. I want this thing out in the open RIGHT NOW. Out in the open for all to see. No more procrastination. No more cowardly Clintonian cover-ups. No more protecting yourself or anybody else. It's time you called a spade a bloody spade. It's not a bloody separation. It's not a bloody parting of the ways, a misunderstanding, an agreement, a trial run, or anything else remotely pussy-footing, bushy-beating, or limp-dicky. You're leaving me, you fucking bastard. Right? And you better stop packing your bloody briefcase and come right out with it and say so. Right? RIGHT?' I was possessed, transfigured. It was *High Noon* and I was the one with the white hat. I put away my smoking gun.

What man in his right mind would answer, 'WRONG'? He agreed with me. Of course he agreed with me. It was time to quit. NOW. It didn't matter that I'd used too many bloodies.

Well yes. A tactical error. I can see that now. I wrote the script again. I just can't seem to help it.

October 9

Must tell the children soon. And there must be no fudging the issue. They must have the truth, hard-edged, cold, like an ice cube to be swallowed whole. Their father is leaving them.

October 10

Decided to tell the children today.

October 11

Changed my mind. This is like tearing each other limb from limb while we are still alive, like some old protagonists in a Nordic myth. Jack can tell them. It is Jack's responsibility. He can put it any way he likes as long as he doesn't tell them he is leaving them.

October 12

My birthday. It is raining. Good. I opened the door to misery and cleaned the fridge instead of writing. At about ten o'clock the phone rang but though I listened and listened when I picked it up I could make nothing of it. Thought at first that maybe someone was trying long distance to play 'Happy Birthday' on an electric guitar. Eric Clapton? Felix in the phone booth at the 7-Eleven? But no. It did not develop into a tune. It began to sound more and more like someone speaking into a vibrating tin can. Eventually made it out to be an automatic recording from the Sears catalogue shop. I left the phone off the hook.

By suppertime everyone had remembered what day it was and they were all exceptionally nice. Entire family overcome by guilt. Jack and I most of all. The children do not know yet.

Just before bed, Marlene called to wish me happy birthday. Said she had been trying to get through all day and was there something wrong with my phone? She suggested lunch tomorrow.

'Oh, I'm sorry,' I said. 'You would not want to be near me.' 'Flu,' I said.

October 14

Jack announced he is moving out at the end of the month. For good. I haven't been out for three days. Have told everyone I have flu. He has an apartment to go to downtown. I shall tell the children tomorrow.

Cannot stop the stupid weeping. Twenty years! More than twenty years to decide he doesn't like me? That's the part I can't get over, the part I can't swallow. Twenty years. That's the lump that won't go down. After all this time, abandoning me at the crossroads. Absconding like a highwayman with any looks or assets or sense of fun I ever had and pointing me down the road that leads to menopause. There you go, sweet thing. You won't be alone. You have the four kids. Twenty years. The knuckly bit of cartilage you find in the turkey stew.

October 15

Annie came by with some aromatherapy oils and kombucha. Said she'd heard I'd had flu.

'It cleared up,' I said. 'All of a sudden,' I said. I'm better.'

She said I should drink the tea anyway and I was to get Jack to massage my chest with Immunissimo and follow it up with Celestial Synergiser.

I said, 'Okay,' emphasizing the *kay* part. 'Or I could drink it,' I said. 'Or a big glass of Liquid Plumber.'

Annie said I had a closed mind sometimes. She said I wasn't helping myself to health, and then she did a sort of double take and said, 'There's something wrong, isn't there?' and my eyes began to water. She said she would take me out for lunch and I could tell her about it.

We went to a new place by the water, all white and green, light and airy. A place to lift the spirits but mine were kept down by the thought of Jack grumpily doing a vapour rub on my chest. It was too dismal to contemplate.

Annie advised nasturtium salad for its tonic effects on the spirit.

'Now,' she said. 'You can tell me all about it.'

Could only shake my head.

'You can. You can tell me,' she said, putting down her fork, though it was more than clear that I couldn't, concentrating as I was on trying not to blub. I had begun to make strange noises. I snuffled to the nasturtiums and the focaccia and then I snuffled to the next course, something billed as white-bait timbale.

Annie reached across the table to hold my hand. I managed to tell her it was Jack but that was all I could say. My noises were getting louder and beginning to borrow from the animal kingdom. Other diners were beginning to look in our direction. 'There, there,' said Annie. 'We all need to let it out,' she said. 'Men are a pain. A pain in the ass. You probably need to leave him. Just leave. Just go. For good.'

At this point I could feel a great open-mouthed bawl rising like some long-trapped air bubble from the *Titanic*. Was saved, however, by the sudden expulsion of my contact lenses as they shot from my eyes on the back of two hot geysers. Jack was momentarily abandoned while Annie and I fished in the whitebait and two waiters checked under the table. Shall have to get a new pair. Again.

.

After lunch, in the parking lot, Annie rolled down her window and thrust a book at me. 'It's been my life preserver,' she said, 'but keep it. I don't need it anymore.'

'*Love Yourself—If You Dare*' did not sound promising. To begin with it did not seem to target my particular problem very accurately. Personally I've never had any trouble with me; it is Jack who seems to have that difficulty. Did not trust this book to reveal the reason but had taken Annie's remark about a closed mind to heart so walked along by the boats and took *Love Yourself* with me. It advocated among other things, 'indulging' oneself in a darkened room with candles and, 'if it has sensual meaning for you,' chocolate. Wasn't sure whether or not these props were meant for their original purposes but was greatly cheered by the sudden recollection of the porn contest, about which I had as yet done nothing. Literary magazine *Rombast* is planning a special issue of what they like to call 'erotica.' The issue is to be called '*Cunnilingua Franca*.' It was the moment surely to capitalize on my talent for raunch without rancid. Threw *Love Yourself* over the side of the fish dock and felt considerably better, confident that I could fire off something altogether more inventive with regard to the contents of my fridge.

Got back in time to pick up the children. Whether it was the gale of tears, or the cheerful antagonism of the gulls, or the sight of *Love Yourself* sinking to the green bottom of the marina, I don't know, but felt much stronger than before. Purged of acrimony. Free of need. Calm.

Announced the new arrangements to the children.

'Your father,' I said, 'is moving out to live in an apartment downtown. He would like to be by himself for a while.' Braced self for reaction.

Miles asked if he would have a TV.

Kate said, 'He'll have an awesome one. Can we go and stay?' and Felix said, 'Cool.' Hettie asked if that was why they are called apart-ments.

Will have to look to my own independence.

October 16

I have it. A food column! I shall not stop at *Rombast*. I shall write to some of the magazines on the top shelf at the corner store behind the 1985 issues of *BC Auto*. I shall draw up a proposal. Erotica—featuring a new food product or a seasonal vegetable each month. Shall send it off tomorrow.

Have finally conquered the vagaries of the consumer system and obtained a refund for my contact lenses. Purchased a new pair at a rival establishment with no trouble at all. I can see clearly now—life stretching away into the distance: single mother of four seeks vigorous, passionate male for uninhibited exchange of laundry. Oh God.

What I still cannot see, with or without contact lenses is why. Jack says he cannot tell me. Does this mean he cannot tell me because he doesn't know, or he cannot tell me because he dare not speak its name? Don't be silly.

The nights have become unbearable. One of us could easily retire to the couch. I don't know why we don't. Is it just that it's too much work? In any event, we soldier on in the frigid climate of the bathroom, taking polite turns at the sink and communicating our displeasure with—oh, *any*thing, a sock, a toothbrush, an accidental brushing of elbows—by the minutest inscriptions of body language. We can read each other with indecent accuracy: the too-protracted intake of breath, the silence before its careful expulsion with an apparent attempt to silence it—but not so much that the other won't hear. We have became a hateful, hate-filled couple too stupid to even laugh at, and for this reason alone I wish Jack were already gone.

October 28

He moves out tomorrow. Am beside myself. What shall we say? How shall we conduct ourselves? There is no script for this, or at least there is a script but it is of the 'Been a trip, baby' variety and is written for other characters altogether, Americans with straight, white teeth, people we don't even know. Fell into a state of panic last night at the prospect of being abandoned like a Victorian wife clutching the baby while the scoundrel husband gallops off, laughing heartlessly. Decided that the only way to avoid that particular screenplay was to go away first. But what about the dog? The waves of panic were Tofino-sized and getting higher by the minute, coming at me more swiftly. I started calling round to places where we might stay. Anywhere except here. Here was only abandonment. Nowhere downtown would do of course. *Oh, look, there's Daddy going into that building with a lady. With a man! With a man and a lady!* Tried some of the places on the Gulf Islands and found them closed, out of business or full. Strange how meeting obstacles only makes the goal more desirable. Was more than ever determined to get away and began to feel like Miles's gerbil gnawing at the cage. In desperation called Annie. I am such a hypocrite.

'Annie,' I said, 'you have to help me. I know you won't mind. You have a heart of solid gold. Annie, I have to get away. I'm desperate. Can I come over to Pender? Bring the children?'

The silence lasted forever. As if someone had put the brakes on the universe. Or as if Annie had just set a wheel in motion and was waiting to see where the arrow would land when the wheel stopped spinning.

'Um,' she said. 'Um, you know Jack's coming over here on Saturday?' My ears started to ring with the futile urgency of a car alarm. 'He called me last night. He can't get into his apartment until Monday and he needs somewhere to stay. Vita? Vita?'

I said, 'Oh, sorry. I think we got cut off for a minute there. Thanks, though, Annie. Listen, I have to run. Thanks again.'

October 29

Friday. Madrona Lagoon. A wet and windy drive up here. Said goodbye to Jack in the garage before we left. Garage has often been the only place to get some privacy. Children all packed and ready to go in the van in the driveway, Jack and I standing face to face in the middle of the oil stain.

Jack said, 'Have you got the Marmite?' Was not sure if this was paternal concern or if he fancied a snack. I said, 'No, but I have the last Syrah d'Oc.' He said, 'Right, right.' It was a long silence. Perhaps we were both taking mental inventory of the booze cupboard. Possible because we both said, 'Right, then,' at exactly the same time.

Saw in the mirror that he stayed to wave, which I thought particularly forlorn and brave until my imagination had him feverishly on the phone to a hot vixen in Victoria as soon as we were out of sight. Or Annie?

Did not see much traffic on the way up. Dark by the time we reached Madrona Lagoon. Hollywood set director had been at work on the resort making sure the sign was broken and the screen door to the office swung in the wind with a rusty squawk. Anthony Perkins did not seem to want to come out in the rain to show us to our cottage but stood in the lee of the door and pointed past a giant satellite dish to what appeared to be a maintenance shed along the beach. An eddy of arbutus leaves blew in when we opened the door. There was no one else in the world who would want to go to Qualicum in late October. Good.

October 29

My last entry proved wrong with the arrival of a family from South Africa. Mr and Mrs Jo'berg had even more offspring than I, all boys and all named after features of the Transvaal. The younger Jo'bergs, Cliff, Rill, and Buck, suffered from a fanatical interest in fishing which rapidly spread to Felix, Miles, and Hettie. Did not attempt to quell it since it offered some measure of relief from the state of festering cabin fever which had until then prevailed in our room. Drove out in the rain to buy a line and a hook. Felix improvised the rod. Left Kate to enjoy supreme dominion over the hulking TV and all its channels and went with Blackguard down to the dock. Wind was at about force nine but the children seemed not to notice.

Returned to keep Kate company. She was busy watching commercials but took the opportunity to complain that she has no money. Said she wants a pair of silver sandals. I drew attention to the weather and tactfully suggested that in any case she has very little in her wardrobe to go with silver stiletto sandals. 'I have cut-offs,' she said. An ambush. No sooner had I begun to point out that wearing silver sandals and cut-offs downtown even in the summer would only lead to unsavoury assumptions on the part of the opposite sex than she was accusing me of being a prisoner of male prejudice and making myself a willing collaborator in their circumscription of her world. 'Like I'd let men decide what I wear. Jerks,' is how she put it, I think. Was saved the need to come up with a response by the entry of the other three, the littles, looking damp and wind-blown and wanting more bacon for bait and Felix, looking chilled, who got straight into bed and pulled the covers over his head, saying it was my turn to go down to the dock. Kate continued her campaign against poverty and launched into her thesis that I was wrong to ban Barbie in her early years and have only myself to blame if she has been sucked into the vortex of the fashion industry. She said she heard it on *Oprah*.

She's right of course. Deprivation only stokes the appetite. 'Rubbish,' I said.

Put on my jacket and went out. The dog refused to join me.

Cold grey sea down at the dock. Plucky gunmetal fish gamely fighting for the chance to be pierced through the lip. Our successes not as numerous as those of the visitors from the veldt but we beat them hollow on spectacle when we hooked the cat. It had come to investigate the bacon. By the time we noticed, it was walking oh so delicately in a circle, its mouth stuck open and emitting polite coughing noises. Clearly it knew better than to panic with a fish hook in its tongue—even with the children shrieking, 'Look, look! The cat has the hook!' But the mind is wonderfully honed by crisis. I would be hard put to describe the exact procedure for extricating a fish hook from a cat's tongue without losing an eye yet we succeeded. Look, look! The cat is off the hook! Dick and Jane rule.

Something of a lull followed this diversion. Emptiness of the late day is always oppressive. In Qualicum at the end of October it is murderous. Lurid light everywhere and murmurings of boredom and dissent in the air. Enforced a late-afternoon walk to look at a ragged, dishevelled sunset as an antidote to the promised evening of greasy pizza and violent movies. Retired to the bath with the red wine while the children lay about the cottage watching the giant TV and arguing hotly whenever there was a lull in the action. Only once wondered if Jack was watching the same movie. Or having a bath. Or. I made a decision. I would cave in to the beauty myth. Kate had and she was nobody's fool. I would shave my legs with regularity, go blond, have laser surgery on my eyes. Create a new me. You know it makes sense.

October 30

Drove back this afternoon in blinding rain to the loud strains of 'Life Is a Highway.' Children finally all in holiday mode at the same time eating, laughing and attacking each other good-naturedly. Malahat pass nerve-racking in the rain. Car behind us begins flashing its lights. Pulls dangerously level with us at first opportunity as we barrel down from summit. Woman in passenger seat looks concerned, urgently signals something. Stomach in a knot. Look in mirror for smoke or flames. Can only see Kate doing her hair. Perhaps a wheel about to drop off? Dare not take eyes off road long enough decipher woman's signals through rainy window. She has her window down, motions me to do same. Rain enters in torrents. We are in the river scene of *Whitewater*. We are hurtling to our doom. Everyone alarmed now. 'Your children,' the woman screams. 'They're throwing wrappers out the window!' I wind the window up. Felix says, '*She's* a good citizen.'

Arrived home without further incident.

House unseasonably cold. Cheerless. Thought I heard someone when we came in. Called out 'Jack?' Stupid of me. Hettie and Miles both said at once, 'He's back?'

It must have been a rat.

October 31

Halloween. Hettie, ignoring all advice to the contrary, insisted on wearing my new swim cap and going as a balloon. Miles was a robot that took two hours to construct and five minutes to fall apart. I carried most of it as we scoured the neighbourhood for toxic, chemically coloured and flavoured white sugar. Will I only miss Jack for these manly things? Lighting fireworks, roasting marshmallows? Sex?

Went up to the fire hall where every year the VFD stage a thermonuclear conflagration in their parking lot and serve hot chocolate and doughnuts to the entire community. It is a time of year when people come together to lose each other in the dark and get their cars stuck in the ditches, a time of year when traditionally our older children take their first steps outside the law in the field behind and make the unwanted acquaintance of the local police shortly after. It is our only truly neighbourhood event. Had to drink the rest of Mother's vermouth in order to get the courage to go at all. Hettie wanted me to dress up so I wore a large hat in the likeness of a spider, hoping the legs would help conceal my identity. Stood unhappily in the darkest part farthest from the fire and was greeted more than once with the words, 'Hi, Vita! Have you lost Jack?' To which I replied, 'Yes.'

Oh, how I longed to be the Wicked Queen and not poor deserted Vita. No wonder we like to dress up in black wigs and red cloaks once a year. The colours of power and might. Such a welcome change from the sunny, the tiresome, blues and yellows of our kitchens. How wonderful to sweep through the world felling with a glance all who oppose, to descend to the cellar of the psyche and summon one's basest instincts in the dread name of vengeance. Oh, it was time, it was really time, to be bad.

November 5

I was right about the manly things. The duty of checking the rat traps has devolved to me. Every afternoon I put on a prisoner-of-war knitted cap and go up in the attic. The dog crawls under the table and cries until I come down. Told Kate the dog was becoming more and more bonded and loyal under our changed circumstances but Kate said, 'No, he's not. He's frightened of your silly hat.'

November 7

Worked all morning on the food porn. I was inspired. I was the Wicked Queen. I had found the cellar at last and the spell that would ignite desire, harness the winds of sexual energy. Threw in all sorts of daft items and still the brew kept bubbling. Had six columns ready by the end of the morning featuring everything from pineapples to rump steak. Normally eat too much when I work, foraging and grazing through the morning, but food porn has advantages. It suppresses appetite. *She took the chocolate sauce and drizzled it slowly between his* ... Nor do I feel a need to question my ethics. *Carefully he cut the avocado into lozenge-shaped pieces and placing one in his mouth he* ...Economic pressure has relieved me of the time to think about it—though I can quite well see that the birth of a movement to protect the subjects of the vegetable kingdom from rank abuse might be just around the corner. Never mind. I need to establish a source of income and this will serve very well for now. Besides, for the sake of decorum I have to put my work away when I stop. Tidiness is so good for mental clarity.

Blackguard spends more and more of his time underneath the table. I think he is grieving.

November 8

Wrote that last entry at lunchtime yesterday. I had super-powers then. Red cape, sexy boots as I sat down to eat my cheese sandwich. Not to be messed with. Then the early dark set in and changed everything. I began to sense a certain emptiness. The word 'hollow' came to mind. And then 'dispirited.' By the time darkness fell I was undeniably downhearted. Lay awake most of last night. Again. Could hear when any of them turned over in bed. Could hear a rat doing a bit of home reno in the attic. Could hear every-thing. The waves sloshing down at the beach. Then the wind decided to rouse some more and push the cedar limbs around a bit. Then it settled. Heard the ridiculous horned owl pretending to be a human pretending to be a horned owl. Heard Blackguard complaining in his dream that the squir-rels climb and he doesn't. Sounds like a nice night when I write it all down. It wasn't. I was adrift on a broken raft made of packing pallets. I was cold and wet and hungry. Oh God, I was hungry and not for food. Have never felt so alone. All of them, all of them warm in their beds, their own lives tucked cozily round them. Mine broken open, in pieces never to be reassembled. My younger self waving with despicable mockery into fade-out. My older self so close, so wretchedly close with her sagging breasts and dulling hair. Her witchy nose. Beckoning. This way, ducky. Over here. No, sorry, there *is* no other way. This is the way you go. This is the way we all go. Sorry, ducky.

Oh dear God. Jack. What a time to choose to do this. You could have done it years ago before this total Mumdom subsumed me.

If you have someone beside you now, Jack. If you do.

November 12

Jack called. Only the second time we've spoken since he left. Called to ask if I could find his old snow boots for him. My heart plummeted. Though Blackguard is not normal by any standards, he is much better than he used to be. The days of his worst misdemeanours are over and, I had hoped, safely buried. It was distressing to think that, like old bones, they were about to be raked up again. It seemed a pity. We were raking up enough ugly little items of our own—all our mouldy old shortcomings, omissions, and cruel-ties—without disturbing the poor dog's dirty past. I had no wish to go over such painful ground again but it was all coming back to me in vivid colour. They were purple. I had been clearing out the basement, finding all sorts of vintage junk, coffee mugs from Mexico, macramé beaded curtains, and yes, purple snow boots while, upstairs, the dog had been standing on his hind legs at the counter snacking on a freshly baked carrot cake. It was when I heard the pan drop that I knew. I raced up the stairs, beat Blackguard with the pan and shut him in the basement so that I could clear up the mess. Before I was finished, however, a publisher called from Toronto. She was interested in my book. The news was posi-tive enough to merit a call to Marlene. When I reopened the basement door some time later, the 1978 purple suede snow boots I had left on the top step were still there, the foot part of them anyway, for Blackguard's impulse to ingest, once unleashed by the lovely carrot cake, had proved unstoppable. The boots were, if you like, remodelled, the dog having made, I thought, a remarkably even job of it. Ankle boots. Though not a job Jack would appreciate. What could I do? I hid them, of course. In the garbage. They were just more old vintage junk. How our sins overtake us.

I said, 'Look, Jack, I'm a bit busy right now but I'll see what I can do, okay?'

Jack said there wasn't any rush. He wasn't going skiing till the weekend.

'In that case,' I said, 'why don't you look for some new ones. I don't think they wear that kind of thing anymore.'

In hindsight I think the dog has been a factor in the disintegration of our marriage. If I were to make a list, for each member of the family, of Valued Items Eaten by Beloved Pet, Jack's would be the longest. My heart bled for Jack, but it was not the moment for sympathy.

Strangely enough it is the dog who seems to be missing him the most.

November 16

Could not remember where I put my food porn. Uncovered one of Miles's comics under a pile of old *Times Literary Supplement*s stashed in the corner. Miles likes to use my desk for drawing and spends hours there in the evening. The drawings he shows me depict unpleasingly overmuscled characters with stubble and outsize weapons blowing each other up. So far I have only seen the men. The comic I found was called *Extasie and Bullette*. It featured nubile females with hair like Tina Turner and sadly impoverished wardrobes. One of them appeared to be clad only in a G-string and a couple of spare parts from a frozen yogurt machine. I shall have to consider my approach carefully. I should not like to discourage him from honing his graphic skills. If only his subjects were not so…well, indecent. Where will it lead him? I worry about my children's future, I really do.

Being single after twenty years of marriage is difficult and not only at home. Word has got about now so that some people I know cross to the other side of the street when they see me coming. These are the happily married. It is not that they fear me as the black cat or the Ides of March. It is just that my situation is all too difficult to deal with in these times of censored emotions. Sympathy might be misconstrued as pity, an emotion we have outlawed. Some, on the other hand, are quick to pounce and grill. These are the recently or soon-to-be shipwrecked. I am the swimmer out here in the open water. 'What's it like? Is it cold?' 'Lovely. Once you get used to it.' 'Really? Promise?' They would like details. But I am a very private person.

November 20
Tomorrow I have a reading. Pre-porn, thank God. And thank God Jack is out of town, otherwise how to stand up there at the mic and read with confidence and verve knowing the fragile, damaged, anxious, failed homemaker not so deep inside could ooze out at any moment? No. Far better he's a million miles away. I can drive myself to the venue. I'm a professional.

November 22
A success. Shared the reading with a writer of great age and distinction whose presence guaranteed a certain charge of excitement. Droves of interesting people had come to hear

his memoirs and make short work of his publisher's lavish spread of sushi and hot sake. There was a great deal of meeting and greeting and elbowing going on and no doubt some exquisitely fine rapiering of reputations. Writers are so insecure. Remembered Marlene's advice to shield the fragile ego with a persona of one's own devising and took it upon myself to adopt certain airs and behave as if this buzz was the least I expected. It's true: confidence is a trick. A great many people who have never heard of me said, 'Loved your last book.'

'Thank you,' I answered. 'And I yours. Here's to many more. For both of us,' and even, 'Let me fill your glass. Do you do reviews?'

But none of that is the memorable thing. The memorable thing was when the poet from Newfoundland materialized beside me in the crowd and said, 'Vita.' Just that: 'Vita.' My persona began to come apart. I said, 'Oh.' But it was an octave too high so I tried again. 'Oh. Have you come all this way to hear Kenji?' I asked. He said, 'No, no. I've come out to see my brother who just moved here but I heard you had a reading so I came along.'

He was shorter than I remembered and his hair was messy. God, but his eyes. And an accent that might as well be Irish.

'It's a fine-looking book,' he said. Felt my new persona falling away like a dress around my ankles.

'Well, oh, well,' I said. 'I can't imagine who will read it.' He was wearing jeans and a grey wool jacket with a black scarf. And soft shoes. Crepe soles. I do like a man in soft shoes. Then we were interrupted. Someone from the university wanted to take me to task for misrepresenting a well-known local environmentalist in the character of my antagonist, Jamie Greely, who runs over her adversary and has the body buried the under the blacktop of a new highway. Lost track of the poet while the professor was telling me the plot of my own book in a very loud voice. He was saying there were many more objectionable passages. I said, 'What! You read it?' He said he tried but failed. My new persona, who had put her dress back on, said, '"Try harder. Fail better."' But he only wanted to lecture. He just snorted and drifted off.

Mitzi came over and said, 'Let me talk to Jack. Where is he? We need some financial advice.'

I said I was sorry but Jack was away. Kayaking.

'Who with?' said Mitzi at once.

'No one,' I said, 'as far as I know. It's, you know, like conception. You don't have to have anyone else.'

God, I didn't mean it. And thank God she was gone before I had finished. Marlene, though, had been watching from across the room and was on her way.

'Ask him back for a drink,' she whispered.

'Who?' I said. 'The professor?'

'Don't be dense,' she said. 'The *poet*.'

But there was the Newfie poet being swallowed almost whole by a woman in a red dress and shepherded away in a little knot of people making their way to the door. Made eye contact just as he went out and he raised his shoulders in a what-can-I-do-about-it gesture. Just as well, then. A weak man is all I need.

Returned to the house for the post-mortem along with Marlene and Dmitri and one or two others.

Dmitri asked how the evening could be possible at all if consciousness was merely a biochemical brain process but we told him to shut up and have another drink. When all the gossip was done and the tales of literary misconduct told, we sat around the kitchen table and listened to my friend

Elaine who is a welcome change from the hotbed of egos and ambition. Elaine has been many things—waitress, industrial nurse, croupier—none of which has cracked her shell of guileless innocence. As a result she lives in a state of constant amazement and sometimes shock and has a rich fund of stories, or as she prefers to call them, 'antidotes,' all studded with subconscious puns and malapropisms, the best last night being the one about the husky truck driver at the traffic lights and what he was doing while waiting for a particularly long lights sequence to change. We all claimed disbelief and were treated to the graphic details or, as Elaine put it, the hard evidence. She said you could see he had proclivities even before he put on the bra. Hers was undoubtedly the best performance of the evening. By 2 a.m. we had finished even the dreadful grappa that Jack had left behind.

November 24

I could lie down for a man with an Irish accent.
　And soft shoes.

November 28

Work on my food porn most mornings now. Have even received an advance—two hundred and fifty dollars for the first piece of five hundred words. Astonishing. It only goes to underscore the fact that I have never understood the world of commerce. Am bewildered by the fact that the nonsense I make up about kiwi fruit and mangoes has a cash value in the marketplace. Bananas have served me well, both whole and mashed. I roam the produce section now with new eyes but fear I shall soon run out of ideas. It is a matter of professional pride to me that I have not yet written about a zucchini. And do not intend to.

November 30

Hettie is trying to whip up some seasonal excitement here. I am resisting.

December 1

I give up. Jack came over today and put up Christmas lights. It was, I supposed, a form of penance for the good time he has had since he has been footloose. The children, though, were disappointed. They would much prefer to go and visit him downtown in his apartment. He said it was rather difficult at the moment. He doesn't have any furniture. I cannot make up my mind whether this is the truth or a craven lie designed to conceal the fact that he has women in crotchless underwear instead of a table and chairs. Could I be losing it altogether?

No longer know who I am. Pathetic, wronged wife, dangerously crossed queen, or a free, broad spirit. A wide-open flower inviting bees, and poets, to dive in. A free broad. Am subject to sudden and wild swings of emotion and suffer alternately from plunging, soul-rotting despair and soaring, blinding elation. The latter usually comes upon me in the car. I turn up the radio, wind down the window, and do high-speed karaoke. Have not yet sung 'Free Fallin'' but anything is possible. Life is an open road, the new horizon is in sight, and all things are possible. Sometimes the urge to keep on driving is almost irresistible. But freedom is the other face of loneliness. It's usually at home that the black cloud descends and most often in the kitchen when it is time to do the dishes. Hettie asked me this morning if my head was sore. I did not understand. 'Where you pulled your hair last night,' she said, 'when you were crying.' Had thought they were all glued to the TV at the time. Thought there was no one to see me slide to the floor in best bad-movie style and bawl like a motherless child. So occupied with tugging my hair out, so occupied with me, I had no idea the whole appalling exhibition was being witnessed from the doorway.

Now there's shame to add to everything else.

December 3

Kate has given an early alert that she has no money to buy presents. The others are well ahead. Hettie bought all her presents for us in August with money separated from me in the Dollar Store in a distracted moment, Miles has joined Columbia House so that we can all enjoy one-cent tapes of Céline Dion and Rod Stewart, and Felix is making some heavy metal art for us all and can be heard most nights hammering in his room. They all have long and impossible lists for themselves, except Hettie. I have been putting all the flyers in the blue box and the TV is not working. As a result Hettie does not know what piece of electronically enhanced plastic the toy industry has decreed she should desire this Christmas. When asked what she wants, she replies, 'Felix.' Or perhaps she does know.

Told all the others they had to prune their lists.

December 12

Dinner was tiring. Dinner is often tiring. Felix told me, and the others supported him, that I practise legislated poverty and they are the victims. He said no one around here agreed to voluntary simplicity. I said 'Oh, change the subject. Please.' Miles obliged with an offering concerning the length of our intestines, prompting Hettie to share the details of the run-over raccoon. Kate soon had the stage with her detailed account of the dissection of a sheep's head in biology and the exciting prospect of cutting up human cadavers at university. I listened politely. I know when I am being goaded. Reminded myself that they are exploring the world around them, that everything is grist for their intellectual mills and that I am lucky they wish to communicate with me at all. 'Look!' said Felix, poking at the fish on his plate. 'Cadaver juice!'

It is times likes these when I think of Jack in his bare apartment, sitting alone at his plank table under the naked light bulb in the total silence of his isolation. Bastard.

Going to bed early now. Nausea. It gave me a headache.

December 13
As I thought, the produce section yielded little inspiration today. I shall have to move to the baking aisle. But at least people have been getting their veggies down them. Or up.

December 16
A long overdue visit to Bangs. Braced for the tiresome question: 'Done all your Christmas shopping, then?' As fatuous as *Have a nice day!* I had my reply ready. 'I've bought a hat,' I said. 'For myself. Performance enhancing.' Keith said, 'Good for you.' He said studies show that the brain's neural pathways conduct information 23 percent more efficiently when the forehead is kept warm. In other words, those who used to wear thinking caps knew what they were doing. I said I was thinking of more literal performance. The hat I bought is soft black felt and will give me presence at readings. It will be the first hat I've worn since my sister's wedding when photographic evidence suggests I crowned a sharp Sassoon haircut with something resembling a boiled cabbage. 'But I bet you felt wonderful then,' said Keith. I said I did and I shall feel the same in this new hat.

A new woman, I thought. A new *single* woman.

'So you've been doing okay?' asked Keith. It was almost as if he'd heard. I made a snap decision to tell him. 'Fine, fine,' I said. 'I'm on my own now, you know. Well not quite on my own. There are the children...'

It was just as I thought. As news, it is not a delicacy to be savoured, not a juicy confession that can be relished as it is passed on. Nothing like: *Actually, Keith, I've moved in with a racing car driver from Montpellier*. It was just a dismal admission, as welcome as a fart at a dinner table and leaving behind the same whiff of inadequacy.

Poor Keith. It was a few moments before he recovered. Then he said, 'Oh, that's hard. That's what happened to a friend of Biloxi's auntie. Been married twenty years. But his auntie said the wife was impossible.'

So. Never mind the seven-year itch. It's the twenty-year something. Continental drift? Tectonic shift? Whatever it is, it's surely better to be the one who leaves. I cannot shake the feeling that abandonment *shows*. The one left behind is not fit for society. She should stay in her cave and chew the frayed ends of her ragged pelt.

But there was to be no scuttling back to the cave just yet. After Bangs I still had the book signing I'd agreed to do at Scanners. The cover of my book is red, holly-berry red, you might say. Over-extended shoppers stupefied by the season would snap it up, I reasoned. Scanners, though, is thirty kilometres from Bangs and by the time I got there it had begun perversely to snow. When I stopped the car, the snowflakes continued past the window horizontally. The prospect of sales did not seem bright. There was not another parked car for two blocks. Decided to view the next two hours as an opportunity to meditate, find my inner centre of calm, as holistic practitioners like to say, in the midst of the commercial frenzy. The irony of my situation did not escape me as I settled in at my table by the door. Nothing I should have liked better than a commercial feeding frenzy. A surprisingly steady trickle of customers scuttled in from the weather to buy *TV Guide*s and chocolate bars in case they were snowed in. Some of them paused briefly at the table to relay the weather conditions—with the clear implication that I was less than wise to be sitting there like that and should be driving home like any other sensible person. After the first hour, legs were numb with the draft from the opening and closing of the door. Kindly staff member moved me next to the radiator, a move which encouraged Clarence the cat to come and lie on the books; this in turn encouraged more customers to stop at the table. Several people enquired whether Clarence was male or female and two asked if he was a biter. I had heard that he was but by that time I was ready for any diversion and said I didn't think so. Went home after two hours. Book sales: zero. Customer casualties: not nearly enough.

Power went out at 7 p.m. At least we had eaten. We built a large fire, played cards by candlelight, and went to bed. We all like it when the power goes out.

December 17
Very difficult to get dressed by candlelight. Trees took lines down everywhere in the storm. No more wind but temperatures still dropping.

Have lost all the Christmas cards, and just as well. *Merry Christmas from Vita. And children.* The pathos. Losing the cards was surely my subconscious reaching out to the conscious world. Shall not send any. Have also lost Miles's and Hettie's lists. Or rather I know where they are. We posted them to Santa. This means that an unhappy minion of Canada Post has grudgingly processed these vital documents and we shall soon get a letter telling us that Santa has noted everything that was in them.

Will play sevens again tonight.

December 18

Phoned Hydro again. It is getting colder. God, it's cold. Our road, having fewest houses, will be the last to be reconnected. Please not sevens again tonight.

December 19

Another cold dark day and I write this by candlelight. I am trying hard not to view this sorry outage as a symbol of loss and deprivation.

Jack is going to come and spend Christmas Day with us. Friends consider this The Right Thing To Do. I suppose it is. It is like taking in a homeless person. Have had to resist the urge to buy him items for the apartment—a placemat, a toaster oven. Or should it be a pair of placemats? *His* and *Her* towels? Who knows how he lives there? Just a bed? A mirrored ceiling? A chandelier? I may be shopping in the wrong places. Satin sheets? I think about Jack too much.

December 20

Power came back on at 8 last night but we were all in bed by then. We all hate power cuts.

Kitchen looked messy, cold, and dirty this morning. A great deal of candle wax decorating every surface.

Hettie said today she didn't have a father. She repeated it tonight.

I said, 'Nonsense. Who do you see every Saturday morning?'

She sniffed hugely and said, 'Phil and Lil.' I said, 'Phil and Lil?' She said, 'In *Rugrats*.' We both cried into her pillow.

December 21

Party at Galeria Toxicana. Came home feeling cross and unwanted. Everyone has a partner. Have we returned to the Dark Ages? My confidence swings and dives. Plummets would be a better word. I feel leaden and unloved, unlovable. I am Quasimodo and must scuttle into a corner by the tartlets. Who could even bear to look my way, ravaged as I am by the devastation of child-bearing? Marlene wandered over to see what was wrong with me lurking by the crumbs like a pariah. I told her I am considering a tummy tuck. She said 'You? You don't even allow your teeth to be X-rayed. Have you gone mad?' I said, 'In the summer I want to be able to lie on the beach. With a man.' She said, 'Well lie on your stomach, then.' So Marlene.

I left early. The noise of conversation had reached a dull roar.

Returned home to find Felix and friends watching a seasonal chainsaw massacre. I worry about Felix. I think he too is in a red and black phase.

December 23

The children are mastering the art of animation on the computer. They have created what appears to be a bondage scene with Santa.

The plague of rats is getting worse. Felix and I have been up there several times to check the traps. Dread finding a live one. Have promised myself I won't ask Felix to knock it on the head. I shall do it.

Have bought Jack a scarf. The sort of neutral gift you buy for those you do not know very well. Everyone has a neck.

December 26

Don't know what strange impulse led me to make fish stew on Christmas Eve. Set it to simmer thinking it would be something comforting to come home to after the carols. The children protested vehemently at the smell but at least it got them out of the house promptly. It's important to be early. The pope has time to modify whole chunks of religious practice between one visit of ours and the next. We are the people who sit when others stand, stand when they kneel, so we don't want to be sent down to the altar steps where the latecomers are seated—facing the congregation.

The wait was excruciating and did not offer the hushed, incense-wreathed moment I was hoping for. Babies crawled under the extra rows of chairs and grade-school children placed bets on when the leaning plaster Joseph would fall into the manger. Hettie and Miles writhed and were, like Felix, whose eyes watered copiously from suppressed yawns, furiously bored. Kate's eyes blazed with indignation at being brought to this public place with her family, in whose company she would not be seen dead. The priest, when he finally made his entrance, confirmed my suspicions that though the church's heart may have been in the right place when it concocted this family affair its brain was nowhere in the vicinity, for here came an elderly stroke victim brought out of retirement, like an old accountant at tax time, to relieve the still sprightly but overworked Father Patrick, who would top the bill at midnight. Before he began the liturgy, he addressed us all, though whether it was a Christmas greeting or an admonishment to keep our children under control was impossible to tell. Perhaps he had forgotten his teeth. Our agony only intensified when someone found the switch for the speakers and gave us all feedback. Priest possibly deaf since he seemed not to notice. 'Ah,' I said, trying to mollify the young, 'a sweet old man.' Received poisonous glares from all four.

Returned almost two hours later to find culinary statement had crawled in glutinous yellow trail down front of stove and filled the house with the smell you get under the pier.

Embarked on a three-stage cleanup operation. Felix said Environment Canada has twenty-four-hour hot-line for toxic spills. 'Right, then,' I said. 'You mop.'

After several cans of Campbell's there was the traditional general outcry about presents and how EVERYONE, ALWAYS gets to open AT LEAST one present on Christmas Eve EXCEPT US. Decided to break with domestic custom since it was anyway in tatters and said okay. By eleven thirty we had opened almost all of them. We were a poor but happy family in a small town in northern Europe opening unlooked-for delights while Sinterklaas—too lonely to stay in his bare apartment—trod the snowy streets outside. Miles said he had waited for this moment all his life. Was struggling to suppress guilt and give in to the warm glow when Kate called out from the kitchen that the dog was eating the cake. Retribution. Did not remember it ever being so swift. 'Look,' I said, 'this does not seem quite fair on your father. You rewrap all these. I shall salvage what is left of the cake.'

Resolved to make Christmas morning more of a success.

Got up at an ungodly hour. Found the oven on. A note from Kate on the counter. She had put together another Christmas cake. It was in the oven and she had set her alarm and gone back to bed. Not only that, I thought, she had found the missing ingredient. The *L* word. I was awash with it. Tears when they have been held back tend to gush like culverts after heavy rain. It was good to be unobserved. Jack's impending arrival was becoming strangely confounded with Father Christmas and Firstborns.

Prepared the house. Worked hard to create a festive aura—heat turned up, music on, a nice fire blazing with the evidence of last night's unwrappings, and hot apple cider on the stove.

It wasn't long before I heard his voice at the kitchen window. 'The bloody chimney's on fire!' Wished I was hearing an ancient form of pagan midwinter greeting, an antic expression of goodwill, perhaps, in the face of dark privation, a call to the cheer of the hearth, but no. 'Get a bucket!' he shouted. I called the children. Felix said, 'This is bigger than the toaster!' They were very good and helped cheerfully with the whole ladder-hose-bucket routine while I flung wet towels on the hearth. Must have caught it in time because as far as I can make out Jack had only to lob a couple of bucketfuls in the general direction of the flames before they expired. He was still up on the roof with a bucket—in case the thing leaped up again like an enraged tiger—when Hettie began to cry.

'Cheer up,' I said. 'You will remember this. Your father on the roof like Santa on Christmas morning.'

She said, 'He's put it out.'

'Of course,' I said.

Hettie said, 'What will the firemen say?' It seems that, during the confusion, she had called them on Kate's new phone and given them our address. They had wanted to talk to a big person but she had said he was up on the roof fighting the fire.

'I'll call them back,' I said—too late. We could hear them coming down the drive. Had time to reflect on the advantages of independence and how nice it was to have sole responsibility even for a disaster and not to have anyone spitting at anyone else: *I told you she shouldn't have a phone.*

So Christmas spontaneously combusted as it were. The volunteer firemen seemed thrilled to be with their mates on this otherwise sacrosanct family day. They stood around in the kitchen for a long time eating mince pies before they moved into the living room where they pretended to talk fire safety with Jack while getting through a case of my home-brew and most of Kate's cake. But one could only be grateful. Their bonhomie helped Jack over his irritation at wayward children and feckless wives.

Once the VFD had sped away, we settled into a soothing afternoon of indulgence. It mellowed into a rich sense of well-being by the time we reached the brandy Jack had brought with him. Seemed such a pity not to be able to comment on the agreeable nature of the day for fear of simpering or, worse, of its sounding like a hopeful prompt. The longer you maintain silence, the more difficult it is to break it. 'This is very pleasant.' Four words. The more I thought about them, the more freight they carried, and the more impossible they were to say. And I could think of nothing else. An estrangement is as insidious and as powerful as a virus. It is a publication ban on the emotions. Every twitch is suspect. Neither of us spoke.

Said goodbye to Jack at the front door last night at about 1 a.m. but he hovered in the snow on the path in a shameless reversal of the Dickensian wife turned from the door. My feet were freezing so I invited him back in. We crept up the stairs like delinquent teens. We got rough and disorderly under the covers and did unspeakable things with our teeth and our icy feet. We put our hands over each other's mouths whenever we tried to speak. And then we were quiet, but only in a monumental way. Like the sea. *And when they were good they were really, really good ...*

Woke this morning to a sense of change. The whole day unusually pleasant and calm. Simply changing the ratio of adults to children is game changing. But I want Jack for more than that.

He's coming back on New Year's Eve. Perhaps this time we will talk again.

THREE

January 1

A day of tears and recriminations. This is no way to start the new year. This is a roller coaster and I want to get off.

Watched last night for a tall dark stranger to appear on the doorstep just before midnight. He called at eleven thirty to say he wasn't coming. Kate and Felix were beside themselves. What? Like we stayed home and he's not even coming? Felix took off for a party. Kate went to her room and cranked up her music so that I could enjoy the explicit and offensive lyrics that the parental advisory advised me of. Hettie cried. And who can blame her? Eventually she went to sleep and I went outside, a little late, with Miles to bang pots and pans and make a noise. I don't think it lived up to his TV-fuelled hopes of irrepressible jollity. Should have videotaped the event and sent it to Jack in place of a red-hot poker for his conscience.

He came over late this morning with some story about an old friend turning up unexpectedly. Right. And I was born yesterday. *Seeing an old friend*. It put me in mind of my British uncle's favourite euphemism when he was off to the pub: *Just going to see a man about a dog*.

'Right,' I said. 'An old friend. Right. Well here's an old family with an old wife and some old children and an old dog but don't let us stand in your way. We wouldn't want you lying awake at night worrying about loyalty and honour and

decency. Not when you could be screwing an old friend.'
Oh God. The things that come out of our mouths when
we're mad.

Jack said, 'Calm down. You're being ridiculous.' The two
most destructive sentences in the nuclear arsenal of domestic
warfare. My rational mind was a mushroom cloud. I could
not reply. I could only reformulate what he said.

'Calm down? I'm being ridiculous?'

And he said 'Yes.' *Yes!* But apparently he had a third
weapon because then he said, 'You're always ridiculous.'

I told him he didn't think so on Christmas night and he
said Christmas night was just an old habit.

I said, 'Oh right. Not novel and exciting like sex with an
old friend.' He said, 'It's not about sex. What is it with you?'
And I said, 'Calm down.'

I love it when that happens.

January 2

Yesterday left a bad taste, and the fact that it did made me
madder than before. He didn't fight back after I said calm
down. He just sat there looking grimmer and grimmer, more
and more haggard and ghastly about the mouth. And the
more hag-ridden and ghastly about the mouth he looked,
the more vicious and harpy-like I became, morphing slowly
from injured wife to harridan complete with fangs, two-inch
fingernails, and a thirst for blood. It is irreversible, that.

To Bangs. On impulse. The place as I suspected half-deserted.
Felt as if I were doing a good deed. A kindness. Most people
get their hair done before the holidays. I was helping to keep
the shop in business. Good old Vita in blue and yellow mode.
Only actually I wasn't. I was there to put an end to all that.

'Make me red and black,' I said. It wasn't Keith but his

business partner, Tristan. *Tristan.* Right. And I'm Isolde. But we have to go along with the pantomime once we step through the door. It's our hair at stake after all.

'Make me red and black, Tristan,' I said. 'I want to be different. I want five bold stripes. A red one in the middle. The new Vita.'

Tristan said in his professional opinion...

I said, 'Professional bollocks, Tristan. I can be anything I want. Where's Keith?'

'In Hawaii,' said Tristan. "He goes every year. Trish and me will look after you.'

'Good,' I said. 'Then make me red and black. It will be my new professional persona.'

Afterwards, Trish, the girl who did me was very sweet. 'You just have to get used to it,' she said, looking at me looking back from the mirror. 'Everyone feels like that, at first.'

Left feeling disconsolate. Trish must have suffered a crisis of confidence with this harpy at the last moment for I was not red and black at all but a rather dull maroon all over. Was not different in any way. Was like the little girls in Miles's class who dye their hair with grape juice, except I was considerably more mature and fifty dollars poorer. And I still looked like me. Not only that, I smelled like a bottle of Windex and had to drive all the way home with the windows down. Shall not make any plans to socialize.

January 4

Kate's school play will require my driving her into town each week for rehearsals. How to consider the two-hour wait 'a welcome respite in my busy schedule'? Perhaps I shall finally have time to write, even to read. Kenzaburō Ōe is taking two years off to read Spinoza to find out why he responds with pain to the world. Too much time on his hands.

January 5

Marlene called to tell me she has a reading in Vancouver in February. She wants me to go. I said, 'What about the—?' and she said firmly, 'Jack. You ask Jack to babysit his children.'

Why not? I shall swallow my pride.

She told me too about a new poetry reading series that has started in town here. Every Thursday night at the Mocha House. I shall try it out on Thursday after I have dropped Kate off.

January 9

To Bangs for a remake. Keith is back. He has given me the hair I want. I told him he had to do something about it.

I said, 'Keith, you have to do something about this,' and he said, 'About what?'

'I am supposed to be red and black,' I said.

Keith said, 'I thought you disapproved of artificial colouring.' Thought he was being particularly difficult.

'Trish dyed my hair,' I said, 'and look at it.'

'Looks great,' Keith said. 'Natural. Almost.'

I said, 'Exactly. If you were anyone else I'd ask for my money back.'

Keith gave me a long sad smile and said, 'You're a funny person.'

I said, 'That's a shocking thing to say. To a client. Some people wouldn't come back.' Confidence rather shaken by his silence. Could that be what he wants? To discourage me. Surely not. I am his only client, am I not?

Resumed relations after Biloxi brought me my coffee. Had a long discussion about the end of the world. Keith said, 'So what do you think? Is the world going to end this year?'

I said, 'Oh that's a TV ad. You can't fool me. I'm surprised you trust such a suspect source of information.'

Keith said it was based on ancient Mayan calculations and their predictions have only ever been off by thirty days. Or was it seconds?

'But doomsday predictions have such a tonic effect,' I said. 'They highlight the transience of existence, correct our moral perspective, and bring our lives into sharper focus.' I said I was always much nicer to the children when there was an asteroid approaching. Keith didn't buy it. He said if a prediction seemed credible enough the criminally inclined would feel they had nothing to lose and would make a point of doing their worst. Obviously we would never agree for this was a case of half-full, half-empty. But I did see his point. We would behave like troops sacking a town when they're in retreat, football hooligans trashing a train when they've lost.

It reminded me of the belligerent who refused to sign my disarmament petition back in the perilous eighties. 'No,' the prospective signatory said. 'No.' He said he'd been watching a long time for the rapture and personally he could not wait for the blaze of glory. Could not wait to be incinerated? With Ronald Reagan? I was deeply shocked but I was always deeply shocked in those days. A fellow pacifist said, 'Don't worry about it. I just tell them they're fucking assholes and deserve to be nuked.'

This story did not amuse Keith as much as it did me.

Considered on the way home how easily global warming usurped nuclear holocaust as our terror-of-the-month and yet just as before we do nothing to change. We are a stubborn lot and refuse come out of the tavern, even though the bombs still proliferate and the leaky power plants limp on. But anyway we can never be saved until we act in unison. Humankind will always be divided into the sheep and the goats. And the crazed consumer goats will always enjoy the world more, ripping through it in SUVs, swilling gas and munching plastic and blackening the grass for the boring old sheep behind them.

It occurred to me that my time as a political activist did not particularly enrich my life. It might even have eaten away a great chunk. And this I think was no ironic accident. I felt some kind of parallel emerging: Jack and I continually confronting one another, exhorting the other to change and in the process demolishing the very structure we strive to save. Decided to think about my hair instead. It's greatly improved. I know it is because the children are united in their opposition to it. Maroon and black, like a vintage jacket.

January 9

Thursday. Dropped Kate off at her rehearsal. She made me stop a block away because of my hair. Says she is not going to get me a ticket for the play. They are in short supply. Went to the Mocha House. At least you can have the hair you want around poets. Arrived late and it was crowded. Found self tucked around a corner beside a noisy fridge. Did not hear a lot of poetry. Much of it interrupted anyway by a man all in black beneath a beige raincoat trying to whisper in my ear. A writer. Saying something about Kant. I thought he was talking about the nature of the poems. He wanted to drink even more coffee afterwards. Flattered but had to say no. He had hard, shiny leather shoes.

Picked up Kate and returned to house to find Felix in the garage with a small cardboard box.

'Rats,' he said. 'Baby ones. Look out.' There were high-pitched squeals coming from what seemed like every part of the garage and all across the oily floor tiny, big-headed, pale pink babies were wobbling on purple feet.

Kate said, 'Eewgh. Don't you dare let them in,' and went inside and locked the door behind her.

Felix said he noticed them when he came out. He was trying to round them up. He had three in the box already, huddling together for warmth. There was much manhandling of ladders and bikes before we tracked down every last squeal. Felix stood holding the box of babies. Eleven. We said, 'What now?' at exactly the same time. 'Well,' I said, 'we have to do away with them. There's no question. We'll freeze them.' We both stared at the freezer and then at the contents of the box. The babies had arranged selves in tidy ball. Some were already asleep.

Felix said, 'It's cold in the woods. It's supposed to be going down to minus ten tonight.'

I said, 'I'll get a flashlight. You carry the box.' And so, like Hansel and Gretel's craven parents, we took them deep into the woods.

I said, 'Just leave them by that tree.' But Felix, shivering in his Megadeth T-shirt, made a nest of dead leaves, scooped the babies into it, and covered them over. I heard him say, 'There.' Perhaps he is not a cause for concern after all.

January 11

A bright and frosty morning. Have not heard from Jack since the row. Well fine. Harpies do not need phone calls. My new status was suddenly sparkling with possibility. It was a morning to relish the fact that I am single and accountable to no one. Cut loose. The drive into town was exhilarating. Rolled the window down and turned up the music. 'I'm a Woman.' Got carried away. A free woman. With an undercurrent of down-and-dirty possibility. Pity I was singing quite so loudly or I'd have heard the siren and pulled over sooner. When the officer came to the window with his book and his pen, the music was still playing. I turned it down. 'Sorry,' I said. 'Koko Taylor.'

'Is that "Mrs"?' he said, still writing.

That is the best thing about being single. No one need know when you get a ticket.

January 13

An invitation to dinner next week at the local pub with two writers from Toronto. It will be a challenge. Years of dining with the children have put stringent limits on my conversational skills. Our meals have evolved into a forum at which their latest nuggets of erudition are laid out for my astonishment, a kind of homespun Quirks and Quarks.

- Each one of our cells has five metres of DNA.
- Total blood vessels in the human body, if laid end to end, would circle the world three times.
- The American jet Peacemaker is armed with enough nuclear weaponry to destroy every major city on earth.
- During mating season the male toad develops nuptial pads on its hands so that it can cling to the female without falling off.

I cannot reciprocate. Years ago I gave away my one Interesting Fact, played my one and only card: the olfactory nerves from the membrane lining a dog's nose would cover the area of a man's pocket handkerchief whereas ours, if spread out, would only cover a postage stamp (a fact one hopes is determined by mathematics and not by practical investigation). There is no recycling such a nut of erudition: it is good for only one telling. Have become habituated, therefore, to listening attentively to the stored wisdom of others.

January 16

Thursday. Drove Kate to her rehearsal. 'Surely, I said, you'll tell me when the play is on.'

'No,' she said. 'None of your biz.'

Went to the poetry at Mocha House. Hardly heard a word. Getting very cross with the man in the beige raincoat. Some people thought we were a couple. He leaned and talked in my ear the whole time. Said his name is Max Marcel. I do not believe him. 'Where is your work published, Max?' I said. He was very evasive. Said he didn't think I'd be really interested. Left early and sat in the parking lot at the school. Read Blake by the light of a nearby streetlamp and felt a lot better. Though I could not help checking every time a lone male walked by. No raincoats, thank God.

January 17

Signed today for another three pieces of gastronomic sex. The magazine is talking about another six. Shall have to keep my particular line of work to myself. The poets at Mocha House are all very young and serious. They carry bags full of papers and read Rilke and Rumi. I don't expect they go home and cry into their children's pillows.

Am I even normal?

January 18

Whatever is happening to us is killing Jack. He came to see the children today. He looks haggard and tense. You could almost say drawn and quartered. We still have not had a proper talk. I refused today and said the children come first. He did not speak much at all after that. He allowed Hettie to make a mould of his face with playdough but he seems to have lost the ludic ability and gone over to full-blown stoicism.

Miles begged to do the same with plaster and bandages, a handy homecraft he learned in grade three, and Jack heroically obliged. He remained preoccupied and serious the whole time, his teeth gritted. When this morbid white mask is dry, Miles wants to put it on the wall. Terrific. We can all eat dinner while the dead patriarch watches over us.

January 23

Thursday. Asked Kate on the way to rehearsal to tell me more about her role. She said, 'I am the lead.' She said she is playing the part of a young girl who has great aspirations and who loathes her family. A girl who feels they are all against her and wants to leave home as soon as she can.

'What a fantastic challenge,' I said. She still won't get me tickets.

The others too are creating pockets of their lives to which I have limited access. Felix has rearranged all his bedroom furniture to resemble the barricades at Sarajevo. I have not made up my mind if he sleeps behind it or if he climbs out of the window and goes elsewhere. Miles has created his private space on the computer where he spends a lot of time refining his animation skills. He only shows me the blandest. There are others. I cannot sneak a look because he will not reveal his password to me. Are they following their father's lead? Removing themselves piece by piece, yielding to the seduction of the dark side?

Went to Mocha House. The man in the beige raincoat was there. He gave me a poem he said he had written especially for me. Dim light made it hard to read but told him politely I felt honoured. He said it was not the usual sort of thing he wrote. Would not tell me what the usual sort of thing was. Read it again at home and braced self for some thinly disguised projections and salacious fantasizing. Did not understand a word. Pity. No one has ever written me a poem before.

January 24

Dinner in town with Marlene, Danny, Mitzi, and the two writers, both called Ian, from Toronto. One of them fortyish and more attractive than I had thought. Everyone—except Max Marcel—is more attractive than I had thought. One of the Ians has a good line in scandal and it is matched by Mitzi. For a while she holds court with tales of dissolution and philandering among the board and tells how the music director and the performing arts director exchanged partners like CDs for Christmas and how the chair is so devoted to the gallery that she claims to have indulged the fantasies of a local banker in the hope of restoring the enterprise to fiscal health and was at this moment attempting to claim expenses for the rather steep pay-per-view charges incurred at the QueeneVee Motel in the process. This leads everyone to trade stories about porn movies they have seen in hotel rooms. I listen attentively, unable to find an opening for the bit about the dog's nose.

After a while they move on to body parts and body products they have tasted. I seize this obvious opening but they are all too busy airing their egos to hear my claim to special expertise in the area of garnishes they could have used.

Listening to Marlene, it seems she has had a more colourful life than I had imagined. Tell her this afterwards as she drives us home and she laughs loudly.

'But I make it all up,' she says, and I detect a note of disbelief at my own credulity.

We say good night and when I am in the house I can only think, Does everyone? Make stuff up? Are they all making it all up as they go along? And everything then is fiction? No truth and lies? And I'm the only one sticking to the boring old truth and feeling naive and gauche? So there are only lies? And resentment.

January 30

Thursday. How many Thursdays can there be in one month? Not a good night. Pouring with rain all the way down. Had thought about staying in the parking lot to read but Kate's rehearsal tonight was three hours so went to Mocha House instead and ordered red wine. An open mic in progress attended by a sparse crowd of black-clad, white-faced young people with very little hair between them. Greatly relieved to see no beige raincoat. Took a seat at the front where I might hear something for a change, but no sooner had I sat down than Mr. Macintosh himself appeared on cue from the washroom clutching a sheaf of poems. Worst fears confirmed when he took the mic and read angry incoherent poems full of vicious images, seeming to direct them for the most part at my lap. He was frothing. Felt decidedly uneasy and my knees were getting damp with the spray so decided to leave. Went to a late showing of *The Madness of King George* who in comparison seemed quite sane.

February 1

Woke up in the middle of the night. Max is a pornographer! Got up and reread the poem he gave me. How I thought it was a poem about the Chilcotin I can't imagine. It was somebody's buttocks. Probably mine!

Couldn't sleep so got up and wrote to Mother.

In the morning, as soon as the children were out of the house, I sat down at the computer to end my relationship with the magazine. Had first to fulfill my part of the contract so worked up three pieces and shot them off as rapidly as schoolboy ejaculations: a clichéd whipped cream fantasy, a bath of Jell-O, and an innovative technique with alternate applications of cayenne and sliced cucumber, the latter more like a naturopathic remedy than an erotic encounter. Shan't oblige if they want more. Have visions of thousands of men in raincoats salivating by the light of the fridge.

It is time I forsake facilitating other people's sex lives and start creating one of my own.

Called Jack to arrange for him to come and take care of the children when I go to Vancouver for Marlene's launch. He might as well get used to it because I'm not signing up to be a single mum single-handedly. I said, 'And Jack, it is time we talked seriously. We cannot go on with this half-and-half sort of wishy-washy, 2 percent arrangement. You may not want a wife, but you cannot divorce yourself from your children.'

There was a terrible silence. Then he put the phone down. What did I say?

February 9

Sunday. Yesterday to Vancouver with Marlene. Jack arrived for parental shift early in the morning. He wore a sombre sort of Clint Eastwood expression, went straight into the living room, and switched on the TV. When I put my head round the door to say goodbye he was staring at the crazed flickering of the screen and looked as drawn as the curtains, still closed from the night before.

I said, 'Don't you want to know where your children are?' He shot me a murderous look so I backed off and called from down the hall, 'Have fun!' Got out quickly. Climbing into the car with Marlene felt like the beginning of a two-woman road movie. Could have driven right on down to California.

Checked into the Sylvia in the afternoon. This is the part we like best about readings. Never mind the stimulating intellectual exchanges in the bar, never mind the possibility of making interesting and fruitful connections, at the moment we have families and the best part is being away from them. It is luxury of the highest order to sleep between sheets that someone else has laundered, to drop fluffy white towels on the floor after a shower, dress unhurriedly and go down to a breakfast that someone else has made. I asked Marlene if she didn't agree.

Marlene said, 'Of course. But only for us. For our families it is daily custom.'

I laughed in solidarity but a secret vision of wet washing and cold leftovers at home was giving me a momentary pang of guilt. I trod it down like an unwelcome roach. They value us for more than clean shirts and hot meals. Don't they?

Had an early dinner and got ready for the evening. Asked the fellow at the front desk how to get to the Carnegie Library. He said, 'Why?' Then he said 'Oh, hahaha. You don't want that. You mean the *Vancouver Public* Library.' Marlene doesn't stoop to argument. She said, 'Just tell us which bus for the Carnegie, if you don't mind.'

As we were leaving, he said, 'Make sure you have plenty of change.'

Took the bus along East Hastings at about seven. Had difficulty alighting at Main, there were so many people jostling at the bus doors, each holding a paper cup for donations. Managed to get into the building with not too many evasive tactics.

'This must be how rock stars feel,' I said, hoping to relieve the tension.

The library is a drop-in centre for the local community and provides an open welcome to the men and women society has failed, people with concerns more pressing than the pursuit of poetry. Marlene excused her publisher on the grounds that they were based in Mississauga and could not possibly be expected to know. We agreed they had probably been seduced by the name.

Still, the library was open and full of patrons, but they were all reading papers or books, chatting, or playing checkers, and generally already occupied in one way or another. No one appeared to be waiting for a reading. There was no one at the information desk in the main foyer and no evidence at all of an imminent book launch. A board behind the desk listed the night's program: rooms 103 to 105, *Legal Aid*, *Chess*, and *Haircuts (Free)*; room 209, *Needle Exchange*; rooms 213 to 216, *Speaker*, *Computer Basics*, *AIDS Update*, and *Women's Wellness*. Marlene said she did not feel well at all. We decided she must be *Speaker* in room 213 upstairs.

It was a large room, a small hall in fact, and to our surprise was already half full of people, many of whom were already asleep.

There was a buffet table at the back with cookies and orange juice and a large urn of thick coffee. On the other side a senior in a blue raincoat was sorting her bags and a wild-haired fellow with a beard was picking at the drapes. Marlene, it seemed to me, was too cerebral and abstract for this venue. Her exfoliating humour might be bracing for middle-class sloths and parasites but it was altogether too caustic for this audience whose lives were bleak enough already. Was relieved when the evening's other writers finally arrived, Belinda, sturdy and homely and full of cheerful good sense, and Doug, big and hairy and with a redoubtable beer belly. There was a salesperson from Buffy's with a box of books but no representative from the publisher nor any host for the event. We took seats among the audience and waited. Marlene looked round to see if any help was arriving. Turned back and fixed her eyes on the empty stage.

'Don't look round,' she said under her breath. 'There's a great big guy two rows back ...' I looked round. There was a great big guy two rows back, a large fellow the size of the giant in *One Flew Over the Cuckoo's Nest*, and he was mouthing *Fuck you!* at anyone who glanced his way.

'Don't worry,' I said. 'Everyone else looks friendly.'

'On medication,' said Marlene.

I said, 'Perhaps they could give us some.'

It was getting late and still no publisher appeared. Marlene got up suddenly. 'Somebody has to take charge,' she said, and strode to the front. Saw her take deep steadying breath as she mounted the first step to the stage. Only a few of the audience were aware of anything happening. Marlene paused, looking across the sea of touques and baseball caps, then she took the mic. The general rumble of voices continued. No one could hear what she was saying. She stepped forward and bent down with the mic in front of one of the speakers. The feedback was excruciating. She smiled and said, 'Good evening, everybody. I'm going to read a very short piece. A very, very short piece, about like this.' She held up one hand in the shape of a thick burger. 'And when I've finished anyone else with a story like this'—she made the air burger with her hand again—'is more than welcome to come up here and share it with us. Seriously.' Her voice was suddenly kinder than I'd ever heard it. 'Seriously. We'll listen.'

Afterwards in the hotel bar we tossed down drinks like commandos after a raid. 'Some of them made me cry,' I said. 'Me too,' Marlene said. 'Me. too.'

The ferry ride home this morning was a last taste of freedom. Blue, blue sea, islands gliding by. Gulls.

.

Jack looked pallid and chilled when I got in. He has a cold. The children seem okay.

I said, 'Did you have a good time? What did you do last night?'

'Watched TV,' they said.

I said, 'But you are trapped in suburbia. Do you know what they do at Hastings and Main in Vancouver on a Saturday night?'

Felix said, 'Score?'

I said, 'Not everyone, no. Some people meet friends. They play chess, checkers, read magazines, books. They listen to music, inform themselves and attend to poetry. Some people,' I said, 'talk to each other.' Kate said, 'Thank God we don't do that. I'd kill myself.'

Jack spent all day in bed. In my bed as I have come to think of it. With his cold. And he is still there. Hettie asked at dinnertime if he was lonely. I said, 'He's taking care of himself.' She said, 'Can't you do it for him?'

February 10

And Jack still here. Sick. Off work. Still lying in my bed. He has the telephone and the fax machine and numerous big black file folders spread out upon the duvet. He is like Louis XIV at a levée. He even had a visitor. A fawning minion from the office brought a report over in a taxi and Jack received her from his pillows. I do not think I can stand it. Hettie goes in at regular intervals to ask him how he is. He smiles bravely and says, 'On the mend.' On the mend! My grandfather said that when he had his leg amputated.

Around noon, he made a feeble attempt to get up. Probably hungry. Why he is here is beyond me. He knows I am not a good nurse. Had to tell him many times to stop sneezing on us. He is so much taller than we. Eventually he went back to bed. Kate said I was unkind. 'When he is in his coffin,' she said, 'you'll probably tell him to close the lid.' She made him a hot lemon drink. Shall put her at the top of my list of future recipients of same.

Shall have to sleep on the sofa again. Do not want to be left with a cold.

February 11

Lazarus got up today. He looked ghastly. Has lost his voice. How convenient. All my aspirations of freedom now dashed. Had hoped to reconcile a few differences before he left, take an inventory of the bones of contention, arrive at serious discussion of divorce, but it seemed unseemly now. A rehash of The Situation might finish him off so offered him an egg instead. He shook his head and pointed to his throat.

When I asked, 'Where are you going?,' wanting to know if he was going to the office or back to his apartment he answered, 'I don't know.' And because he said it in a hoarse whisper it somehow seemed as if he was revealing his greatest secret.

To Bangs. Keith very bright and breezy.

He said, 'So what about Bill Gates, then?'

I said 'Who?'

'Bill Gates,' he said, and made me repeat my response for Biloxi who was sweeping up. They both thought it was very funny.

'Windows,' said Keith. 'You know.'

'Oh. Right,' I said, 'right.' But Keith knows a vacant look when he sees one. Perhaps he sees it as a professional duty to keep his clientele's knowledge of current affairs up-to-date. He does not like to see puny unfledged specimens like mine.

He began patiently to recount the intricacies of Mr Gates's business affairs, frequently repeating the sum of six billion dollars.

I said, 'These figures, Keith, mean very little to me.' But he was undeterred. While he persisted with net investments and projected global profits, I gave myself up to reflection on the enslaving nature of technology. Such a feeling of elation that comes with doing without it. Being without Windows means being free to enter the world on the other side of a real one, to contemplate the beauty of the view beyond the window. It means being free to walk, as it were, in the open air. It means regaining full use of one's senses and, through them, one's sense of reality, being able to tell the difference between the real and the virtual, the immutable and the transitory, the substance and the form. It is no coincidence that economics, which is a virtual science, has developed such a close bond with technology. Economics enslaves us with its myths, technology enslaves us with its hardware. It was a comfort to think that, like the Atari and Pascal of my youth, Windows too will pass away without having consumed a moment of my time outside the minute's attention I was just giving it.

Keith could see I was drifting. 'You must use a computer, surely?' he said. I said only as a sort of muscle-bound typewriter. I did not have a use for any of its other functions. I said I tried the internet once but it was a disappointment. I thought it would be a valuable research tool for a story I was writing on the four-thousand-year-old mummified mountaineer who was discovered in the Austrian Alps, and I searched the internet for *Ice Man*. The computer offered me many returns—*Ice-T*, *the Beatles*, and *The Attack of the Killer Refrigerator* among them. After about an hour of this exercise in futility, I changed my search to *Tyrolean Man* and was rewarded with three documents, one of which—from a San Francisco gay bar's newsletter—told me that the Ice Man was gay. Keith said 'How did they know?' and at once, I could see, wished he hadn't.

I said everything was perfectly preserved. Inside and out. It was all becoming rather delicate, or indelicate, for Bangs at ten in the morning. 'In any event,' I said, 'it put paid to my story idea about an Ice Age man who leaves his clan, his wife, and his children and so on—rather like Jack—and takes off over the mountains.'

'Oh, I don't see why,' said Keith. And suddenly *I* could see. I could see that there were indeed possibilities I hadn't even considered. Keith has this knack. Sometimes I see Keith as the child playing blind man's buff in the long-lost parties of my childhood. He is the blindfolded player who stumbles within an inch of the prize and then goes the other way.

For the rest of the day I tried not to think about the Ice Man implications. It was hard. Just to get through the evening suggested a movie for tonight. Fair to say the lot of them were dumbstruck. 'And I get to choose,' I said. No one argued. '*The Magnificent Seven*,' I said, because I had seen it at about the same age as Felix. Kate went to bed early.

February 12

Not many days to Miles's birthday. I miss Jack's shopping skills, not to mention his gold card. My unique, hand-crafted gifts—the djembe drums and the rainbow socks of global trade—never go down as well as shiny CDs and crisp twenty-dollar bills. You can hear the little bleats of disappointed surprise they elicit. These things never escape me. Miles wants a computer game. No doubt when Jack is better he will go out and spend a lot of money on one and it will be a huge success.

February 13

Thursday. A wet night. Drove Kate to her rehearsal. Sat and read for two hours. Not used to consecutive or coherent thought processes. Felt quite light-headed.

February 14

Valentines from Hettie and Miles.

Kate asked where I had hidden their chocolates. Could not remember.

Felix said, 'Under the—,' realized his error at once, and promised to buy some more.

February 18

Miles's birthday. Eight-year-old boys and puppies have a great deal in common. All organized activities eschewed in favour of hurling themselves upon one another in the middle of the floor. It was difficult to get their attention, even for food.

Jack called in the middle of the mayhem to say happy birthday and that he had hidden a present for Miles in the living room. This intelligence drove them all to new levels of idiocy as they rearranged the furniture in the search. A watch! Miles was ecstatic. He put it on at once and went back on the phone to thank his father, his exact words being, 'Thank you Dad oh thank you Blackguard ate some of the cake again.' And sadly it was true. Lightning does indeed strike twice—thrice in our house—the cake having been savaged by the dog but kindly remodelled by Felix to produce, with the addition of a LEGO man on a piece of string, a fair rendition of the ascent of the North Face of the Eiger. It was a big hit.

I said, 'Give the phone to me, dear, and go back to your guests.'

Jack said, 'That dog ought to be put down. I'll do it myself.'
Now we see your true colours, I thought.

Afterwards, drank a glass of red wine and ate cool, limp pizza amid the wreckage of potato chips and bent straws. Exhausted. Orchestrating the happiness of others is a terrible drain. And were they happy? Was it worth it? One is always left with the question. I was never happy at birthday parties. From the time I noticed everyone was wearing fluffy pink angora but me, to the later days when I lived in terror of having to be kissed by my cousin with the polyp in his nose, parties were a sickening blend of dread and disappointment. And perhaps they are still.

February 19
Woken at five thirty by Miles asking how to stop the alarm on his new watch. Said I didn't know. Did not say he could try throwing it out the window.

He spent all day timing us at our various activities and giving us hourly updates. There were no surprises.

Called Mother to thank her for the money she sent to Miles. Told her all about the cake and what Jack had said he'd like to do to the dog. Mother said, 'Never mind the dog, I should think it's your throat he'd like to slit.' Rather strong language, I thought. No one had mentioned bloodshed.

Pondered the meaning of it all until the long list of my transgressions, omissions, errors, and misdemeanors came into focus. Cock-ups all. I admit it. I shall have myself branded with a hot iron: the words *Mea culpa* in raised welts on my forehead.

·

The play is this week. I shall die of curiosity. Asked Kate, as I dropped her off for her last rehearsal, if she was going to relent and get me a ticket. I said, 'Look, the hair's faded now. I'm innocuous.'

She said, 'Like I care what that means.'

I said, 'Well at least tell me why.'

She said, 'Because you're so, oh...ugh...so...*you* know!'

Well yes. My mother was that way, too. All the women in our family are. But I persisted.

'So...what exactly?'

And she said, 'So...*annoying!*'

Just as I thought. We are all tarred with the same brush. I pursed my lips and said, 'Fine, fine.'

February 21

I am lonely. Have taken to reading the personals page, mauling the columns the way shoppers maul the bins of socks and underwear on Scratch and Save day: Anything I might fancy here? But of course I'm looking through Jack's eyes too as I scan the columns. Which one would he go for, perhaps has already contacted? The one with a thing for leather or the one with an endowment? He might even be in there himself, in disguise, lurking greyly as a fun-loving forty-something into salsa, sumo, and swinging. Good lord. These pages are not the last resort of the lonely. They are a monstrous parlour game for sexual gadflies. A party! No, it is another world I shall never be able to enter. I would never be sure what is code and what is not. Would be too afraid of making a terrible mistake. Have only just realized that DWF does not refer to a person of restricted growth and so is not in bad taste after all. Miles too reads them over his Cheerios. I do not like to make too much of it but I do wonder how much of it makes sense to him. What does he understand by *hunky, funky and all yours*, or *well-endowed and up for fun*? Some of it by any standards is inexplicable. What is one to make of *Gore-Tex kind of gu*y? That is when I start trying to deconstruct the message and get to the subtext. Today I was completely baffled. I'll have to copy this one word for word: *Do you love to wear hats? Let's gather informally for an hour or two of millinery drama—people who love to see and wear hats.* Or did they mean *only hats*? Hope my own passing interest in the hat around Christmas time was not the beginning of a powerful forbidden obsession. Discussed it with Marlene over lunch. Her teenagers, male and female, currently wear knitted caps pulled down over their ears. They look like safe-breakers or perhaps POWs from an old British war film. She asked me why I was reading these pages anyway. She said wasn't I just relieved to be having a break from that whole male / female tussle? *Relieved?* On the contrary, I am desperate. Right now I would tussle with the recycling man.

February 23

Kate's play was last night. She is a hard-hearted young woman and did not relent. I drove her down and dropped her off at the playhouse where parents and grandparents were milling in an anticipatory buzz. Felt another cliché coming on about being never so alone as when in a crowd and would not have been surprised to hear the excruciating strains of 'Downtown' any minute. Took myself and the great abyss of my heart to a dreary romantic comedy at the Capitol but at least I did not have to sit next to any doting parents.

Afterwards went back to the playhouse and waited outside for Kate. Her friend Asta's mum asked me what I thought of the production. It was hard to say since I'd only seen the stage door. I said I thought they'd worked tremendously hard. Tremendously. She said Kate had been just awesome through this whole thing. I said, 'So has Asta. She'll go far.' Asta's mum walked away without a word.

For God's sake. Why didn't anyone tell me what had been going on? Why didn't Kate tell me? Voluntarily sacrificing her role to Asta? Asta slated for surgery. Asta with a potentially terminal illness.

The gist of it was hissed in my ear by a passing parent and followed up with, 'You'd know if you had more interest in your children.' Couldn't make out who it was. Eyes too blurry with sudden tears.

When Kate came out she looked more elated and wonderful and, well, alive than anyone in the movie I'd just watched. I said, 'Kate, you are awesome. I heard what you did. I wish you had—' She said, 'Mum. I don't want to talk about it, all right?'

Such a long drive home.

A phone call earlier in the day from Mitzi at Galeria Toxicana. An invitation to take part in an erotic reading. Never mind that not all of the poets have their own teeth. Hundreds will come to listen in much the same way the nation might tune in to CBC were it to announce an erotic party political broadcast. I should probably write something special and not the usual nonsense from the supermarket aisles.

February 27

Have been meditating on the state of singleness. I have been celibate now, with only one exception, for twenty-nine weeks. Not only that, but the house seems to be slipping into dereliction. Two of the doors are broken, the fridge has stopped, Hettie's window is stuck, the laundry sink is plugged, and the toilet will not flush properly.

Have written a poem especially for the reading. It is based on a newspaper account about a German restaurateur serving sushi on naked models lying on top of tables. It begins with Hood's famous dactylic dimeter, *Take her up tenderly*, and maintains the meter right through to the final words, *drizzle of soya sauce*. I am calling it 'Sushi on Broad.'

February 28

Annie came today to read my tarot. It all seemed to revolve around the man and woman yoked together by a chain attached to iron rings around their necks. Annie pointed out the size of the rings and the fact that both parties could quite easily remove them by slipping them over their heads— if they wanted to. Annie says I must become proactive in removing my ring. She says I am not single yet, only separated. I say I am single. I do not need a court of law to uncouple us. My marriage is annulled. By me. The only authority in a marriage is the will of the partners. Annie on the other hand, in a most unAquarian way, favours litigation. When I began to say that lawyers are superfluous and that the situation of marriage is exactly parallel to the situation of borders and passports, that the earth belongs to me by right of being human and that national boundaries are arbitrary limitations imposed on us by the greedy, she said she could see why Jack left me. She said it was time I joined the real world and had I ever thought of getting help. And then she said another thing. Just as she was getting into her car she stopped and held the door open long enough to say, 'He's seeing Liz, you know. You know that, don't you?'

When she had gone I meditated some more. Crying meditation. There was only one question. How many people know? Liz! It hurt more than anything yet. Liz. From more than twenty years ago. The equivalent of the love of his life, then. Do I feel stupid four childbirths later? No, that is not another question. That is a statement. I feel stupid. A dupe. A stupid dupe.

You can feel wrath getting born. It is like *Alien*. There is something inside. Not in the uterus. In the stomach. In the stomach and clawing to get out.

And it will.

March 1

All right he's gone. Never mind that I heard it from Annie. *I can see why he left you.* Why he left you. Past tense. Not ongoing. Not why he is leaving you, why you are splitting up, or any of that in-process stuff at all. Why you are having a trial separation. Not a present participle in sight. Why he left you. Why you have been left. Done. Finished. Over. Over to Liz to dangle the participles over there. *He's seeing Liz, you know.* Fine. What I've always wanted. Some clarity here. Some light on the picture. Good. He's seeing Liz. At this moment. In the present. So yes. I'm a free woman (have I said that before?). I am putting all thoughts of Jack out of my mind. No. I *have* put all thoughts of Jack out of my mind.

Another birthday (evidence that I too once experienced actual sexual activity in my life) looms. Hettie's. Negotiations have begun in earnest. They have been open and honest. I have agreed to fourteen guests for pizza, a movie, and a sleepover, and Hettie has promised to remember to feed the dog. I think the dog's behaviour is deteriorating. Yesterday neighbour informed me that it had 'mouthed' one of her chickens. Thought 'mouthed' a strange choice of word, bringing to mind a toothless eighty-year-old mumbling milksops. It does not seem to bear any relation to the dog's impressive dental equipment.

I said, 'Oh, dear. Is it all right?'

'Yes,' she said, 'it is now.'

Afterwards, when I told Felix, he said come to think of it, he had seen a lopsided hen down by the gate.

March 2

Erotic Reading at Toxicana. The gallery had accommodatingly hidden its conceptual art behind bedsheets and projected a giant blow-up of a male torso so that the event seemed to be promoting name-brand underwear, or lack of it. The power of the imagination! Mine must be impoverished. Could not imagine any of the poets, apart from a nice young man who was gay, engaging in a single one of the activities they so feverishly described. Come to think of it I could not imagine engaging with any of the poets. There were two tired old stallions reliving their magnificent moments, a student who could not hold anything back but seemed disinclined to leave the stage until the lights went up, a young woman with a taste for violence, and a middle-aged lady in a cardigan who read her stodgy fantasies in the creaky voice of my British primary school teacher reading *Five Get into a Fix*. She had a filthy cold. It was best to listen with the eyes closed. It was best in fact to imagine another poet altogether. Sometimes to imagine another poem. A pity the poet with the soft shoes had to cancel. Mitzi said he was going to come out especially.

But have thought of some more nonsense. *Nudes under Noodles.* Men this time. It is a consolation.

March 4

Saw Matthew S. today. Hettie let him in unannounced. He came to invite Jack and me to a party to celebrate his new breed of pig. He is a busy man with no time for gossip and clearly had not heard. I must have looked very foolish, caught as I was unawares, still holding the baguette I was sawing, unable to think of a response except, 'Oh, Matt, oh, Matt.' He came over to me and took the loaf out of my hands and put it down. I picked it up.

'Don't you want any?' I said.

He took it out of my hands again and put it down again very gently.

'What's wrong?' he said. 'You're troubled.' So I told him. I said, 'Matt, Jack isn't with us anymore,' and then, because he sounded too much like a dead pet, I said, 'We've decided to part.' He seemed so put out I didn't know what to say next so I said, 'Oh Matt,' a few more times and he said, 'Vita.' And then Hettie came in from just outside the door and said, 'Miles is timing you. You've been holding hands for three minutes.'

March 5

Matt called to see if I was all right. He said if I needed anything he would always be there. Matt is one of the staunchest people I know. He said he'll drop by again and make sure I'm okay. Matt is one of the staunchest people I know. I said that already.

Went to select a video for Hettie's birthday.

'Not this one,' I said, reading the back of *Cruise to the Apocalypse*. 'It says, "Warning: violence, explicit language and swearing."'

'Oh, bloody hell,' said Hettie, 'we can't see it.'

March 6

Hettie's birthday. Jack called.

I said, '*Jack!* After all this time! How wonderful to hear from you!'

He said, 'Stop it, Vita. It's important. I really need to talk to you.'

139

I said, 'Get this. You're just going to have to wait until it's convenient. I have a life too and it is crammed with importance. There are important visiting five-year-olds, important regurgitations of strawberry ice cream on the carpet, important near-death experiences with two-pin plugs, important earaches and sudden longings for home in the midst of hilari—'

He said, 'Vita, please…'

'Hettie!' I called, 'Come back and talk to your daddo again.'

Rest of her birthday went by in a flash flood of pop and drinking straws. Remember very little. Mind was somewhere else entirely.

March 7

Called Matt but his son answered. Can't think why I felt I had to put the phone down.

Toilet is broken altogether. The little girls yesterday pumped the handle right off the tank.

March 8

He called. He called! Said he had something to bring over and could he drop by. I said, 'Of course.' I put some coffee on. He is very nice. Staunch. Have always thought he is very nice. We stood in the kitchen a long time performing the diving-in-each-other's-eyes cliché, then he put his arms round me and just in time because I was beginning to think of commercials for telecommunications. He was a big woolly sweater, a warm blanket. He was the pillow to lay my head. Oh, and I had been on my feet for so long. He said he did not like to think of the pain. And that made me moan just a tiny bit. So he stroked my hair a little and then he did his own tiny moaning. Then he said he did not want to hurt anyone and he removed me from his person. Oh. I had forgotten how it's done, who lets go first.

I said, 'Matt, what were you going to bring over?'

He said, 'I can't remember. I'll come by again.'

March 9

Lunacy. He has four children. A son and three daughters.

March 10

Saw Matt in the hardware store. I was checking out the handles for the tank.

He said, 'Vita! Hi!' in a sort of oversurprised way.

I matched that with, 'Matt! Haven't seen you for a while!' and then he was there at my side saying, *sotto voce*, 'I can't bear to think of you doing your own plumbing.'

A dozen retorts sprang to mind. I said, 'Thinking is getting difficult.' And we looked at each other for a considerable time and might have gone on except that an assistant with a stack of plastic chairs came through saying, 'Mind your backs.'

March 11

Lunch with Marlene who wanted to show me some reviews of her new book. The best bits were highlighted. She spread them on the table in a fan. I could not read. I said, 'Marlene, I think I'm having an affair.'

She said, 'Surely you know.' And then, 'Not on the internet, is it?'

I said, 'No, of course not. And yes, I do know. I am.'

'Vita!' she said. 'How wonderful!' She was still looking at her reviews, I noticed. 'What does he write?'

I said, 'He's a farmer.'

'No!' she said, but not with much conviction. She was rifling through her purse. She pulled out a pink highlighter and carefully drew a neon streak through two sentences. 'Missed that,' she said, and then, 'No really! A farmer? Haystacks, dumb beasts, the lush valley, the heave of the sod?'

I said, 'Marlene, sod off. I'm in love.'

She looked up. 'Have you told Jack?' she said. 'He's been telling people you won't talk to him.'

I said, 'Which people?' but she was reading again. She said, 'Listen to this: "Glatter's work gleams through the gloom of late-twentieth-century global consciousness. It glitters."'

March 12

Matt called. Said he had remembered what it was: some chicken manure. I had asked him for some last year. I said it was very kind of him. He said he could bring it over. 'Great,' I said, thinking damn damn damn damn damn. Wanted very much to tell him that Miles was home sick but somehow it seemed a bit fast. Why should he care? Why should I care? Who said anything about jumping into bed?

Sweating with nervous perspiration by the time his truck pulled up. Hoped his farm fragrance would mask it. How to wait for someone you want so much to see? How to greet them with gay nonchalance, or even steady composure, and never a trace of unplumbed sexuality?

'Hi!' I squeaked. 'Miles is home.' Could have died on the spot for my indiscretion except that I saw his smile vanish for a moment. It did, it vanished. He had to paste it back on. Felt better at once.

'Shame.' He smiled. 'Sick?'

I nodded. Smiled. 'Coffee?'

He said, 'Great.'

I said, 'Cream?'

He said, 'Thanks.'

'Sugar?' I said.

He said, 'Sure.'

We didn't say much for a bit. Then he said, 'Okay?'

I said, 'Yes.'

Then I said, 'Thank you.'

He gestured towards the bathroom.

'Toilet?' he said.

'Fixed,' I said.

He said, 'Great.'

He took a sip of coffee and said, 'Hot.'

I nodded. 'Burnt my tongue,' I said.

And then there was nothing more to say for a whole long time.

'Don't let your coffee go cold,' I said.

'No,' he said. 'I'd better be going.' And he got up without drinking it.

Went outside with him. At the truck he turned and dropped his voice the way he had done in the hardware store. He stood very close.

'Vita,' he said, 'I have to tell you. I wanted us to be alone. Together. I was thinking about it the whole way here. I've been thinking about it all week...'

He didn't get any further because Miles began calling from the front door that he felt better and where were his socks.

I said goodbye and went back in.

Miles asked who had come by.

'Matthew S.' I said, and realized he had driven off without leaving the manure. 'He called in to see if we want any chicken manure.'

'Do we?' asked Miles.

'Yes,' I said. 'Lots.'

March 13

'It.' He said he'd been thinking about 'it.' 'It,' us? Or 'it,' it? I think I prefer it.

Miles is back at school.

March 14

A call from Jack today. He wants to meet. He says what he wants to talk about is too important to discuss in an atmosphere of domestic hostility and confusion and antagonism. I said, 'But that is my milieu, darling. It's where I live,' and he said, 'Vita, for God's sake. This is not a joking matter.'

I said, 'I'm sorry, Jack. I'm really, really busy. I'll call you back.' *Jack, darling. I told you. I am having a life. I have joined the company of the present.*

March 19

A black day. Kate came home demanding to go on a ski trip.

'Everyone knows how to ski,' she said. 'They all go with their families. Everyone except me.'

I said, 'Everyone who?'

She said, 'Nicky and Andrea and Courtney and Graham and Darcy. And,' she said, 'Laurie S. is going away next week with her dad and her sisters. For three weeks.'

'Laurie S. is older than you,' I said. 'She probably has a job and pays for the trip herself.'

'No,' she said. 'Her dad's taking her whole family. Her whole entire family for three weeks. And they're pig farmers.'

'Three weeks,' I said. 'That's a long time.'

That is a very long time.

March 22

So April 13 when they get back. I've counted.

March 23

I have to take my mind off it. This weekend have thrown self into a blizzard of wholesome family fun. We have been to the pancake breakfast for the Limpet Preservation Society at the fish dock, swum every day at the Rec. Centre, hosted four visiting Mexican students for a traditional Canadian St. Patrick's Day marshmallow roast, ridden our bikes on the new cycle path, or the psychopath as Hettie calls it (she has a uniquely TV-based vocabulary), shopped for new running shoes, and walked 10k for Guide Dogs for Everyone.

I shall die waiting.

March 24

Hettie fell off slide in school playground.

Life continues dull as ever.

March 25

Same.

March 26

I think I shall go mad.

March 27

I am going to read Ficino. It will be something to do.

Hettie came out of hospital the day before yesterday. She's okay.

March 28

He phoned!! He said he's coming back early. His farm hand has had an accident so he needs to come down from the mountain. 'For the pigs,' he said. His ex-wife has gone up to the ski hill to be with the kids. He will be by himself. Except for the pigs.

March 29
He called again. Said he'd be here tomorrow. I said, 'Good.' This chicken manure thing has gone on long enough.

March 30
Jumped a mile when the phone rang today.

He said, 'Vita.'

I said, 'Matt.'

He said, 'How are you?'

I said, 'Fine. How are you?' thinking: we are true Canadians. In a vast prairie of repressed desire.

He said, 'I'll be right over. No one sick?'

'No,' I said.

Felt sleazy and foolish waiting. Like a cut-out from a fifties magazine. Why not run upstairs and slip on a little black lacy number? The adulterous housewife splashing cologne into the feverishly heaving cleavage. I didn't have either. And no bouffant beehive to tease.

Decided the house was altogether too claustrophobic. Went outside to pull up some weeds.

I know the sound of his truck. He didn't say anything when he got out, just came over and put his arms round me. Well, tried to but the dog nosed him vigorously in the groin.

'Why don't you come in?' I said.

We sat across from each other at the kitchen table and held hands while the dog grumbled underneath.

'I've thought about you a lot,' he said. 'Are you okay?'

'Oh, I'm fine,' I said. 'Fine. Fine.'

Matt said, 'Vita, you and I have a lot in common. Every

time I talk to you it's like connecting up with someone who speaks my language.'

'We don't say much,' I said, wishing it was possibly even less.

He said, 'I just like being with you.'

'I like being with you,' I said.

This could be a rally of Wimbledon standards, I thought. The ball may never stop moving.

'You know I got hurt, too,' he said.

And then—I don't know why—I hit that bloody ball again. 'Tell me about it,' I said.

So he told me in great detail about how his wife had a lover and who did what to whom. And then he said, 'Look at the time.' He kissed me. 'The neighbours will talk,' he said. 'Goodbye.'

'Come tomorrow night,' I said.

He said, 'Tomorrow night.'

April 1

Spent the morning thinking a lot about yesterday's outpouring. Am I his revenge on his wife? Or the consoling bosom. Hadn't planned on being either. He is coming over later. Felix and Kate are at friends'.

April 2

Spread the chicken manure today. It's not very mature and stinks of ammonia. Felix covered his face with a white bandana to take out the garbage and the other three will not go outside at all.

Matt came over at ten thirty last night. Hettie and Miles were fast asleep. He said he'd left the chicken manure outside. This time I did not think I would let him have the ball at all.

'Matt,' I said. 'Let's not talk about the chicken manure. Or your wife. Or the plumbing. Just let's not talk.'

Took him by the hand and went upstairs. Stood for a bit with our foreheads touching, like conjoined twins.

I said, 'Tell me what you're thinking.'

'I think I need some help,' he said. Feared he was going to request some boots and leather routine or even some banana cream pie or, God help us, Viagra, but he said, 'Can you give me a massage? My shoulders,' he added quickly. 'I've been shovelling *all* day.'

'Of course,' I said. 'We'll get really relaxed.' Was thinking warm oils, lotus blossoms, but Matt put his hand in his pocket and said, 'I've got some liniment.' Tried my best not to think of horse handlers.

'Let me put some music on first,' I said. Found some Holly Cole, who is probably lucky enough never even to have heard of liniment. Matt sat on the edge of the bed and stripped off his shirt. Unwelcome suggestion of doctor's offices. Or toddlers playing doctor and nurse. Opened the bottle and caught a familiar smell. The vet! The vet had put something like this on the cat's abscess. Thought of the sheets permanently impregnated with it. I'd never sleep again.

'Let's do it on the floor,' I said, but was saved the trouble for I had chosen the very words that aroused him most. He groaned. I had found his sexual faucet. 'Put the lid back on,' he said. 'Lie down right where you are.'

He was, I must admit, quite energetic for someone initially so fatigued, but for me the whole situation was beyond rescue. Somehow just could not rid the mind of exhausted vets and physical labour. Artificial insemination.

Stayed awake a long time afterwards. Matt slept well. He didn't snore but sometimes he changed rhythm and did an

in-out, in-out snuffle like, well yes, like a pig in potato peelings. Drank three-quarters of the wine and eventually fell
asleep.

In the morning he was gone, and so was the liniment.

April 3

Matt called to say he hasn't been able to sleep or eat. Says he
realized driving back to Whistler that this is the Real Thing.
He is mad at all the wasted time. Said he had to go but he
feels trapped on the mountain. He will call in a few days.

My hands are covered with tiny bumps. Something from
the pigs? Chickens?

April 5

He called to say he is going to come back down, on the tenth.
'For the pigs.' He will be by himself again.

Saw Marlene. She says of course you don't get chicken
pox from chickens and anyway it starts on the chest and
didn't I remember the children with it, or had I forgotten I
had any children, for God's sake?

A barb? From Marlene? My only friend? Probably. She
followed up with another one as she was leaving. 'Thought
of something for your food porn,' she called from the car
window. She knows about the food porn? 'Breakfast sausage!'

But the trouble is I haven't forgotten I have children. Oh I
have not forgotten. They are both the scissors and the glue.
And I love them more than any man. And that is the whole
trouble.

April 6

Jack dropped by to pick up a tire from the garage. He was in a hurry. He said he had swung by late on the first but there was a truck blocking the door. Demanded to know why the yard smells like a latrine. I kept quiet. What happened to his need to talk?

'The tire's at the back,' I told him, 'under the shelf.'

In the garage he began pulling apart my careful midden, cursing each item methodically: broken skateboard, bent tent poles, paint rags, rotting runners, crushed box spilling rusted hardware, frayed doormat, mildewed carpet, two burnt toasters. For making burnt toast? Kept mouth shut.

'So whose damn truck was it anyway? One of Kate's friends?' I didn't answer. Fishing tackle box crammed with hard playdough, stringless tennis racquet, armless lawn chair, legless ironing board . . .

'This place is a dump,' he said. 'Like the yard.' He is not happy with my yard maintenance? Our lives are self-destructing, sliding into a chasm of bottomless black disintegration and he cares about yard maintenance? I pointed out that the kale has never looked better. 'The sod,' I said, since it seemed to be the word of the season, 'is already turned for the potatoes, and I shall soon have manure on the whole vegetable garden.' An unfortunate prompt. He said, 'Shit on the vegetables. They're always full of holes anyway. Look at the rest of this place.' He was standing now where the flower bed used to be. I think he was unhappy with the tangle of dead brambles and the unruly look of last year's leaves heaved up by the new growth underneath. An unruly garden, I thought, is what John Donne loved.

'And who rode through the fence?' he said. Miles's bike was still stuck there, so there was no denying the occurrence but since Felix had been riding it at the time I simply said, 'Not Miles.' There was an unwholesome undercurrent to it all. It was not the garden he was looking at. It was us. It was the heaved-up marriage. Where I saw burgeoning life and riotous growth, he saw entropy. Rampant chaos and disorder.

'I'll deal with it,' I said.

He said,'You won't.' He said, 'You never do. I'll get someone to come in. Every week.'

I said, 'I do not want some mad-eyed anal-obsessive with a leaf blower in my garden.' Urged him to see the reason we have so many leaves in the first place is that we are on all sides surrounded by mad-eyed, etc., etc., blowing their leaves over to us.

He said, 'Fine. You get someone. I'll pay. Just get someone.' He left the subject alone but I know he was not appeased. He kicked the abandoned gerbil cage as he went by and the door fell in. Looked at it lying there after he drove away. Thought perhaps Miles and I might try converting it to an outdoor aviary. Budgies. At least I'd have someone to talk to.

To Bangs for another long overdue cut.

Keith said, 'What happened to your hands?'

I said, 'Too much work in the garden I suppose,' and hid them under the black cape. 'Or worry,' I said. 'Let's change the subject. What are your latest worries?'

Keith said he was not dreaming enough. He said studies show that the average healthy person needs to dream for three to four hours every night. Lately he said he had not been dreaming much at all and had been quite happy about it until he read the study. He said he used to have very vivid and frequent dreams, mostly involving panic attacks—a shop full of customers and all the scissors being taken away in the back of a dump truck, rows of men from Revenue Canada wearing black capes and waiting outside the door, that sort of thing.

I said, 'Kate Pullinger regards dreaming as theatre, her own private theatre of the absurd waiting each night to interpret her life.'

He said, 'Well I bet she's a writer, isn't she? What sort of dreams do you have?'

'Me?' I said. 'I am a much more vulgar and simple soul. My dreams are more like IMAX and involve huge volumes of moving water, Technicolor, and choirs.'

'Always?' he said. 'You must be exhausted.'

I said, 'Well no. It is exhilarating but lately, I must admit, I have suffered one or two really boring re-enactments of my daily life. Such a waste of time.'

Did not tell him that last night I dreamt I was in bed, waiting for M. to come over. In the dream, he arrived, to my great excitement, and then sat down with the kids to play crazy eights. I had to get up, dress, and go make them all peanut butter sandwiches.

April 7

Got someone for the yard today. My good friend Larry is managing a group home for youth with addiction issues. They will come and do a cleanup for a donation. Six of them. A great deal and a good cause.

April 8

Warts. It is warts, I know it is. Made a doctor's appointment for Friday but cancelled all other appointments. Seeing M. on Saturday. The tenth.

April 9

Dreamt I had another baby. There was a party, the throbbing, humming sort of affair with a pounding pulse and carnal energy strobing the room. Dancing with the man I wanted, though I couldn't see him. He was behind me. Noticed a small child crying, so I stopped. Picked it up and dropped out of the dance. Comforted the child. Party swirled on all around. I was the only one being responsible and I was missing all the fun. The others knew to leave it alone.

April 10

A phone call today from the hospital in Squamish. It was Matt. He was there with his ex-wife. She has broken her leg. He is staying there with her this weekend.

Took the children out to dinner. I think I was celebrating.

Miles tells me he is going to be a peer counsellor. 'You know,' he said, 'when kids' parents get divorced they'll come and tell me all about it.'

Felix told me his friend Corey really digs having divorced parents. He gets to stay in both houses and he gets two of everything.

'That's because they're not cheapskates like you and Daddo,' said Kate. 'I don't know how Dad can stand it, living in that hole. It sucks. He hasn't even got his own TV.'

'That's why he likes to comes here,' said Hettie.

I smiled benignly. My children! My children and me and not a bag of chicken manure in sight. Where have I been these last weeks?

Rest of the meal strangely transfigured. Children could say no wrong, do no wrong, though they were, I must admit, bemused by sudden renewal of maternal interest. Could not stop looking at them. Hettie told me to stop staring. I said, 'But how did you get that dreadful scar on your forehead, darling?' She said, 'When I fell off the slide, silly. You took me to the hospital, remember?'

April 11

Spent a remorseful night, mostly awake. Decided I have been driving dangerously close to the edge of the precipice where this family seems to live. Hettie! In the hospital! Of course I remember but I've just been reading back. It's almost as if I didn't care. Didn't care! I love her so much. I love them all so much, but it's real love. At the time, I was in stupid love. In stupid love with stupid Matthew S. And look what we did. Made fools of our stupid lonely selves. Good God. Humans are idiots. Such a narrow escape.

Made an appointment at the Tuesday wart clinic.

April 19

Wednesday. I cannot go out. My hands are still in bandages. I knew I was in trouble as soon as I saw Dr Fell-Cropper in attendance with a flask of liquid nitrogen bubbling and smoking on the desk in front of him. Vincent Price at his peak. Dr Fell-Cropper is past retiring age and his eyesight is worse than mine. He should not be allowed near the stuff—or the patients.

'Now whereabouts are they?' he said. A superfluous question, I thought, to ask of anyone sitting there across from him with fingers like dill pickles on his desk. He was dipping into the flask with his little stick and he pulled it out smoking and hissing. He took another look at my hand.

'Ah, yes,' he said, 'I see.' Clearly a lie. He applied some of the liquid nitrogen to my bare skin.

'This will sting a little,' he said.

'Actually a lot,' I said. 'And you're in the wrong place.'

'Am I?' he said. 'Ah, yes. I see. There it is, now.'

Liquid nitrogen makes you yelp. 'It isn't,' I said. 'It isn't there at all.'

He tried again.

'Look,' I said, 'why don't you try another one?' Thinking, good lord, man, there are enough to choose from. We went on in this fashion for five minutes or so until I said, 'Why don't you put your headlamp on?' thinking, you bat, you stupid old blind bat this is not pin-the-tail-on-the-donkey, you silly old bugger—and his score improved. Somewhat.

The blisters did not come up straightaway. They developed slowly in the course of the evening. By morning some of them had filled with blood so that you might say, if you had a medieval turn of mind, that my hands are now bejewelled, pendant with limpid opals and with rubies. Or you might say I have bubonic plague.

I have wrapped them and shall not be going out.

April 20

Felix has formed a band. He writes songs delivering abuse to the industries that exploit the earth and the governments that encourage them. He has constructed a sound room out of cardboard boxes in the garage and jams there often with his friend. Sealed off from the public gaze. Occasionally, empty pizza boxes fly over the barricade.

My own immurement is more depressing. Spring is depressing. My new exciting life has vaporized like liquid nitrogen. Spring without something—someone—to look forward to is cheerless, like a healthy stir-fry without dessert. Oh and it is dessert I crave since we are having so little of it. Hands still wrapped in the last of the bandages. Very weepy. Me and the hands. Children refusing to let me prepare their meals. In case they catch it. Everyone eating frozen burritos and pizza.

April 22

Had to go out for milk and bread. Hands a little better. Gloves too irritating so have wrapped hands in colourful strips of torn sweatshirt leaving fingers free for making change etc. Hope to be taken for eccentric Vivienne Westwood type.

April 23

The yard crew came today to clean up: five young offenders and Larry in a white minivan. Some needed encouragement to climb out, and one went straight to Miles's swing and sat down shakily, patting at his jacket as if looking for smokes. I said, 'Let's let him stay there,' but Larry was keen to give them all some experience. He did most of the work himself, I noticed, and was exhausted at the end of two hours. But the yard looked better than before and the guys enjoyed the dog, who is now as exhausted as Larry.

April 24

Jack's birthday approaches. The children have their presents ready. Shall invite him up. Summoning the courage to call. Every little action, even the most basic acts of human friendship are fraught now with emotional baggage, real or perceived.

Marlene and I are planning a joint book launch. She is a closet impresario. When opportunities wing their way in her direction, she knows what to do with them. My skills lie in other fields. I expect. She calls me up at breakfast to remind me of the task in hand, or in the evening to update me on developments. She seems surprised when she calls that we are all still eating at eight o'clock and I get the feeling that she is at these times already in her bathrobe while Danny is wiping up the last crumbs of the day before winding the clock and putting the cats out. She once asked me what I do until midnight each night. 'Do?' I said. 'It would be easier to tell you what I don't do.' Sometimes I think I'd like to be Marlene. Often I think I'd like to be Marlene. I'd especially like to go to bed at eight thirty. It is becoming one of my life goals but it may remain elusive. I suspect a genetic flaw in my makeup. I am to be always late and always behind. When opportunities decide to wing their way in my direction I shall not be there yet.

April 25

Took a deep breath and called Jack. Said, 'The children would like to celebrate your birthday on Saturday. Will you come over?' Jack said that was very kind. Of course he would. He was hoping to come anyway to pick up his kayak but that would be a special pleasure. Oh, but we are civilized. Bite each other? Never.

April 26

More exciting news of cells. Miles told us in the car on our way to the Rec. Centre. There are fifty thousand million cells of different kinds in the human body and each human eye alone contains over a hundred million rods. Felix said spiders each have two rows of four eyes. Miles said, 'Oh, yes. I knocked over your science project, Kate, and the fruit flies escaped.' As I had anticipated, a row of volcanic magnitude erupted and continued in the car almost all the way to the Wind-Down Swim.

As the lava roiled, the words "For fuck's sake" inadvertently escaped my lips and pretty soon the expletives were thick as said fruit flies in the air. I glanced in the mirror.

Miles was white-faced, white-lipped. Was afraid that the eruptive atmosphere might push him to the brink of psychic collapse. He might never speak again.

I had had E-NUFF and braked to say so but only got as far as the *E-* when the steering wheel came away in my hands. Had braced against the seat, tensed to bear down on the final syllable when there it was, the steering wheel separated from its column, cables still attached like strings in a severed chicken neck. Kate and Miles shrieked with laughter and grabbed each other in their mirth. Consoled myself with the thought that at least I had brought them together.

April 28

Jack is coming over tomorrow. Kate has promised to bake a cake and Felix has cleared the drive. He offered to make a NO DUMPING sign but I said not all of us would find it funny. Miles has created a birthday card depicting two mutant superheroes clawing each other to bloodied shreds. He is very talented. When you open the card the combatants pop up. One of them has lost an eye. Hettie has painted a picture of herself. She has her arms wide open.

Perhaps Jack and I will get a few things sorted out.

April 30

I do not know how things went the way they did yesterday. Hettie came and woke me this morning, saying, 'Look. There's Daddo out in the kayak.' Went to the window and yes there indeed was Daddo himself, Daddo the man paddling away from the shore with a very determined set to the shoulders. That was at six thirty. It's 9 p.m. now and I have to decide what to do next. What began well enough yesterday degenerated last night into a toxic dump of recriminations. He had come over in the late afternoon. Kate's cake was a superb double chocolate cappuccino, and everyone behaved impeccably. Afterwards we untied the dog and went for a walk through the woods. It had been raining most of the day on and off but the clouds had parted just before the sun went down. Air fragrant with green. Walked a long way without talking. Jack very quiet. Sometimes seemed about to speak but didn't. Neither of us wanted to disturb the peace. When we got back we stood by his car. A great wave of loneliness swept over me and I said things I hadn't planned.

'Don't go,' I said. 'I mean don't go right away. Come in for a drink.' He smiled.

'I thought you'd never ask,' he said.

We went inside and I found a nice bottle of Côtes du Rhône. Dark like a September blackberry. It was as if we'd done this a hundred times before. Actually ...never mind.

Keith once told me there is a chemical component to red wine that triggers a hostile neurone. It may be true. It was after Jack opened the second bottle when I said, 'We could be talking, you know.' The younger kids were in bed and the older two had gone out. It seemed like the moment we had been waiting for to get to grips with The Situation. Jack said it was too late to talk.

I said, 'It's only ten thirty.'

He said no. It was too late, too far down the road. He had wanted to talk. That time he came over and there was a truck in the yard. He really had wanted to talk. He had needed to but now it was too late. Way too late. The thing was decided. He said he had had to work everything out for himself but now he knew what he had to do. He had just needed time.

'Oh, right.' I said. 'Let me know when you've made all the decisions.'

He said it wasn't to do with us. It was his affair.

'As it were,' I said.

He said, 'Vita, how many times. I am not having an affair. Not like some people.'

I said, 'I'm not having an affair either.'

He said, 'Right.' Then he said, 'I just need time. I need to go away for a while.'

I said, 'You are away.'

He said, 'Really away.'

'Fine,' I said. 'But as long as you're here we can talk. And if you're not having an affair and I'm not having an affair we could even go to bed and talk.'

He smiled then and said, 'Before or after?'

I said, 'We're married. We can do it when we want.'

Jack said, 'Or we could have an argument about it.'

'Sex is good for you,' I said. 'We should be employing its healing powers. Let us throw off our egos with our clothes, sit naked in the light of each other's souls.'

Jack said, 'Have you got anything to smoke?'

It took me a while but I managed at last to remember where I had put the Sharpe's toffee tin. It was very old stuff. We turned up the heat and I went to find some candles. When I came back, we spread a blanket down and lit them, then we undressed, switched off the light and sat across from each other. Jack lit up. 'We need an ash tray,' he said.

I put on a robe and went to find one, came back, disrobed, sat down, and we started again. After a little while Jack said, 'Are you sure this isn't tea?' He said, 'I think we should open another bottle of wine.'

I got up and put on my robe again. Jack got into bed while he waited. It wasn't my fault the cork broke. Miles had been picking bits out of the top for his combustibles experiment. By the time I got back with the wine and the glasses Jack was fast asleep. So I woke him.

'What do you mean get up?' he said. 'Look, you drew blood.' And he wiped his mouth. 'It's the middle of the night.' Then I think he said, 'Bloody vampire,' but I ignored it.

'So go and find Liz,' I said. 'She might be able to keep you awake.' The dynamics of marital hostilities are so predictable. A point is always reached when combatants fling aside their elegant fencing foils and start to throw the furniture around.

He said, 'It's two fucking thirty. Do you think I'm crazy?'

I said, 'I am the crazy one around here so look out. I'll call her and tell her you're coming.'

'What are you talking about?' he said. 'She's out of the country.'

'Oh, really,' I said, everything suddenly becoming horribly clear, present, like a dead fish on the sand when the wave washes out. 'That explains everything. Especially why you're in my bed. *My* bed. The one you don't sleep in anymore. Not unless Liz is away. Gosh darn, it's lonely without her. Think I'll just mosey on back to the little woman.' We called each other some less than flattering names and then the dog, sensing bad vibrations, began to howl. Miles woke up and came in saying he had an earache. Hettie woke up and said Miles had woken her. It was about three thirty when we all settled down again, Jack in the kitchen with a blanket wrapped round him, the rest of us in our beds.

It was not a long night. I got up early when Hettie came in the second time. She said Miles was throwing up. That was when she said she had seen Daddo out in his kayak. 'Why is Daddo out there?' she said.

May 1

Spent yesterday washing sheets and nursing a vicious headache. Strangely dizzy too as if I've been turning my head constantly to find Jack. My whole life, like a gerbil's, is a metaphor. Miles threw up everywhere he went. Fortunately Miles is a good patient. When the worst is over he simply pulls the covers over his head and retires into oblivion until his body tells him it is time to leap up and start raiding the fridge again. Hettie spent most of the day at the window looking out to sea. Told her he would be back before dark. Empty reassurances have a habit of turning into betrayals.

At nine thirty called his apartment but there was no answer. Didn't really expect one because you don't kayak into town. It seemed sensible to make a few more enquiries before assuming that he had met a watery end.

Pender Island seemed the most obvious destination. Two possibilities, Annie or Liz. Called Liz's place first because what if he had lied. 'Out of the country' might be just a decoy, code for otherwise occupied or having a headache. If she answered I would say the children wanted to say good-bye to their father. Forever.

A house sitter answered. She was sorry, she said. Liz was in Brazil.

So Annie? A thought occurred. Maybe *always* Annie. Maybe Liz was just a decoy. It was Annie after all who told me about her in the first place. Why would she do that? And it was Annie he went to last fall. Annie and Jack. Not Liz and Jack. Not Daz and Annie. Never Daz and Annie. Annie and Jack. Jack and Annie. It made such sense.

Had to sit down and stop shaking before I could dial. Took a deep breath and tried not to sound like a Valkyrie coming down the wire.

'Annie?' I said. Very measured, very controlled. 'It's Vita. It's okay. I know about it.'

She said, 'Well you probably do. We're trying to be very out about it. But you don't have to sound so straight. It's the nineties, Vita.'

It was like the TV without the cable. I could see a kind of picture, but not the one I'd seen before.

'Oh, I'm sorry,' I said. Why does everyone know what's going on except me? 'I'm sorry. Did I sound like that? I'm just a bit stressed. You know. PMS. Something. What I meant was I'm pleased for you.'

Annie said, 'Well thank you. It's always good to pass on good thoughts. It builds karma.'

'Have you seen Jack?' I said.

Annie said, 'No. I was going to ask you the same thing. Mitzi wants some help with the books, don't you, Mitz?'

And I heard Mitzi's voice, very sleepy, very close, say, 'Mmm.'

Sat and considered the state of play and in the end called Marlene.

'No,' she said. 'You should not call the coast guard. There are any number of places he could be. You don't drown, Vita, in a dead calm sea. You don't just roll over and go under.'

I heard Danny say something and I knew that they were in bed too and he was sitting next to her trying to read his book.

I said, 'What did he say?'

Marlene said, 'Nothing. He's just being an asshole.'

'What's he saying?' I said. 'He's saying, *Not unless you want to*, isn't he? Is that what he's saying? It is, isn't it?'

Marlene said, 'Sort of.'

The nice young woman at the coast guard was very apologetic. Said there was not a lot they could do at night anyway but they'd have their patrol boat take a look around all the same and they'd put out an alert to boaters in the area. She said not to worry. Cases like this, the paddler is usually holed up somewhere safe until morning. But she'd take the details anyway. Went to bed about twelve and slept fitfully.

Woken at six thirty this morning by Constable Trudy. She had a Constable Retchett with her. She said he was just starting out and would it be all right if he asked me a few questions. It was routine. Constable Retchett was everyone's idea of a Mountie and no one's. He could have made a living selling aftershave. I moved the cat and settled them at the breakfast table. Then I made them coffee: black with two sugars; white with one and just a tad of skim milk. They both said it was very kind of me. I thought so too. Constable Retchett took down Jack's name, birthdate, occupation, and citizenship. Then he took down my name, birthdate, occupation, and citizenship.

He said, 'And Mr Glass resides at this address?'

I said, 'He did.' He raised an eyebrow.

'He has an apartment,' I said.

'And he lives there,' said the constable.

I said, 'Yes. I guess.'

'And, er, Mr Jack Glass is your husband?' Constable Trudy reminded me of my days in England playing netball. I would run up and down the side of the court like a crazy terrier behind a fence and eventually snag the ball only to throw it back where it had come from.

'Well yes. And no,' I said.

'He is not your husband?' said the Constable Retchett.

I said, 'Yes, I suppose he is.'

Constable Retchett said, 'But I take it you and Mr Glass are separated.'

I said, 'We're just not living together.'

'I see,' he said.

He drew a thick black line across the form and then he turned the page. I saw the microbyte of a glance that zipped between the two officers.

'Ms Glass, your husband left at what time yesterday morning?'

'At about six thirty.'

'Did he say where he was going?'

'No.'

'You didn't ask him?'

'No.'

'Did you speak to him at all?'

'No, actually I didn't see him.'

'You didn't see him?'

'No, only when he was already out on the water. It was early.'

'Ms Glass would you say your husband was an experienced kayaker.'

'Yes, I suppose so.'

Miles who was on his second bowl of cereal to refill his emptied stomach said, 'He went out in it all the time.'

Constable case-for-the-prosecution Retchett turned his beady eye on Miles and said, 'All the time?'

'Well not all the time,' said Miles. 'Only after a fight.'

Constable Trudy had her hand up to her face and was pretending she had an itchy eye. Her protégé didn't seem able to speak for a moment or two. 'Did Mr Glass usually say where he was going, when he went out in his kayak?'

'No, never,' said Miles.

I said, 'Miles, will you go and get ready for school?'

But it was a losing battle, for Kate, who had just come in from the shower, said, 'He never told us anything. No one ever knew where he was.'

Constable Retchett swivelled to take her in but for some reason could not seem to formulate a question.

'But he was here last night?' said the terrier.

'Yup,' said Kate. 'He comes here to watch TV and then he goes away again.'

'So this is not unusual behaviour for Mr Glass?' said the terrier.

I said, 'But he's been gone all night,' and looked to Constable Retchett to do his duty. But Constable Retchett was staring at Kate and her hair wet from the shower and now dripping down her back. Knew that I was going to get about as much interest out of him now as a little old lady who had had her purse stolen. He wrenched his eyes away from Cindy Crawford.

'You were saying, Ms Glass?'

'I was saying he's been gone all night.'

Constable Retchett made his jaw go sort of crooked and looked down at his lap. Constable Trudy dropped her chin down a little so that she was looking at me under raised eyebrows. She pinched in one corner of her mouth and didn't say anything. She just looked: *And you say you left this purse, the one with the five hundred dollars in it, in a phone booth?*

Well brusque was the only response to that sort of look. I said, 'Well. If you have everything you need for now, I'll show you out.'

But Constable Trudy's radio was talking to her and she was seeing herself out in a hurry. Constable Retchett was shuffling and reshuffling his two pages of notes.

'I'll see him out,' said Kate. 'I'm just leaving. Follow me.'

Called Jack's apartment again when the children had gone to school. Had a blistering speech searing the tip of my tongue but even though I let the phone ring and ring there was no answer.

Called his office at 9 a.m. sharp. Message on his machine said: *You've reached Jack Glass. I'll be out of the country for a while. Leave me a message or press one to speak to my assistant.*

He paddled out of the country?

I pressed one. His assistant's machine said: *Hello. The office is closed for the next three weeks. Clients who wish help should contact Glen Glottentrot at the following number—*

I called Glen Glottentrot. Glen's machine said, *Hi. You've reach—*I put the phone down.

May 2

Glen Glottentrot's machine called me back. It left me instructions on the use of its extensive menu.

Marlene came round. To straighten me out, she said. She said there were two possibilities. 'He's run off with Liz, or else he can't live with himself anymore and he's ... you know...paddled off the event horizon.'

I said he might have told me.

'That should tell you something in itself,' she said. I waited for her to tell me what it was. I am not always very quick.

'It tells you,' she said patiently, 'in case you didn't get it the first time, that he doesn't want to have anything to do with you. He is cutting you off from his affairs.'

'His affairs,' I said.

Marlene said, 'Probably.'

'Like a gangrened limb,' I said.

She said, 'Yes. If you like.'

'But we had sex,' I said.

'You didn't?' she said, sounding interested.

I said, 'Actually no, but we were just about to.'

She said, 'Doesn't count. No,' she said, 'you've got to face it. He has a plan of his own. And it doesn't include you, darling.'

She asked if I had called his assistant. She said we should try her home number. I said I didn't know it. 'What's her name?' she said. It took a while. There are two and a half pages of Mitchells. Some of them are very friendly and some sound as if they have irritable bowel syndrome. Finally just before lunch we got a lead. 'Oh, 'Carson?' Mr S. Mitchell said. 'Yes, she's my granddaughter. No, you can't speak to her. She's in Hawaii.'

Marlene said, 'Now there are three possibilities.'

I said, 'Marlene, you really think so? His assistant? If we are having a life crisis here at least let it be original.'

Marlene said there is no such thing. It's all biochemical fizzing and if that upset me I needed to find a support group for victims of mid-life banalities.

No consolation at dinner either. Hettie would not stop asking about Jack. Truth and lies, truth and lies. And what about evasion? In the scheme of things it is rather like heaven, hell, and purgatory. When they ask me questions I direct them round the corner to evasion. You'll get to the truth eventually, you will, dear, only not just yet.

I said, 'He is just taking a break from everything.'

She frowned at her peas.

Kate said, 'He's having an affair. You're so slow.'

Felix said, 'Make everyone feel good, why don't you?' He said Daddo wouldn't do that. He said he probably stayed out too long and got hypothermia and didn't notice when the *Queen of Esquimalt* came up behind him and mowed him down. He said, 'You know what they call those yellow kayaks, don't you? Speed bumps.'

Hettie laughed and then she started to cry.

Miles left the room.

I said, 'Felix, I've had just about enough of you.'

He said he was only trying to cheer everyone up.

May 3

Annie came by on her way to the gallery to see Mitzi. She said Marlene had told her what had been going on. I have the answer, she said. 'We'll do your tarot.'

We made some tea and she laid out the cards. She assumed a look of serious concentration like a wartime radio operator and she manipulated the cards, in a way that, had it been crazy eights, I'd have called cheating. The Hanged Man I noticed was rather central to the whole affair.

'All is in process,' Annie said. 'There is no cause for concern or intervention. Jack has his own plan.' And there was the Devil card again with the man and woman chained together at the neck. 'And you still wear your neck ring,' she said. 'Jack has slipped his but you choose to wear yours. You are linked but not linked,' she said. 'Patience and love are the keys to the dungeon, the keys to freedom.'

I said, 'What about truth and lies?' She picked up the unused part of the pack and fanned the cards until she came to the World: the naked woman dancing in a wreath of flowers, the emblems of the four seasons surrounding the whole.

'The thing about Truth,' she said, 'is that it is hardly ever revealed. But you will know when it is because it will be without veils. And it will always be solitary. When you know the Truth there will be no one to tell it to. All will be one.'

In her garbled way she's right. We are all alone. Together. We cannot manipulate each other's lives or perhaps even our own and if we try it is a door to disaster.

'And the Hanged Man?' I said.

'You notice he is hanged by the foot,' she said. 'He is, to use the ancient terminology, baffled.'

May 4

Tried to assuage guilt and make up for my distracted

parenting by taking Hettie and Miles to the circus. Drove down with considerable misgivings, all my ethical fixtures in disarray. It was the last show to feature performing animals, for which I was glad, and would not have taken them at all, but Hettie had cried with broken-hearted longing to see a real live elephant and neither of the children had ever seen a circus or smelled the dusty, woody, metallic, dieselly, greasy, sweaty, dungy smell. It seemed like a gap in their experience though I know that, for their children, the fact of never having experienced a circus will be neither here nor there. The idea of the animal circus will have passed into an illustrated volume of historical entertainments alongside bear-baiting and public hangings. And they will be glad of that. They will have their own dilemmas to face.

We were almost there when I thought we passed Jack going in the other direction. My stomach tightened. I waved like a lunatic. It is like seeing an old boyfriend, I thought, a lost lover who can still make your heart turn over. Imagined his car pulling into the parking lot. He would have made a U-turn and followed me down.

Jack! I would say, and go over. He would roll down his window and then I would lean in and kiss him. And Jack would say, *God, Vita. Sometimes it's hard to keep going in the opposite direction.*

I'd put my hand on his and say, *I have to go. I need to get the tickets.* And he would say he would call and explain everything and I would say that would be really nice.

Later, I cried when the elephants came in. Trapped in their bulk they are so sad. I think they know we love them despite our inexplicable behaviour and that is why they do not step on us. Shared the thought with Miles. He said no. It was because the trainer has a poky thing.

'Well,' I said, 'circuses always make me sentimental.' I could not bear to watch the bears at all. Someone had dressed them in schoolgirl mini-kilts and ties.

On the way home Miles said the best act was the motor-cyclist. 'Wasn't it, though?' I said. 'Far more thrilling than the sad animals. But wait till you see juggling with chainsaws. That's *really* exciting.'

'It will probably make you semi-mental though,' said Hettie. I said it probably would.

That is what I am waiting for. A U-turn. I hate the way a crisis turns everything into a cliché. I want to turn back the hands of time.

May 5

Followed the phone instructions on Glen Glottentrot's answering machine and took the tortured route to his assistant. She said yes, Glen Glottentrot was dealing with Mr Glass's affairs while he was on sabbatical. She hoped he was enjoying it.

May 6

Hettie said she saw a kayak at Meg's house. I said it was probably Sue's. 'Sue's a kayaker, too.'

Sue is a kayaker, too. Am I dense?

No. Surely not Sue. Hettie will see Jack's kayak every-where now. It will be like seeing the face of a dear one in a crowd—while his woolly hat still sits in the basket in the hall like a faithful pet waiting for his return.

May 7

I am the one lost at sea. Feel as if everyone is drifting apart from me. Flotsam. Flotsam all of us, on the surface of a heaving sea. Slipping away on the glassy swells.

Ruby called from England this morning to say she has found the answer: Latin dancing. She has purchased a tight red dress and joined a club called Salsa-cha! I said I was very happy for her but perhaps I would call her back later because it was only 3 a.m. here. She apologized. Did she wake Jack? I said, 'No, no. He's...no.'

Did not get back to sleep for a long time. I know I should have told Ruby. Mother, too. It is hard conducting conversations in the bright voice I used to have. Hard holding on. But I do not want any long-distance therapy sessions. It was a long, lonely night. When I finally drifted off, I dreamt about the gates of heaven. They looked like the entrance to the VIA Rail terminal. All my friends were going through carrying portfolios. I knew what was in them: registration forms for dance classes. But I had no portfolio. Stood at the gates and watched them disappear down a long track. When I looked at my hands I was holding a bunch of ear candles.

Wondered when I woke up about the meaning of this. I am a good listener? I am not a good listener? Called Annie to ask her. She said, 'You are certainly not a good Jungian. The meaning is clear. Your friends are searching for the secret of existence. You, the artist, do not search with them. You search within. You would like to call them back but they have no ears for you.' Then she said. 'And by the way, you know it's only seven-twenty, don't you?'

The rest of the day very thought-filled. Drove downtown without any music, the better to think. Is everyone searching for Truth? Is everyone baffled? Have felt a good deal calmer about Jack's disappearance since I have tried to cultivate patience. Everyone must work out her, his own destiny. But

172

still. Cannot equate a New Age search for Truth with the complexities of tangling legs with a short Latin man.

I looked in on Bangs as I passed on my way to the library. It was looking very bare. Keith offered me a coffee. He said he had sold all the paintings. He said the world was hungry for art. I said, 'It is starving. Look how people cast about for food for the soul.'

I told him about Ruby. 'People everywhere are searching,' I said. And I wondered, though not aloud, if that is what Jack is doing. Not eloping at all. 'Men,' I said. 'Especially in mid-life—' Then I coughed a bit to hide the fact that my voice sounded a bit strangled.

We discussed this searching thing at some length, ranging over astrology, channelling, Stonehenge, and drumming in the woods.

Keith said, 'What about your children? What do they think of all this New Age stuff?'

I said, 'It's not for kids. The kids are okay with their souls. Kate feeds hers with music. And Felix is going to take his to Australia as soon as he can. Not to search. Just to be.'

'What did you say to that?' said Keith. 'Great,' I said. 'I asked him if I could go along, too.'

Keith was appalled. 'You were supposed to react,' he said. 'Say things like, "Over my dead body" and "How're you planning to get there, kiddo? On your bike?" You know all that stuff,' he said. 'You're the parent.'

'But it is a good idea,' I said. 'Better than school. Anyway,' I said, 'You'd learn so much. *I'd* like to.'

Keith said, 'You'd really like to do that?'

I thought not but I said, 'Yes. I really, really would.'

Keith shook his head and said, 'I'm having trouble with that. You really should start learning to lie.'

.

Arrived home to find the gerbil cage repaired and reinstated in Felix's room. Poked about inside and found two babies small enough to have spontaneously generated from the sawdust. From the science lab, I suppose. He'd better take them to the Outback when he goes.

May 8

Hettie announced she and Miles want to join Little League. I said she was too young and the uniform would be too big and it was too far to drive and it took too long to play and I was too busy and it was too expensive. She kept glancing at Miles as I spoke. He was her heavy hitter.

'Daddo would let us,' he said.

Marlene came round with the local paper. Said her book had not arrived yet, 'But look at this.' She showed me a full-page spread. 'They called you, apparently, to set up an interview,' she said, 'but you weren't in so they gave me double space.'

'How lucky is that,' I said.

May 9

Mother's Day. Kate and Felix both camping. Miles in tears because he left his present at school. I suggested he help Hettie fix breakfast in bed. Such a nice lie-in.

May 10

Went to register for Little League. A windy day. Everyone was cold. We lined up at tables that had been set up outside. Papers blowing everywhere. Was processed, when it was my turn, by a blond woman with parrot earrings.

'Birth certificates,' she said. 'Take the forms home to read. Sign here, here, here, here, and here.'

'Goodness me,' I said jovially, 'this sounds like serious business.' Nobody smiled.

Parrot earrings said, 'Fundraising. You're down for bingo. Saturday the twenty-first. Nine p.m.'

I said, 'Who put me down?' thinking, *I'll kill her*.

She said, 'It's automatic. Same as the concession.'

Konsession? Was ist Konsession, bitte? Exempt myself on grounds of foreign nationality? Decided to try to be friendly instead and said, 'I like your parrots.'

'They're angels,' she said. 'And I've got you down for french fries every Wednesday night'—she handed me the sheaf of indemnity forms—'for the next six weeks.'

Took Hettie to Dusty Sue's to play with Meg. Hettie was right: Jack's kayak. There is no mistaking it. Blackguard's four-claw signature streaked across the bow. So Dusty Sue? Really? A fourth possibility? In a jumble of entwined limbs and woolly socks, a dozen scenes of hale outdoor adultery competed for the screen in my head. 'Oh, yeah,' said Sue when I asked. 'Jack left that for my boyfriend while he's away. Real kind of him.'

'Oh,' I said in a vague and hopeless way. 'Oh.' And my brain fog must have been apparent because she continued.

'Well you know he came round, Jack, that is, the other Sunday? I guess you knew that. So I said I'd help him out, you know, with a ride back down to his apartment.' Felt the beginnings of that chill sense of exclusion that comes from knowing you are not it; you have no role: neither confidante nor consolatrix. But then she added with a certain kindness and warmth and nothing like pity, 'I don't expect he wanted to bother you. You know.' She put her arm round me.

An act of kindness can be devastating when you're low. Suddenly saw the world peopled with men and women all struggling with great knotty problems of their own, all with their backs to one another, all so intent. So alone. I gave Sue the sort of smile a dental anesthetic induces and made a few strangled noises that I hoped she would recognize as gratitude.

May 11

Went to Scanners to see if they have any news of my book.

'No,' said the girl behind the desk. 'Afraid not.' I could not help noticing the large cartons beside the counter.

'It would have only just arrived if it was here.' I offered a meaningful glance in the direction of the boxes the way Blackguard looks at his food bowl when it's empty.

'Afraid not,' said the girl again. 'Those are Marlene Glatter's.'

Went home and phoned her to relay the good news.

May 12

Annie came round, unannounced as always. She is moving in with Mitzi but is not sure when. She is waiting until Venus enters her house after the full moon. She had a van full of hand-me-downs for the kids including a skateboard and a computer. I said, 'Annie you are always distributing material wealth wherever you go. You are like the reverse of a travelling salesperson.' I like this about Annie. She is doing her best single-handedly to undermine the capitalist economy. The model economists have confected for us out of thin air is like a car without wheels, a useless fabrication. Worse than useless. We are shut in the garage with it and the engine is running. If we all behaved like Annie we might eventually switch it off.

She sat down and offered to read our tarot with her new feminist pack, the cards of which are circular. Eventually even Miles was drawn in. Watched with admiration as she engaged each of my children. Noticed that they attended to the readings with all seriousness, though, had I tried it, they would have dismissed me outright as a demented hippie.

'It is a game,' she said. 'Like life. You make it up as you go along.' Admired her even more for seizing the moment when she saw she had their attention. 'Only three rules in life you have to remember,' she said. 'Only three rules and they must never, ever be broken. Brush your teeth, have safe sex, and eat a carrot every day.'

May 18

Called Torrance the environmentalist organizing the Islands Festival that we shall attend after the launch. Like Hornby, it will be a trip. We will enter a colourful time warp where ponytails are long and grey and people address each other as 'man' and only the weed moves with any speed.

He said yes everyone was welcome, even the dog. We can camp in his field. Everyone seemed pleased with that, except Kate. She said, 'Environmentalists suck.' I said someone in the audience made a similar remark to a well-known performance poet while she was performing her work and the poet replied, 'Poets suck harder.' Said I'd like to get a bumper sticker made and attribute the quote in the bottom right-hand corner where born-agains put chapter and verse. Kate said, 'What are you talking about? No one's *listening*.'

May 21

Still no word from Jack.

And still no book. Launch is in ten days' time.

Everyone asking if they can do jobs for money to spend at the festival afterwards. I said there will be nothing to buy. The people there are all wearing the same tie-dye they wore in '74.

Everyone said, 'Cool.'

Hettie said, 'There will be ice cream.'

I said, 'Yes. Guar gum and soy curds. They look after their health.'

'And drugs,' said Felix. 'There will probably be drugs.'

I said, 'You buy, you die.'

Jack, if you've any heart at all come back. Come back now and rescue me.

May 25

Kate's birthday. He called. He's there, too. Brazil! He called from Brazil. He's up the bloody Amazon. Her bloody father. It is the end. It is the absolute end. 'What the bloody hell are you doing in *Brazil*?' I said. 'I suppose you're in Brazil *not* having an affair. With Liz.'

He said, 'Not now, Vita...'

'Not ever, darling. Not fucking ever. Never. This is it,' I said. 'It's too much.'

He said, 'Vita, I'll explain everything, I will. Only not right now. This is Kate's call.' I hesitated. I had enough adrenaline pumping to tackle a whole gang, a whole squad of delinquent mid-lifers and their therapists. But what could I do?

Went to the bottom of the stairs and coo-eed. 'Kate, darling! Your daddo's on the phone!'

'Tell him to hang on,' she said. 'I'll be right down.'

Relayed her message sweetly and left the receiver dangling against the wall. With any luck she would be waiting for her toenails to dry.

God.

Did not ask her what he said. Up the bloody Amazon! Do not want to know. He is finished. Gone. Out of my life forever. Forever. Done with. Shall focus on the children. Shall devote myself to their every need, their every want. Shall become the Poor Clare of motherhood. My children will be my raison d'être.

We had to celebrate Kate's birthday without her. She took off for a Flaming Lips concert in Vancouver and is staying overnight at a friend's house. Drove her to the ferry feeling crushed with responsibility. Wanted to give motherly advice on the way, talk to her on the way about personal and sexual safety but it was impossible. She has glimpsed the open road. She would not even let me tell her where the bus stop was for the return trip. Worried about her out late at night in her silver sandals. But perhaps she would not wear them. She had a ninety-pound backpack with her.

Felix is in a foul mood. He says Kate gets to go places and he doesn't. He is going to leave home.

I said, 'Soon?'

Publisher called to say I will not have a book in time for the launch. They are making a mock-up for the occasion. 'Ah,' I said. 'I thought for a moment you said something else.' The plan is this: my cover is to be wrapped around the body of another book: *The Politics of the Satiated Society*, I think she said. 'No one will know it is not the actual book.' I am to slip some poems inside for the purpose of the reading and no one will be any the wiser. 'Great,' I said.

Hair is a mess. Less a mock-up than a mockery. Must do something by Saturday.

May 26
Annie dropped by again. She went straight to the kitchen

and made tea with a raspberry leaf tea bag she had brought with her and alerted us all to the fact that we were in the presence of a menstruating woman. 'You've been warned,' she said. But Miles had quickly vacated the room. She had come to pick up the tarot she left last week. Asked if I wanted a quick one. I declined. When you can see the pouring rain you don't need a weather forecast.

Before she went she gave us a set of nesting tables painted with the coats of arms of the western provinces and an inflatable neck support like a miniature toilet seat to wear when travelling. Will need to rethink my ideas on the new economy if this kind of thing continues.

May 27

Dropped children off at baseball game and discovered I was expected to stay despite unseasonably cold weather. Parents are supposed to watch and not swan off to poetry readings as I was doing. Told the Team Mum I do not watch sport of any kind.

'You don't support your children?' she said. 'I'm shocked,' she said. 'Frankly.'

'I don't expect they mind,' I said. 'I wouldn't have liked my mother to watch me miss a goal.'

She stared a bit and then she said, 'We don't have goals.'

I looked around in vain for a rogue cougar to wrestle her to the ground and tear her throat out. I said, 'I see.'

Was particularly unhappy driving into town. Felix is right: I am a wuss. I care what people think. My soul, which would otherwise be blooming like a Japanese plum tree, is constantly being withered and blasted by society's frost. Yet another reason to withdraw from the world.

May 28

Another game. Could not with decency absent myself again. Took a notepad and pen so that I could write to Mother but was too embarrassed to bring it out. Several generations of players' families filled the bleachers. All paying attention. Some of them had cushions and blankets, a white-haired gentleman was watching through binoculars, and all had a repertoire of praise and blame beyond my powers of invention. 'Good' was high on the list, as in, 'Good eye!' 'Good going!' 'Good swing!' 'Good arm!' and 'Good leg!' 'Way to' was equally popular, with 'Way to go!' 'Way to wait!' 'Way to stay cool!' and even 'Way to fool them!' Felt conspicuously silent. Eventually, when a little fellow hit the ball a respectable distance, I tried: 'Good strike!'

'That was a hit,' said the large woman next to me.

'Yes,' I glowed. 'Great, wasn't it?'

'A strike is when you miss,' she said. It took me a minute. When I got it I was more tongue-tied than before and spent the rest of the game in shamed silence.

'Do you like it when everybody yells?' I asked Miles later.

'Not really,' he said. 'It puts you off. But it doesn't matter anyway,' he added after a minute or two. 'We can't hear what you're saying.'

May 30

To Bangs for a last-minute appointment before the launch in town tomorrow. Bemoaned the fact that appearances matter. Keith didn't bite. Understandably. I am not blessed with tact.

'You know,' I said. 'The beauty myth?' Digging myself deeper.

'Well they don't matter to you, do they?' said Keith. A bit uncalled-for I thought.

I said, 'Of course they do. But we all have such a double standard. We all swear we don't judge by appearances but we're sure everyone else does—so we all keep the beauty industry afloat.'

There was an uncomfortable silence. Both of us avoiding more provocation. Then Keith said, 'Well let's just blame Barbie again.'

After that we turned with relief to the Middle East.

May 31

The day of the book launch. Also my day for the concession. Not a happy alignment. After three hours in the afternoon serving burgers and onion rings, came home smelling like a Full Meal Deal. Worse, Blackguard had got into the garbage. Cleaned it up and put pizzas in the oven for the kids. None of them interested in the launch. They are happily staying in with a movie. Barbarians. Dog regurgitated a half-digested Tetra Pak and a chicken wing in the middle of the living room floor. Cleared that up too and served the pizza. Neighbour called to say there was garbage all over his lawn again. I said, 'I shall send a child over at once.' To set fire to your garbage can. Did not feel composed. Virginia Woolf said Life, if it is to be compared to anything, must be compared to being blown through the Tube at fifty miles an hour. I think it bears a pretty good resemblance as well to being dragged through the town by a crazed steer. What hope is there of presenting a sparkling public image from the end of a manure-caked rope? Blood in your nose and grit in your hair. Marlene and Danny were to come and pick me up at 6:40. Had just made it into the bathroom to change at 6:31 when the phone rang. A stranger's voice said, 'Ms Glass? How are you tonight? My name's Travis. I'm with—' I said, 'We don't have any carpets.' Dragged some clothes on. Black. Everything black.

No time to start being creative. God, where *is* Barbie when you need her? Managed to get one contact lens in, dropped the other in the soap dish. Decided to go without. Checked for efficacy of single lens. Pleased to find that I had created my own bifocals. Could spot Felix's Hacky Sack over on our neighbour's roof *and* read the parts per million of toxins in the toothpaste tube. Phone rang again. It was Marlene. Wanted to know if I was ready. 'It is six thirty-five,' she said. 'We will be at your door at six-forty.' I said, 'I know that. You are a very punctual person. I on the other hand am still trying to be. Now I really have to go.' 'Six-forty,' she repeated. Thought, 'It will be in a minute.'

Almost ready when Hettie and Miles came in to demand arbitration in their latest dispute: whose turn was it to have the remote control. Suppressed the first response that came to mind, and said instead, 'I know. Why don't you toss for it?' 'We haven't any money,' Miles said but Hettie, easily distracted, was now in the closet looking for some shoes for me. 'High heels,' she was saying, 'because you're going to your lunch.' 'Launch,' I said. 'Launch.' She emerged in a flurry of dust balls with some old familiars from the very back.

I said, 'Those? Those are late seventies.'

Kate came in and said, 'Cool. Can I have them?'

I said, 'Not yet,' and teetered out.

Hettie said, 'Mum! Mum! Before you go ... ' Hettie is always full of love. Teetered back, vertigo severe now. She flung her arms round my neck, put her lips to my ear and whispered, 'Bring me back some cake.' I said, 'Of course. Cake for everyone. Wish me luck.'

'No,' Kate shouted, 'don't say that! Tell her to break a leg.'

Miles was appalled at the malevolence of the suggestion and began telling her she wouldn't get any cake. Could hear the beginnings of a new dispute as I left.

Got outside just as Marlene and Danny rolled up in Danny's mother's big black car. I got in. Marlene and Danny too were wearing black.

'Look at this,' I said. 'It's a funeral.'

Marlene said, 'Yes. Oh, yes. It's perfect. Stop the car, Danny.' He stopped the car and she leaned over and whipped the purple silk handkerchief from his top pocket.

'What the fuck?' said Danny. Marlene got out and tied it for a pennant to the aerial and then got back in.

'Now put on your dark glasses,' she said. 'You look the part.'

'That had better be a proper clove hitch,' said Danny. 'That's raw silk.'

We started off again. Marlene said, 'Perfect.' Danny shot her a sidelong glance and muttered something about a fucking chauffeur. Marlene came back at once with something about fucking a chauffeur. Watching them both fling poison gave me a sense of gathering hysteria.

'I shall have to have a drink as soon as we get there,' I said. Danny stopped the car with a screech of brakes.

'What do you want?' he said. 'Brandy?'

'Yes please,' I said. He got out and went to the trunk and returned with a half bottle in a brown bag.

'Go for it,' he said.

I said, 'Danny you are magic.'

Felt considerably more able to cope by the time we arrived at the venue.

Met with some good friends in the bar, glad to see familiar faces. Gerry was there to introduce us. He looks and behaves like a mildly demented professor. There is a vagueness about him that extends even to his hair.

The launch was scheduled as one of the cultural elements

in a tourist promotion, called MayDaze, a municipal extravaganza that, it was hoped, would act like a giant magnet on unsuspecting Americans and their pocketbooks. I could just hear them: *Hey, Lucinda, babe. Switch off the godamn Rangers. They got Vita Glass and Marlene Glatter up there in Canada. Hell, I'm gittin the truck out right now …*

Tents had been erected at the harbour and gaily coloured flags were standing out rigidly in the breeze off the water. Outside the bar, the tent where we were to read was filling up. I said, 'Oh, look. The tent is filling up.' Danny covered the side of his mouth, leaned in, and said, 'They're looking for shelter.' The sky was getting dark and a large purple-black cloud was approaching fast from the west.

'Wow,' I said. 'What a colour.'

'Funereal,' Marlene said. 'Vita brought it on.'

'Is that rain?' said Norman. He is a keen gardener and always watching the weather, and yes, indeed, it was. The tent was encouragingly full. Norman said his beans would be smiling.

'Who's up first, then?' Gerry is always a little bit last minute.

'I suppose it's me,' I said, 'since it's my cloud.' Silly thing to say really, because the cloud opened just as we were making our way to the tent and the rain came on in torrents. It was unfortunate that some keen meddler decided to tighten the guy wires just as we ducked inside. Gerry was just ahead of the resulting cascade from the puddle on the roof as he ducked inside. I in my heels was slower. It is a strange coincidence in the ducking scheme of things that the space between the back of the neck and one's clothing is large enough to accommodate a fair-sized puddle from a roof. And it is one of the less agreeable quirks of this part of

the country that rain in May is almost the same temperature as rain in February. Lucky I was warmed by the
brandy. Stood at the back for a moment to catch my breath.
Book table groaning under the weight of Marlene's book.
Clutched the single copy of my fake book, the mock-up that
the publisher had sent over with apologies that she wouldn't
be able to attend—she must have had a premonition—and
minced damply to the stage. Was concentrating so intently
on ascending the three steps without the aid of depth percep-
tion that it was only on the top step that the terrible truth
like another puddle from the roof broke over me. The pages,
the actual pages from my actual book that I was supposed
to actually slip inside the cover of the mock-up and actually
read from, were, actually, at home on my desk.

I had no choice. Opened *The Politics of the Satiated Society* camouflaged beneath my cover and turned to chapter 3:
'Trimming Budgets, Trimming Needs.' Modulated voice to
a laconic nasal drawl and was thankful for the noise of the
rain on the tent. Picking out alternate lines of text and breaking them up at random seemed to work. Came to the end of
the page and paused, not sure whether to turn over. Audience, assuming it was end of first poem, applauded. Drumming of rain on canvas increased. Raised voice to compete.
It was not going to matter what I read. Turned to chapter 4:
'Breaking the Mould.' Managed to piece together another
five or six fakeries—*In the cold light of analysis / with only
ourselves to blame / the future will condemn / will condemn will
condemn will condemn*—to appreciative applause though
none of it made sense. Decided to stop while I was ahead.
Had become increasingly aware of an unnerving crunching
underfoot rather like standing in spilled Cheerios. On the
way down the steps and back to the bar for the intermis-

sion, there was a distinct crumbling sensation like miniature earthquakes going on beneath my feet. On investigation, found my six-inch seventies heels now down to about two and a half and still in the process of decomposition.

Marlene said, 'But Vita, don't you see? This is the perfect metaphor. After the pinnacle of achievement...'

I said, 'Very funny.'

Then she said, 'Oh look! They are buying my book. I expect that is because yours has not arrived.'

I said, 'I'm getting another drink. You'd better not have one if you're up next. What will you have, Danny?' While I was ordering, the rain stopped and the sky began to look a little brighter. Gerry had the sides of the tent opened up. By the time Marlene stepped up to the mic a brilliant ray of late sun pierced the cloud and a perfect rainbow framed the tent.

Gerry said, 'Your teeth are chattering. Do you want my jacket?'

I said, 'No, I'm fine, thanks. Fine.'

FOUR

June 2

The Islands Festival came and went as any island festival would. Performance artists of all kinds vied for our attention and were for the most part eclipsed by the fifty-two-year-old Tormentil, a nude dancer who leaped over our heads at midnight as we sat in a hushed and bemused circle on the floor of the hall. So glad Hettie had fallen asleep by then. The others, not at all interested in broadening their horizons, made sure they were nowhere near the spectacle and remained outside under the canopy of the stars.

June 3

Mother called in the middle of the night with the perfect pick-me-up for a life that has reached record lows. The lawyers for my aunt Ada's estate have been in touch and are asking for my bank details. Money! They want to give me money! Even in the middle of the night that is good news. It is not a fortune but it will be my own. The really good part was when she said, 'Why don't you and Jack bring everyone over here for once?' My mind lit up like Christmas. 'Oh, Jack's far too busy,' I said. There would be ample time to tell her face to face. 'I'll bring them on my own then and we can go somewhere together.' Mother is the perfect childminder. She actually enjoys children. 'Good idea,' she said. 'You need a holiday.'

Went back to sleep. Woke again with a start. Smiling. Could not believe my good fortune.

A note came in the mail. Life gets even better. It is from the poet. Tom. The one with the soft shoes. Tom Murphy. The note was to congratulate me on the new book. He says he wanted to be at the launch to help me celebrate but he had been helping out at a postmodern interpretation of a medieval mystery play at the university and an ass trod on his foot. *But you know I would have been there for you, Vita, I would. Only wild horses, you know*, he wrote. *All that.*

I could hear his Irish accent bleeding through the ink. It gave me that disemboweled feeling. I had forgotten how it felt. Stars must be in the ascendant.

Have to go away again tomorrow. Miles's class is going camping and have volunteered to accompany them as chaperone. A behavioural aberration on my part but his teacher was desperate. Peggy, my faithful housesitter and one true love, will come here for a few days while Miles and I are away. Miles himself not at all thrilled with maternal involvement. He was hoping for three days of unbridled licence to run amok with his hyperactive little friends. But he is out of luck. Am taking this opportunity to repair my poor relations with the school.

Read the note again tonight. I've put it in my backpack for camp where it will act as a charm against the turbulent world of the prepubescent.

June 7
Arrived home exhausted yesterday. Blackguard bounded up and showed his joy by dragging his claws down the side of the car a few times.

A postcard from Jack. Says he expects be back in Canada by the end of the month. *Much to discuss with you all. J.* Well, *Jay*, darling, we are not all holding our breath and don't you, either.

Also a note in the kitchen from Peggy.

> *Everything is OK. Your Hettie has tonsillitis and is at Sue's. Your Kate might need picking up at 4:30 if she has another detention. Felix (quite the lad, isn't he?) stayed out a bit late last night. Didn't seem to want to go to school this morning but I made him all right.*
>
> *Peggy*
>
> *P.S. Dog is round the side.* <u>*Contained.*</u>

Did not really want to look 'round the side' and see how Blackguard had escaped his containment but went anyway since she'd underlined it twice. 'Round the side' is a narrow dog-run between the house and the fence. A doggy prison cell. Oh, the curse of a stupid animal. He had not eaten his way out through the gate like any other self-respecting brute but through a corner of the house itself, tearing off siding and chewing up a sizable chunk of a post until there was a gap large enough beside the gate to squeeze through. Decided the only solution would be to pretend ignorance. Me? Know about it? New rule: Never go 'round the side' of anything.

Went to pick up Hettie. Sue as competent and capable as always. Unruffled by the peaky child under her roof. 'No,' she said, 'no problem at all.' Immune systems in her house were right up there. In fact, she said, Hettie was feeling better already.

Asked Hettie on the way home if anyone had used the kayak.

She said 'You sound funny, Mum. Have you got tonsillitis, too?'

Picked up Kate from detention. She said, 'Don't try asking me about it because I'm not telling you anything.' Thank you, darling, oh, thank you. I love you.

June 9

Waited for Felix to come home yesterday. An afternoon of festering unease made worse by a call from the school attendance reporter: Felix had not been marked absent. Called around to his friends to no avail but Dunk said he was just fine. But what did Dunk know? Finally the call I wanted.

'Mum?' The call I dreaded. 'Mum, I'm not coming back. Okay?'

'No, *not* okay, not...' But he had put the phone down.

Marlene was good. Very clear and rational as always. *Obviously*, she said, he had found a safe place ... The mere fact that he called *showed*...He would not have called *if*...What you have to remember *is*...Until I had things in perspective by the time she left. Went to bed feeling reassured—only to wake an hour later.

Ragged and desperate this morning.

Hettie beside herself. 'Daddo and now Feeli,' she wailed.

'No, no, no,' I said. 'Felix is just with some new friends, that's all.' Truth and lies. Opposite ends of the tightrope walker's pole.

I do not have a phone number for Jack. It is too remiss. Of both of us. Jack would have called the police by now for sure. Decided to leave a message on his work machine. His preferred mode of communication with the world he has abandoned.

Saw Corey's brother at the corner store. And a good thing I did. He asked me if I was following the Nanaimo protest. I was embarrassed not to be keeping up with the news. I said, 'You bet.'

He said people were calling them eco-terrorists now but as far as he could see they were well within their rights. Passive resistance. You know.

'Something we all do when it suits us,' I said counting out my change and thinking of Monday mornings. And Felix.

Watched the local news at six for coverage of the camp up at Nanaimo. The area about to be developed for an access road was a melee of dogs and protesters, machines and police. There were close-ups of tunnels that had been dug overnight, the faces of activists peering out. There was a close-up of protesters giving a police officer a hard time, a close-up of several police officers giving a protester a hard time. There was a long shot of giant trees lying at odd angles on top of one another like the fallen on a battlefield. There was a shot of some protesters being led away. I don't know why it hadn't occurred to me.

I know my son's back when I see it. The way the body carries itself identifies us like a voice print, a fingerprint. There is no room left for doubt.

So does that mean I have to worry less now? Or more?

Phoned the police at the station up-island where the protesters were taken. No, they could not release the names of minors. No, not even to the minor's mother. They were sorry but no, not if the minor was over fourteen. Was on the phone for fifty-seven minutes to no avail. I think they cut me off.

At bedtime Miles gave me a note from his teacher: *Many thanks for your help at the camp. It was much appreciated. We hope to see you at the lunch for our volunteers on June 14.* Lunch? I was hoping for the Order of Canada. The experience of Miles's camp was such a trauma that I see I made no entries for it. They ate mountains of chips and cookies, broke several limbs, flooded the washrooms, and barfed in their sleeping bags. Their teacher's tolerance and occasional collusion can only be explained as brain damage.

June 10

Momentarily stunned this morning by a male voice asking: 'Where are my socks?'

I said, 'How did you get in?'

He said, 'Bedroom window. Same as before.'

Felt better knowing that, for Felix, for a little while longer, heroism was not as compelling as comfort. Should have liked to ask him about his adventures and shall one day, but mothers know as well as fathers how to embrace the prodigal. For now we have resumed the rhythm of daily routine without so much as a hiccup. Thank God.

Mother has booked the flights. We leave on June 28. Reminded everyone to save for the trip.

June 11

Baseball concession. On fries again. The noisome vat of grease that fries the fries is reheated each day so the job becomes only more odious as the season wears on. Petrified objects lurk at the bottom and resurface if the temperature gets too high. Some of them look as if they might have fallen in from the lost and found. Might it one day yield the jock-strap Miles lost before he went to camp? Profited from my time there by attending to the conversations of other parents, all of whom seem to know each other well. Such rapid and efficient exchanges of information taking place over the slurpies and hot dogs. The concession is a data bank, a stock exchange of information. Sleeping, feeding, and work habits of entire households are revealed along with Visa charges, exam results, breakthroughs in acne control, and current preferences for boxers or jockeys. Did try gamely once or twice while at the fryer to contribute to this pool of experience but only got as far as, 'My—', 'We—', and 'I—.' It was like trying to jump into a turning skipping rope and it reminded me of school days. Timing is everything. Gave up and decided to feed from the pool instead. It was all most enlightening. This is how it is done, I thought: we share experience, we exchange information; we do not go home, shut the door, take the phone off the hook, and write in our journals. We get on the phone. To each other. *Val? Are they in bed? Good. Well remember the pipe bomb last week? Well they found out who did it. Yes, expelled. No, Greg wouldn't tell me. I got it from Cassie. And you know what else . . . ?* We have a complete cast list of the neighbourhood. We do not wake up at two in the morning helplessly beset by vague but heart-stop-ping suspicions. We collect and collate information. We file and cross-reference. We know the last day for payment of tuition fees, the first day for soccer registration, the cost of a replacement orthodontic appliance, and the whereabouts of our children at any given moment, even when they run away. By December 24 we have wrestled the great beast of the year to the ground, contained it in a net of handcrafted seasonal decorations, and sit triumphant astride the exhausted mass ready to distribute our seasonal confections baked on a rainy day in fall and kept, labelled, in the freezer. In our homes the recycling is put out on time, the kettle shines, and yea even the garbage can is odour-free. There are bunches of dried flowers in the bathroom and they are not dusty nor are they faded. Our kitchens are clean and ready for action, our muffins swiftly, obediently rising in the microwave. When our husbands and children come home they leave their shoes neatly at the door in pairs facing east and our dogs always say thank you for their cookies. Home-baked.

The question now: should one break the custom of years of non-participation and begin attending coffee mornings, or would one be so crushed by one's own inadequacy, so consumed with guilt at the years of maternal delinquency, that one would go home and burn down the house?

Still trying to find a place for Blackguard when we go away. I do not think any will suit him.

June 12

Overheard Kate asking Felix how the protest went. She is on the side of reasoned argument along with rigid observance of the law, an unusual position for one so used to violating it in the home. She said she hoped everyone got what they deserved. Felix said it was wicked. There was a lot of chanting and he made placards and there was music all day and mountains of free doughnuts.

June 15

Last week of Little League, thank God. As a destructive

factor in the quality of life it is second only to sacking and pillage. Games and practices are so numerous there is scarcely time to address basic human needs. Drove to the diamond yesterday with Miles and Hettie eating pizza in the back of the car. They each wore a tea towel to save their uniforms from the colourful stains of mozza grease and tomato. Ferociously hot, the weather. We should have been at home lying on the lawn, lemonade by our sides, books unread at our heads. Thought again about Virginia Woolf and how she probably did quite a lot of lying about on lawns in between complaining. It does not do to compare lifestyles. Better to remember that Milton was blind, so all things considered I'm ahead.

Still have not found a place for Blackguard.

June 20

Miles is keen to earn money for the holiday and is offering all kinds of manual labour and demeaning domestic service at extortioners' rates. Paying wages is not quite what I had in mind when I urged 'saving.' But must not be discouraging. Felix's lifestyle has taken a more monastic turn lately and he has discovered abstinence. It can only be good for his health. Kate on the other hand is willfully thriftless. She has spent all her money on concerts and music. She announced coolly yesterday that holiday money is no problem: she will sell her hair. Was seen last night with her head over the scales trying to weigh it. Felix said he had done relative brain capacity in bio. Kate claims that she will be able to get two hundred and eighty dollars. 'Kate,' I said, 'there are people who would give you two thousand for your hair, only you will not find them in beauty salons.'

June 22

Invited to a solstice party by new American neighbours along the road—two Texan barbecues, crockery the size of bathroom fixtures, and a seven-metre-high bonfire on the beach ignited at sunset by helmeted Norsemen with crossbows launching flaming arrows from the top of the steps. Hosts can never know the number of questions I'd have to deflect afterwards, all beginning with *Why don't we ever...?*

Two hundred guests (who even *knows* two hundred people?) were served giant hamburgers as appetizers, while the hostess filled a small wading pool with strawberries from the farm. Miles and Hettie were convinced their vegetarian purgatory of repression and restraint had ended with a glorious ascent into heaven. Felix consumed two hamburgers and then went home in protest against capitalist excess and waste. Kate, though, was not eating. She languished moonily under a string of lanterns. She wore the kind of bored look that wardens in Bedlam probably assumed when it was time to feed the inmates, until the barman, in sympathy perhaps, slipped her a Caesar.

Eventually, as they do for most parties round here, the police and the fire department showed up. They always seem to enjoy their work.

Hettie said on the way home that Kate was in love with the barman. Maybe—but not with the barman.

June 23

Decided to go along the road to help clean up. Kate said she would come, too. 'Coming, Felix?' she called as we were leaving.

'No way,' he said. 'There's a cop car along there.'

'Just because they're watching you,' she said.

Asked her later on if that was true. She said, 'Of course not.' They treat each other as contemptible jerks but the seed of loyalty lives.

June 24

Felix has won a hundred dollars. Something to do with a radio station. There is no justice. I've always been the one to say you'd have to pay me to listen to that.

His win precipitated the day of reckoning for the trip. The results were discouraging.

> Felix $101.75
> Miles $13.50
> Hettie $3.18
> Kate   owes me $11.00

Found a place for the dog. It is run by a charming lady who is quite probably daft in the head.

June 25

A blazing row with Jack, the telephone wires overhead beginning to sizzle and fizz until they started dropping blobs of burning rubber and finally went up in a spectacular fireball over the trees. He called from Brazil.

I said, 'Never mind. It doesn't matter anymore. The crisis has been and gone. A bit like you, darling.'

He said, 'Vita, I'll make everything right with you. I will." He said he was coming back in ten days. I said I would leave a key out and he said what did I mean and I said so he could get in and he said what do you mean get in and I said in the house with no people in it. Then he said for Christ's sake what was I talking about this was long distance and I said England. I was talking about England and England was long distance, too. I said I was talking trips, I was talking getaways, I was talking making off. 'But you know all about that,' I said, 'only in my case I am taking the children.'

He said, 'You can't. Not without telling me. You can't take them to England without my consent.'

I said, 'Too late for the head-of-household routine now, darling.' Thought it remarkably injudicious of him, in the circumstances, to even allude to it. I'm sure he could see my point by the way he banged the phone down. One can always tell.

June 26
Clothes, suitcases everywhere. We are not organized. How that happened I cannot imagine.

June 27
Nightmare. All day. Was taken by all of them to be a depository for complaints against the management. Complaints about clothes, about backpacks, about siblings, hair, lack of money, lack of underwear, lack of socks, uneven number of socks, injustice, wet towels, health food, TV censorship, workload, sleep deprivation, harsh words, harsh life. Told them they should all live in Central America. Or Eastern Europe. Or Brazil.

June 28
Drove dog to the kennels. Bills itself as a boarding house. Correction: a boarding home. Pooch Perfect. Dogs all over the place. A small bungalow. Plywood doggy cut-outs on the gate. A St. Bernard with a barrel mailbox. Several dogs potter-

ing in the yard like the spryer residents of a retirement home. More inside languishing on the vinyl and lolling on chintz. Had never seen so many dogs so . . . uncontained. Wondered if she drugged them. Performed secret surgery at midnight. There was a pine-fresh scent in the air holding down something hotter and more hairy like gauze over a bad leg.

Blackguard outside in the van was washing the back window with a steaming tongue. Whole vehicle was rocking with excitement.

Beset by doubts.

'He's a bit of a handful,' I said.

Hilda Gascoigne begged to differ. She had that particular stance. The taut pectorals, the thrusting chin. 'Not to worry,' she said. 'They all like to think they are. He'll be no trouble with me.'

She repeated it when I handed him over. 'No trouble at all. SIT!'

Just as I thought: daft. Not harmless daft, but daft in the dangerous manner of retired colonels and wing commanders. People like Hilda know everything. I bet when they are born they know everything. *No, you don't have to show me that nipple, thank you very much. I know where everything is.* Blackguard still learning to sit as I drove away. He will probably spend the coming weeks sitting on a low stool in the corner, in solitary and wearing a dunce's cap. Hoped he would get the chance to steal some cookies. Blame it on an inmate.

Tears from Hettie on the way back. Oh, my heart! Had trouble convincing her it was not possible to stay with the dog for six weeks. Mrs. Gascoigne would surely notice. Mrs. Hilda Gascoigne was the sort of person who did notice things. Besides, Blackguard impossibly happy with so many friends.

.

Late to the airport. Very late. Not my fault, not my fault, not my fault at all. Had everything ready, bags in hall, taxi booked, military-style cross-check on lights, windows, doors.

'Taxi's here,' said Kate.

'I can't get out,' said Miles, and the bathroom door began to rattle. My heart seemed to rattle in response.

In the taxi, turning onto the airport road, Miles said, 'Do you know I was in there for thirteen minutes before anyone noticed I was missing?'

I said, 'Why didn't you say something sooner? Our plane is at one.'

Miles looked at his watch. 'That's in six minutes and thirty-five, no, twenty-five seconds. Twenty seconds. Six minutes and fifteen, no, ten seconds...'

I said, 'Miles...'

Taxi driver said, 'Ma'am?'

I said, 'Do you think you can go any faster, our plane leaves in six minutes?'

'Sorry. Radar,' he said.

I said, 'We have to make a connection.'

Taxi driver said, 'You'll be lucky.'

You, too, I thought, if you get a tip.

Check-ins were choked with lineups for Reno and I knew we had no chance of getting on the plane—our connector—in three and a half minutes. Had that dreadful sick feeling that might easily have risen to full panic had I not seen Peter. He was waving us over to his counter. He was our beacon in the dark, our home port in the storm. He was the empty check-out on Christmas eve in the liquor store.

'Peter,' I said, 'you are the best.'

'You never change, do you?' he said. 'Here.'

A second attendant stood by.

'You'll need an escort,' he said. 'Pilot's already on board.'

Ushered through at high speed like celebrities, across the tarmac, up the boarding stairs. A shame they were at the front of the plane. Every eye was upon us as we entered. We are a rabble, I thought, my kids and I, a crew, for in contrast to this planeload of neatly dressed and pressed commuters we were a little ragged at the edges. Felix was the worst with his long orange locks and his *RAGE AGAINST THE MACHINE* T-shirt. But, to tell the truth, none of us looked markedly groomed. Our seats unfortunately were scattered about the plane, causing passengers to glance nervously at vacant places, trying vainly to conceal them.

Transfer in Vancouver for the UK flight was a re-enactment of the whole procedure. Late again. Miles needed fresh air after throwing up in each washroom in the terminal and we all looked even more dishevelled than before by the time we entered the plane. Most of the passengers already settled. The attendant looked at our tickets. I felt she took her time reading out the numbers and had perhaps something of the sadist about her. 'Hmm, 6A. No, sorry, that should be 8A.' and so on.

No sooner were we up in the air than Hettie began to wail that she wanted to go to Brazil. Dear Hettie. Heart on her sleeve.

The flight was the usual dismal mix of unrest and tedium. We changed places many times just to keep our fellow travellers on their toes. Hettie broke her headset and spilled her cup of tea. Kate was upset by everyone who came within a five-metre radius. Miles was sick but brought nothing up. After that he slept.

Everyone is sleeping now. We are at Mother's.

July 1

CANADA DAY. Much more restful in England where there is no such thing as England Day and very little patriotism at all unless the country is at war. It is such a rest.

July 4

There has been a change of plan. Mother has been contacted by the hospital for two long-awaited appointments and she absolutely must keep them. She has ceded her role in our holiday to her older sister, the children's great-aunt Philly. Ruby will take care of mother's needs.

Our role is to take Aunt Philly to what she calls 'The Continent.' For today, we are disposed about the lawn, making the most of each other's company and hoping on my part for a resemblance to something out of Chekhov. The weather is fine. Have no calendar, no watch, no newspapers except last Sunday's spread on the grass beside the deck chairs. It is already a holiday. Marmalade for breakfast and Earl Grey tea. French windows standing open in the morning and the cats wandering in and out. Milk in bottles on the doorstep and fresh bread at the baker's in the village. Never mind that we have to walk under a motorway to get it or that the bread itself is like cotton wool, there is always a bottle of something nice at lunch. And it is peaceful! Hardly even know I have children. Mother—always in tune with the needs of the young—keeps three or four stacks of old *Beano* annuals crammed with all that is vulgar, vile, and disrespectful in the British schoolchild, the very lowest form of puerile humour, books capable of lobotomizing the overactive child as effectively as any TV. She relied on them when raising us and has never forgotten their worth.

Ruby tells me today she has literary aspirations of her own. She has been writing a composting column for the local paper and hopes to find a publisher to bring out a collection.

July 5

Learned the details of the French trip today. They are complicated, *mon Dieu*, beyond belief. Aunt Philly has strong connections to France. She would like to stay in the hotel where she took her honeymoon. Unfortunately she would like to travel there by boat and by train as she did sixty years ago. Once there, she would like to stay in the same hotel, *naturellement*, but the hotel is fully booked—*Zut alors!*—for the week except for a single room, but—*Courage, mes enfants!*—there is an annex nearby owned by one of the housekeepers and, *regardez*, the basement suite is fully empty. What luck! The travel arrangements are so complex they don't even bear thinking about. We leave on the eighth.

July 8

Survived the ferry crossing, though only barely in Miles's case, and now tightly installed in Hotel Nano just outside Calais. Establishment named for its miniature rooms. We have two of them, each with an area the size of a tablecloth. Kate said, 'What? I'm sleeping with you two old people?!'

I said, 'Sweetheart, we are all making sacrifices.'

She said, 'No way I am.' She said, 'I'm sleeping with the guys.' This caused Hettie to wail that it was not fair. At which point Philly emerged from the closet where the builders had installed the bathroom and said, 'I'll go with the boys. I'll be safe with them in the event of an intruder in the night.'

'Ha!' said Kate.

'Besides,' Philly added, 'they are altogether less trouble.'

Kate said two words I prefer not to record and we all pretended not to have heard. It is after all only the start of the holiday.

July 9

Took the commuter train into Paris. The motion did not agree with Hettie. Or Miles. He said, 'Why does everyone stare at us wherever we go?' I looked around at my family. With the exception of Kate, we all look as if we have dressed in a hurry. Some of our clothes occupy a sort of no man's land between on and off. Shoelaces trail, sweaters dangle from shoulders and bums, socks are indecisive. We have that North American Nike stamp about us—the baseball caps backwards, the running shoes—with none of the crispness; our lunches and breakfasts become inexplicably attached to us and our luggage straps are always broken.

Entering the Gare de Lyon, Hettie brightened considerably at the prospect of food vendors. Aunt Philly bought her a chocolate croissant against my wishes and said it was the emptiness of the stomach that was causing the reflex action. She said her old border collie used to do the same thing just before dinner. In any event our next train was the *grande vitesse,* the famed TGV and smooth as silk. Hettie was as right as rain. Might have admitted as much to Philly but she was asleep with her mouth open. Did not wake even at Poitiers where train stopped long enough for me to get off and catch a flight back to Canada. The thought!

Went instead to buy lunch. Found a real fruiterer in a back street, a virgin Frenchman unscathed by the British tourist. A genial soul—as all the unscathed are—he added extra fruit to each brown paper bag and was inviting us all back to his family before he realized we were still en route.

'*Mais Biarritz! C'est loin!*'

'*Oui c'est loin, très loin!*'

'*Mais le TGV, il est vite!*'

'*Oui, il est très vite! Il est très, très vite!*' In fact so *vite* it was hardly *loin* at all. Oh, it was a delightful conversation and entirely composed of just six words, not counting proper names.

The rest of the journey went as smoothly as the train. Woke Philly ten minutes before the station, organized the bags and the boys and our plentiful rubbish, and flung ourselves from the train before it sped away.

The train may be fast but we are not and it had emptied and the taxis had all departed before we had got ourselves off the platform.

'No need to disturb me,' said Aunt Philly when we finally stepped off the bus at Hotel Alexandre. 'I shall rest tomorrow morning.'

That is not how Mother would have managed things.

Felix and I carried her bags up the steps for her and waited until she was safely checked in while the others got ratty in the heat outside. Continued on to Chez Ronson. But I am exhausted and cannot write any more about the rest of the day right now. Shall do it tomorrow. Have to be up early for the beach.

July 10

Cannot believe only one day has passed. It seems like a week. To continue.

'*Quatre heures!*' said Madame Ronson when we arrived. '*Mais c'est vite! C'est très vite!*' And we were off again on the ten-minute, six-word exchange. The French are very proud of their *Train Grande Vitesse*. Like one of the *Grandes*

Horizontales she is treated with awe and admiration by those who do not have the occasion to get on her.

'*Bien sûr,*' I sing, boosting the word pool by 40 percent. Madame was next astonished to learn that we had walked from the Hotel Alexandre and we were off again: '*Oui, c'est loin. Très, très loin,*' etc. And once again I had to agree, for it had taken us fifty minutes and—but now Madame was pre-empting me and trying out her English, which was altogether as uninspired as my French—yes we were tired, very tired, yes and very hot, very, very hot, and Hettie was demonstrating the degree of her own hotness and tiredness by standing on one of the beds and removing her clothing and Miles was telling us it was 6:43.

At the sight of the dusty shoes on the counterpane, Madame quickly snapped out of automatic and went into overdrive. None of us understood a word but we grasped the drift and when things had calmed down we stood in a chastened group ready to have our dirty feet cut off at the ankles while Madame pointed out the special features of her basement—for this was where we were staying—and reeled off the aptly named inventory. The net effect was to instill in us a special kind of despondency. It was, if possible, more constricting than the Hotel Claustrophobe for all the windows were barred and there was only one way in or out. Most of the rooms, including the bathroom, seemed to be located conveniently in the kitchen so that we did not have to stir far for our tour. 'And this'—Madame took half a step forward and paused at the table—'this the dining room.' Felix muttered something about being able to watch his toast while he was on the john and Miles said he was going to watch TV when he was in there. When she had finally finished, Madame, all professional smiles, bade us *Bonnes vacances!* and turned to go. She paused in the doorway and turned back.

'*Il n'y a pas un monsieur, Madame?*'

'No, Madame,' I said. 'There is no monsieur.'

She smiled noncommittally and started to go again but could not manage it. She put her head round the door a second time.

'*Je suis jusqu'en haut,*' she said, pointing to her celestial apartments. '*Jusqu'en haut. Je suis toujours là.*' And it sounded suspiciously like a warning.

'What did she say?' Miles asked.

'She said she's got your number,' I replied.

Would have liked nothing more at this point than to have lain down on the besmirched counterpane and woken up the next day but the children had never been so hot in their lives and so we set off for the beach instead.

Caught the last of the sun on the warm sand and then retired to the bar at the back of the beach to wait for Kate. Children ate *les pommes frites* and *les hot dogs* served by grubby waiters while I had a glass or two of excellent red as the sun went down. It could have been perfect. It was almost perfect. And yet. And yet over all the magenta and rose of the moment there was an unlovely grey smudge: I was the transatlantic lonely woman, born in the Gilded Age and kept alive by movie makers ever since. Well I wasn't. Thank you very much. I had the children to save me from a quickie with the singleted *artiste* of the *pommes frites*. No, I didn't even need the children to save me. I had more than that. Life for instance. The sea. All of it. The clawing surf had tired of climbing up the beach and the waves had rocked slowly to a gentle swell, like water in a basin. Pink. Who could resist? Kate was still swimming a lazy, luxurious backstroke. Swam out to join her, the water cooling. Perfect. It was almost dark when we got out. Returned to Chez Ronson considerably restored.

Spirits sank somewhat at the sight of our rooms. Electric light not enhancing the effect of the heavily barred windows or the dispiriting decor. The furniture, which can only have been posing as something else when we arrived, now revealed its dismal late fifties provenance. Nothing is more depressing than grey arborite with stars and the uncomfortable, spiky-legged look for which the term 'contemporary' was coined. Fit only for Ken and Barbie.

'Cool,' said Felix.

'Totally,' said Kate, and curled herself up in a wide wicker cone on legs.

July 11
Breakfast beach lunch beach dinner beach.

July 12
Beach breakfast beach lunch beach dinner. Beach.

Heaven.

July 14
Saw Madame's face this morning peering in through the bars. It flashed away again as soon as I lifted my head from the pillow. At breakfast Hettie said, 'I saw a burglar this morning, looking in.'

I said, 'That was Madame.'

'Snooping,' said Miles.

I said, 'No, dear. She was making sure her tenants were still alive and able to pay.' Shot a look at Kate intended to lance her conscience.

She said, 'You've got jam on your nose. It looks like a booger.'

Kate and I had words last night. Loud ones. Can't remember how they started but they revolved around some ongoing dispute she has with Miles about whose turn it is to sleep in the bed with the reading light. Pointing out her superior age, size, understanding, worldliness, wisdom, maturity, and intelligence only seemed to incense her. Equal rights is her rallying cry and no concessions to—well, anyone. As our tempers rose, so did the decibels. It became a row of operatic scale and prompted Felix to put a pillow over his head. I gave up and went to bed but Kate continued the performance solo until without warning there was a loud explosion followed by another. And another and another. Closer and closer they followed on one another until we seemed to be in the midst of one huge crackling eruption. Kate was struck dumb. My heart stopped for what seemed like a minute and no one said a word. 'What's the time?' I said.

Miles looked at his watch and said, 'Midnight. Look, the date's changing. July the fourteenth.'

That's okay, then,' I said. 'It's our neighbours. They're letting off fireworks,' I told Hettie. 'Just like us.'

Woke refreshed as after a thunderstorm. Breakfast of fresh warm bread and apricots. *Boulangerie* the only shop open for business. When the French have a holiday they really have one, but no one goes without fresh bread. The fact that all the other shops remain closed marks the day as something extraordinary. I do not understand our present national fear of going without. At home the local supermarket is open from seven until midnight three hundred and sixty-four days in the year in case any of us gets caught short without the canned pineapple or the aluminum hot-plate guards.

.

Attended the surfing festival. Felix liked the cool young men. So did Kate. I liked the part that featured prodigious acrobatic stunts performed by Hawaiian families on longboards, three generations arranging themselves in a human pyramid above the racing surf as it tore towards the shore. The very epitome of reconstructed domestic life just before the next crisis. At the end of the day a group of Hawaiians performed exotic sunset ceremonies on the beach before heading off for the casino. Felix booked some surfing lessons at an outfit run by more cool young persons the colour of sand.

Wandered the streets in the evening eating crepes and watching local talent earnestly performing American songs in marquees in a parking lot. Much of the local talent was watching Kate. Left the older ones to achieve communion with the milling crowd and retired to a bar with Hettie for coffee and ice cream.

July 16

A surprise. Invited by Madame and Monsieur to dine. A meal to be remembered, simple and delicious, prepared by her simple woman in the kitchen, who was toothless and not entirely right in the head but a culinary wizard. Children behaved impeccably. Monsieur lit some leftover fireworks for them. Hettie told him that her father was up the Amazon. Monsieur took it for a euphemism and nodded sagely. The French invented these things. A man is not a man without his indiscretions, his infidelities. 'Ah,' he said with discreet understanding. 'Ah.'

July 23

Home early. It is a long story. Felix had his surfing session. A black day he'll not forget. The weather was changing that morning when we woke, wind swinging round to mess up the sea. After days of settled weather something serious was coming in on swift-moving cloud chased by a lowering sky. Kate went back to Chez Firetrap to read Aunt Philly's *Harry Potter*. Aunt Philly gamely took Hettie for hot chocolate in an expensive Italian bar. Miles and I sat on the beach shivering under a towel while Felix and his group went out to confront a chunky grey ocean. And he was doing so well. Felt that inexplicable pride—for what, after all, what *really* is it to do with us as progenitors? But still. There's that irrational glow. Missed being able to share it with Jack. Sorry too that Felix did not have him there to witness. But Felix was in the moment. Felix wouldn't have cared. And then suddenly, unbelievably, Felix wasn't there. Nor was his board. Then his board was there. And Felix wasn't. A barrel wave of *No!* rose in my throat and all of time stood still while I begged and pleaded for it to change course, for it to release me from the fated moment, for it to deliver us safe to another planet where none of this could be happening. It was the longest five seconds of my life. That's how long Miles tells me it was before they had three rescue boards in the waves. Ten seconds before they reached the spot. He was timing it. For a moment it was hard to see what they were doing, the waves were so choppy. And they were taking their time. Did they have him? Why weren't they bringing him in? They were taking so long. I couldn't understand it. I was on my feet running and yelling against the wind, 'Bring him in! Bring him in!' I was the distracted mother of all tragedies ever, with no witness but Miles. He said quietly, 'They can't hear you, Mum.'

And then here they came, paddling, the boards in a raft formation with Felix on his back on one of them, a lifeguard kneeling to hold his head steady. I took Miles's hand and we ran. They were paddling parallel to the shore and then they turned to float in past the break. At first I thought he must be dead. He had his eyes open and was staring straight ahead. Knelt down on the sand where they set the board. He blinked and said, 'I'sh okay, Rum.' Blood flowed abundantly from his mouth as soon as he opened it. Couldn't think of anything to say so settled for, 'Shh.' Thought of every possibility in the next few minutes—brain injury, broken neck, internal bleeding, spinal-cord damage, paralysis . . . It's why mothers are always exhausted.

An ambulance took him to the hospital and we followed in a stranger's Citroën. People so ready to help, people so lovely, when you're in need. People everywhere. I learned that much at least, over the course of that wretched day. Learned too how the French health-care system operates and what a broken clavicle is called and a wrecked acromion and how to recognize the signs of concussion or of nerve damage and how to reach medicare as soon as they are up for the day and who I needed to call to change our flight. Learned too that the French are afraid of people who look worried or on the verge of hysteria and they will not readily speak to them, so learned to deport self with calm and dignity and agreeability—with a smile even and a hint of charm, like a real Frenchwoman—while I asked my questions, shoving the gibbering wreck of me deep down out of sight, where she couldn't be heard repeating the only question that really mattered: *But will he be all right? Will he be all right?*

Felix for his part had a state tour of the Biarritz *Urgences*. Was treated to every available MRI and scan until the whole world and his mum were 100 percent sure he hadn't broken his neck or curdled his brain when the surfboard reared up to strike him on the shoulder and then returned to hit him again the face.

Nurse, kindly speaking gruesome English to me, said when they were through that I could see him in the 'Shock Room.' He was on a high gurney in the centre, one arm inexplicably held aloft, the other bound to his side, a cervical collar still holding his head in position. He looked at me from the corner of his eye. And said, 'Shorry, Rum.' His mouth was still full of blood and his lip was the size of a dahlia tuber. He had lost a couple of teeth. I said, 'Oh, Felix. Oh, Felix,' until he said, 'Cool it, Rum.'

He said, 'Rhere are vee ovvers?'

I said, 'In the waiting room, with Kate. She's doing a great job.'

He said, 'You fink she *rouldn't*?'

A medic came in with the results. Told us we were to wait for a doctor to consult about treatment in the morning. They were keeping him overnight. I said, 'Oh, Felix,' a few times more and he said, '*HRum*! I're not kidding!'

I know I do not make the best company for a casualty: eyes like giant cue cards announcing *My God you look terrible!* and *You'll die before morning!*; observations and questions—*Is that air bubble in your drip okay?*—better left unspoken.

There were many more phone calls to make and appointments to arrange in the next few days, but we did it, between us all. Arranged a flight for treatment in Canada, while the other three, accompanied by Aunt Philly, made the journey back to England to wait for the original booking. But here is the thing: thank God for the teen-woman, competent and smart and responsible beyond her years—for in truth it was 'the other three accompanied by Kate'—and thank God for the grace of strangers. A crisis is transformative. I always knew that, but now I *really* know it. People step up, they rally. Even Madame Ronson, who was transformed. As if dinged by some Disneyesque fairy godmother, she turned into our devoted roadie and ferried us tirelessly to hospital, train station, airport, dismissing our thanks, swatting them away like flies with the back of her hand: *Ah, mais non! C'est normale!*

So Felix flew business class all the way home, though it was wasted on him for he slept most of the way and would have only railed against the capitalist construct of prestige had he been awake. I visited him often from the back of the bus. Crept in through the dividing curtain. Just to check. Who knows how painful a wrecked acromion might be. Who even knows what it is.

Sixteen messages on the answering machine when I got home. Only listened to the last: a new contact number from Jack and a cryptic assurance that he would keep me posted. Did not have time for all that again. There were arrangements still to be made. Left him a message of my own.

July 24

Listened to the rest of the messages this morning. Two from Marlene, one from Jack saying he had a flight home in two days. Marlene's message said they were going away for a week. She said Jack had called several times in the last few days wanting to know if we were all okay. He was worried about us.

Had an inexplicable urge to cry, to howl, in fact, like a baby. Called Jack's new contact number again but couldn't get through. Decided to try again when I had up-to-date news of Felix. Thought it better than bawling into the mouthpiece.

Felt decidedly strange. Altogether 'shaken,' I think, is the word. Had a sudden overwhelming and irresistible urge to get the dog. The comfort of animals.

Tremendous commotion when I rang the bell at Pooch Perfect but no evidence of a response. Was contemplating leaving, when the front door flew open and out shot the dog, followed by Hilda Gascoigne in horizontal fashion, hanging on to the leash.

'Mind those stitches!' she bellowed as the dog ripped the leash from her hand and leaped to greet me. Stitches? I wrestled him to the ground. He lay on his back and sure enough he had stitches. 'Fifty-three,' said Hilda. He looked like an old teddy bear that had been poorly repaired or perhaps—since he had very little hair on his belly now and it was a ghastly plastic pink—something out of a grisly hospital kit: *O.R. Fun for Tots*. Hilda said he had jumped a fence and torn himself wide open.

'He really has got no brain at all, have you, Blackie?' said Hilda. 'And I'm afraid the bill is pretty steep. Seven hundred and fifty. Plus GST.' She had the invoice in her hand to prove it.

'I'm afraid,' she repeated, as if it would help. 'Anyway. He's right as rain now. Just pop him two of these three times a day.'

She bent down, expertly opened his jaw and flung a couple of small blue pills to the back of his throat. But Blackguard was too quick. As soon as she let go he seized the invoice and ate that as well. Who said no brain?

I wondered about 'the last straw.' Does such a thing in fact exist?

Went back to the hospital in the evening, spent some time with Felix until he said, 'You know you're making things worse?'

Of course I was. Scuttled away home much like a beetle found in the kitchen. Spent a very fretful night and was woken this morning at seven by a phone call from the hospital. Felix's surgery is postponed while they wait for the right screw.

They couldn't order one up like they do at the garage? But seriously.

A good thing I have Blackguard. Still could not make contact with Jack.

My whole family is beyond my reach. Are they loving it?

July 25

Can scarcely believe what I am about to write. I am in the hospital. With a bed of my own. Got out of the shower this morning to find a message on my machine. Hospital had the screw and Felix's surgery was slated for first thing this morning.

I felt the wonkiness as I was driving in. Felt better when I saw Felix. Held his hand and wished him well and told him I'd be there when he woke up. Could not stay calmly in place so went to buy groceries. Kate and the littles arrive tomorrow. Did my best to ignore the wonkiness but it progressed to bumpiness. If a heart had feet mine was hopping and skipping. Kind of disappearing for a moment and then reappearing. Playfully. Ignored it while I got the groceries. Ignored it at the checkout, but could not ignore it on the way back to the hospital. Wound all the windows down just to breathe. It was a cartoon rabbit running in my chest—at high speed—and spouting jibberish. By then I was in the parking lot. Fellow nearby said 'Ma'am, your windows,' and then pointed skyward to the black cloud. But I could not answer. The black cloud descended and settled on my eyebrows. But my heart. My heart. The timing mechanism of the whole world was out of whack. The mad rabbit was running a mile a minute while my feet and legs were ploughing through a viscous, slo-mo gel towards the main entrance of Emergency.

'See a doctor,' I said, mouthed really, when I reached the front desk. It wasn't quite what I meant but it was all I could manage.

'Take a number,' said the front desk.

Shook my head, except 'shook' is also wrong word. Head was the size of a watermelon and swung heavily, slowly from one side to the other. I seemed to have morphed into King Kong.

Front desk looked up and then a made a phone call, *sotto voce*.

Door behind her opened and an aide came through with a wheelchair. Scooped me into the chair and steered away into Triage.

Can't remember who did what to whom in there but I know I said, 'My son is—' a few times and I know my chair was juddering, the walls were leaning in, and the room was getting progressively darker.

Triage nurse said, 'Lucky you. Heart rate of 175. You win. That'll get you a bed in no time.'

So here I am, after an hour or two of checks and monitoring and tests, sorted out now, put to rights and stabilized without resort to electric shock. They unhooked me and let me go down the hall to see Felix. He too was successfully put back together and opened his eyes long enough to tell me I was late. Again. Declined the opportunity to do a version of the *Pietà* beside his bed since he was such poor company and made my way back to here to my bed to wait for the doctor to sign off on me. Am writing this in the white spaces of a *People* magazine and will copy it into my journal tonight. When I get the final word I can drive myself home.

July 26

It was very peaceful—between shifts, I suppose—when I went back to my bed yesterday after seeing Felix. Tried not to think of Blackguard roaming the kitchen. Was enormously tired, even though it was only eleven, and there was nothing more to write and I just could not keep my eyes open while I waited for the doctor.

Had begun to give in to the urge to let go, when I heard Jack's voice on the other side of the bed curtain.

'Glass,' it said. 'Jack Glass.'

A woman's voice said, 'You're the third one today.'

Could feel the newly stabilized HR climbing. Couldn't speak. Something strange was happening to my throat. Could only listen.

'You have my son,' Jack was telling them.

'Right. Felix Glass? And we have a Vita Glass, too,' said the woman's voice.

'My wife,' said Jack. 'That's my wife.'

Wife. Such a medieval appellation. *My* wife. I was glad I was it, I wanted to be it forever. Eyes—closed—started leaking. Badly.

'We'll get you that X-ray,' said another voice behind the curtain. My eyes flew open. I was wide awake. 'And then maybe you can take that collar off if it comes back clear. Here. You can chat as long as you don't turn your head.'

A pair of hands pulled the dividing curtain back and there was Jack in a neck brace. He was lying on his back and looking like a Tudor whose ruff had been too long in the freezer. He tried to look sideways but his eye was too swollen. The alarm sounded from my monitor and suddenly our reunion had two additional attendants, one of them with the dread paddles in her hands. No one spoke. Fortunately the beeping stopped and then we all engaged in an unnecessary exchange of names. Carly said to Nina, the keener with the paddles, 'I don't think we'll be needing those.' I was not so sure. Jack's face was beaten up a little. Quite a lot. Carly watched the screen at the head of my bed. The rabbit in my chest was doing a bit of foot thumping. Asking Jack if he was all right didn't help because he was asking me the same thing and we fell silent at the same moment. We settled for dry-mouthed smiles while the nurses did their fiddling with leads and tubes and wires. I reached out my hand. Jack put his hand out too and winced.

'Careful,' said the nurse by his bed. 'He had a bit of a bicycle accident.'

Carly said, 'Here.' She took the brake off and gave my bed a nudge to the left. 'This needs to move over anyway so we have room for the lab work.' Both of us knew the lab work was already done.

So there we lay, Jack and I, extending our extremities in silence until the activity in my chest and around our beds subsided. It was hard then to know how to begin. Whispering each other's names seemed the easiest.

Eventually I asked what happened.

He said, 'I hit a bollard.'

I have always thought that a funny word. I'm still sorry I laughed. He was telling me he had been trying to reach me to no avail when he arrived at the airport so he got a cab home. He knew from my messages on his work machine that

Felix was in hospital. When he got in he listened to our own machine and realized Felix's operation was only just taking place, deduced that I was at the hospital with Felix, and jumped on Kate's bike to come tearing over, cutting across on the bike path through the park and needing to swerve on three occasions to avoid kids and dogs and balls. On the third occasion he was concentrating so hard on a dog that he failed to see the bollard dividing the path in two. It seems he hit it hard enough to crack his helmet on the concrete when he went over the handlebars.

We are at home now. I shall return for Felix in the morning. His mates are with him. Jack's X-rays were good or at least did not call for screws. He has a fractured collarbone and a very sore shoulder. I am now officially termed 'stable' and shall remind the family of it often.

There is so much to talk about, so many cryptic messages to explain and we have only just started.

July 27

Up early to get organized before the arrival of Kate and her charges. Felt amazingly calm and collected and thought I might learn to love pharmaceuticals, though I would have my fingernails pulled out before I profess it in public.

Over coffee Jack said, 'I was worried about you all, you know. I missed you.'

Tried to match his reserve. 'Well we missed you too. Terribly. We didn't do very well without you.'

He smiled.

I said, 'You could give up your job and hire yourself out as a guide, escorting the naive and the troubled on tours of Europe.'

I walked the dog and then got ready to go to the airport. Jack came, too. On the way, he said, 'What were you saying? The stuff about being a guide, what were you really saying?'

'You know,' I said.

He said, 'So tell me.' Anglos. God we are pathetic.

I said, 'We need you.'

He said, 'I need you, too.' So there we were a couple of cats kneading away at this old sofa of the heart.

I said, 'All this needing.'

He said, 'Yes.'

I said, 'And we still need to talk.'

He said 'Tonight.'

Hettie broke into a run coming through the barrier. She disappeared between legs and luggage and re-emerged where Jack was standing. How infallible are the instincts of the young. She flung herself upon him and commandeered the moment, for which I was grateful. Miles looked at his watch and said, 'Eleven hours six minutes and twenty-three seconds.'

Kate, pushing the cart he rode on, said, 'Where's the car for God's sake?'

Kate beautiful in her new role of competent young woman, shepherding the small and vulnerable through a maze of anxieties and excitements, to deliver them, untraumatized, home.

She thought nothing of it. Said, when I tried to thank her, 'Whatever. It's only Hettie and Miles.'

July 28

Up early. Toilet leaking. What is wrong with us? Called several plumbers. None passed my rigorous screening. Trick is to find one who is competent as well as willing. Turned the tap off underneath instead. Did not want a plumber in the house anyway. We shall draw our water from the well each day and carry it back in gourds.

And last night? Last night. Oh God, to lie with the man who stood by your side all those years ago while you publicly avowed your love for each other in front of all your friends. It is something. There is such comfort in the flesh. It is limitless. There was moonlight coming through the open window. It was very warm and we lay and talked. Or Jack talked.

It was a long story. More than twenty years long. All the way back to Whistler Mountain before it became Whistler Mall. All the way back to that crisp New Year's Eve when the snow was squeaky underfoot and the air smelled of pine needles and woodsmoke and when abandoned revelry did not mean that your husband had just left you and you were ringing in the new year for your seven-year-old out on the deck with a milk saucepan and a wooden spoon. Such a good time I had that night in crisp, white Whistler enjoying age-old Scandinavian customs that I never thought of Jack or wondered what had become of him. And certainly he never gave a thought to me, because he was out of his mind—and his long johns—with Liz.

And next morning it was just on with the long johns and down the hill again. No questions, no confessions. Love like a body could stand up to all sorts of abuse; it trained for it. It could stay up all night drinking and smoking, and then go for a jog in its sweatpants and terry-cloth headband before sitting down to a healthy bowl of granola. Except that poor Liz started going off her granola altogether a couple of months later. She was working on the cruise ships when

226

she found out, and she had just left Canada and gone to Rio to live with someone she thought she couldn't live without. The last person she wanted was Jack—or his baby. She waited it out and had the baby adopted. And then she closed that chapter of her life and she never did tell Jack. She came back to live in Canada eventually. Then just last December, her daughter, Elena, the child she gave up, traced her. She wanted to meet. She wanted to know both her parents. She had been searching for three years.

And that's why Liz called on New Year's Eve. Jack said he wanted to tell me. He said it was the most difficult time in his life, and remembering his ghastly demeanour, I believe him. He said he had wanted to come back, had been planning to, but here was this child—this child of his—blocking his way. When he said that, I could see how the image must have come to him like a visitation, the barefoot child abandoned on the road, arms outstretched. Only that is not it how it is. Elena is a gracefultwenty-one-year-old, mature beyond her years. The people she loves and calls, with pointed logic, her 'real-time parents' still live in Rio. Jack has met them. Elena now lives and works nearly three thousand miles away from them. I was crying by this time. And for once it was not for me. I was crying for Jack and for Liz. I was crying for children who lose their parents and for parents who lose their children. I was crying for Elena and for Elena's mum and dad, for the goodness that can heal wounds and for the knowledge of its unfathomable random nature.

I said, 'We're lucky, Jack. We're all lucky.'

Jack said he hadn't thought of it like that.

And that's really all there was to it. He is moving back in on September 1.

I said, 'What about the apartment?'

He said, 'I've already given notice.'

I said, 'That would come under Important Information, wouldn't it? You know, for The Wife, I mean.'

July 29

So we are going to conjugate again. We are going to yoke and shackle ourselves by the neck but remain free like the couple (we shall do that, too) on the Devil card. No use trying to explain to anyone else. We'll just do it.

Meanwhile Jack is making use of the apartment until the lease is up. And why not? Independence in marriage is a fillip. It will save on gas.

Family are tolerant beyond belief. They seem to know that as adults we have forgotten how to live true and simple lives. They are very patient. Jack has told them about their half-sister. They like the idea. Hettie said, 'Elena can sleep with me.' I said she will not live with us. She is all grown up and has a fruitful life of her own. She is going to work in Belize with the man she wants to marry.' Kate said, 'Oh, cool. This is like a soap.' She is right. There are no new stories. Only the same one and we each have a part in it.

Felix said it was a coincidence that Elena was in Belize. He said he's always wanted to go there. He has a thing for trees.

Asked him if he would try out his thing right now and pick up all the fallen apples. Enough early transparents to feed the nation.

August 1

To Bangs. 'You haven't been in for a while,' Keith said, looking at my hair.

'I've been away,' I said. 'France.'

'So how was it?' he said.

I said, 'Thrilling.'

'You went to EuroDisney?' he said.

'No need,' I said. I asked him how business was and he said it was slow. People get their hair cut short for the summer and don't reappear for months. He said this is strange because studies show that hair grows faster in the summer. Thought of the grass and how I ought to be mowing it. Had to make a conscious effort not to let my mind wander on to the apples and what to do with them. Made a special effort to talk follicles. Always get the feeling, talking to Keith, that I am his only customer and feel driven to do more than my share to help conversation along. It is a terrible burden of responsibility. Deserted craft stalls have the same effect. My heart goes out to the lonely vendors who have spent countless winter hours making twig cabins for miniature mice or hand-painting boxer shorts with killer whales. I know that on occasion I have made an appointment at Bangs on a mere whim, a vision having come to me of Keith alone in the salon idly flipping back through his appointment book, a wistful look on his face. As I said it is a terrible burden of responsibility and lucky that I have a lot of hair.

Marlene phoned. She is back. She said she will come over tomorrow.

Phoned Mitzi at Galeria Toxicana. Astonished to find that a great deal of hanky-panky has been going on, and I missed it. The chair has quit. The music director has left his partner to go and live with the performing arts director. The chair's partner has moved in with the performing arts director's ex and the secretary has come out. The gallery itself is about to be seized by the bank and only a huge benefit will save it. They are looking for ideas. Suggested a pantomime.

Mitzi said, 'We are all so tired.'

I said, 'I'm not surprised.'

August 2

The man of my dreams: plumber who can fix things. Maybe be the only one in the yellow pages I have not used before. (None will come a second time, not even to fix the things that they have broken.) This one arrived within twenty minutes, did not take all day, and did not once say, *Who put this thing on like this?* or, *Whoever installed this was a dickhead*, or, *Can't get the part*, or, *If I were you I'd take it out and get a new one, might as well do the job right, knock this wall down, get yourself a new bathroom* . . . Instead he talked political philosophy. He is a charming man from Croatia with a profound concern for the state of the world and a clear vision of what is wrong, which he illustrated with wads of toilet paper on the lid of the seat. Heer is smoll contree. Heer is ozzer smoll contree. Heer—tearing off reams and balling them up—is superrpowerr. None of them in the end escaped the septic tank but were all flushed away together in a whirling, cleansing vortex.

Marlene came over. 'Well?' she said.

I said, 'Jack is coming back.'

She said, 'Surprise, surprise.'

I said, 'But there is more.' I made a great show of patting the dog. It seemed easier to say while I was busy. 'He has a twenty-three-year-old daughter. In another family.'

She said, 'That's okay, isn't it?' It threw me. I looked up

to see if she had heard or if she was fondling the spines of her books again. She wasn't.

I said, 'Yes. You know what? It's really okay.'

She said, 'Why wouldn't it be?'

I said, 'Marlene, I love you.'

She said, 'Why wouldn't you?'

Spent a convivial hour catching up. She filled me in on all the details of Toxicana. I said it had taken me quite by surprise, all those aesthetes, with their devotion to Art, getting steamed up over the biannual grant proposals. I had always left the meetings early, thinking myself clever for avoiding the tedium. Clearly the interesting parts of the meeting happen after it is declared closed.

Marlene said, 'You didn't know that? You really should get out more—and stay longer.'

She said if a cheap flight comes up I should go with her to Toronto. She said if Jack has moved back in by then it will be easy; I could even go standby. I really ought to think about it, she said. For professional reasons. Her publicist has arranged five readings; it will be good exposure and I can do some networking. A strange word. 'Networking.' Know I am meant to think interactive exchanges, a web of live contacts, links in cyberspace, but can't help thinking tatting, crochet, *Whistler's Mother*. People who are better left alone. On standby.

It is about time for a party.

August 3

Have not had a proper conversation with Jack but I shall go ahead with the party anyway. It will be the weekend of the air show. Told Kate she could invite her friends. She said,

'Like they'd want come. The place will be full of old people.'
I was pointing out the Theory of Relativity and that anyway
this would not be true were she to invite some friends of her
own but she was already outside where her own friend Asta,
thriving after successful surgery, was doing her best to blow
the muffler off her mum's car.

August 5

Called Mother today and found her well. She said Aunt
Philly can't believe how smoothly the holiday went.

Phone call from Vancouver. The organizer of a fish benefit is
in a fix. Wants me to read in Vancouver at short notice. One
of the poets has cancelled. Zozie Louiz-Louiz. Organizer is
sorry the publicity can't be changed at this late stage but it's
probably better left as it is. 'You know,' she said, 'the pull of
the big name and everything . . . ' It is on August 13. Oh, and
she was sorry again but they wouldn't be able to offer more
than a small honorarium, in fact most of the other writers
had donated theirs back to the cause. Anyway, August 13.
Had to agree. Marlene says it is an unbreakable rule: 'Never
say no.'
   I shall be missing Toronto.

August 6

Jack called. He is going back to Rio. With Liz. They are
going to sign some papers and then they are going to fly
to Belize to attend Elena's wedding. He says it is only for
a week. Is this a thing to say to The Wife? Doesn't the
wife have more than a question or two? Does he *have* to
attend? Of course he does. It's grown-up. It's atonement.
That doesn't require an explanation. But he must know a
week sounds a like an unnecessarily long time. To the wife.

And what about accommodation? I've got a few questions here. Do I really have to ask? Why didn't he volunteer some information. Or does he just feel safe? With this good medieval wife of his.

But my own instincts are contrary to all that. I have to trust him. Sometimes we're so ready for the lie, we muddy the truth with own projections. I'll trust him. I will. I'll trust him because—ugh—I love him. He's just a bit deficient in certain departments.

He said he will be back the day before the party.

Had to look up the place where the wedding will be in the atlas. Page 129. Mouths of the Amazon. Like the title of an erotic poem.

Shall have to call Peggy for the thirteenth and see if she is willing to risk another night in the domestic wild.

August 7
Yes! Travel pornography! An erotic poem drawn entirely from the atlas—Tongue of the Ocean, Dripping Spring. Kissamou, Kissame, Kissidougou. All place names! An entirely new line in travel literature! Erotic destinations.

August 8
Have been busy for the last two days. Sent out invitations for the fifteenth, the date of the air show, a spectacular display of human folly in its thriftless consumption of resources and willful destruction of the ozone. But it does take place right in front of the house. The planes come in over the bay and swoop and loop and dive and circle one another in a kind of kinetic metaphor for social intercourse while we sit on the deck and thriftlessly consume our own resources.

Poem going well. With the right accent and a lot of breath, the index to the *Sunday Times Atlas of the World* is a hothouse, a global greenhouse of erotica. Neck, Long'an, Lean, Kollum, Arve, Dees, Zaire. Tay, Qu'an Long, Wild Bight.

August 10

Met Keith in the Italian deli. He said he had my invitation. 'You must come,' I said, 'It's the day of the air show and we'll all watch it from the deck.'

He said he never would have guessed I had an interest in aeronautics.

I said, 'You know I do not but, Keith, these are front-row seats.'

He said, 'Great. I'll bring my partner.'

A phone call from Ruby. She says she is a bestseller and her book comes out next week. I said, 'Ruby, surely that is not possible. It is all in the wrong order, like saying it is an eight-pound girl and you are pregnant.' Nevertheless it turned out to be true. She says her publisher pre-sold the entire first print run to the largest gardening club in the UK and as a result it has been picked up for excerpts by the *Daily Telegraph* and in consequence two different book clubs have expressed an interest. I said, 'So did you think of a title?' She said they hadn't liked my own suggestion of *Hot Heaps*. It was to be called simply *Compost: Get to Know It!* Just before she hung up she said, 'Oh, wait.' She had a second piece of good news. They wanted her to do another: *Drainage*. It would be the second in what they'll call the *Get to Know It!* series.

Have almost finished the poem. Shall read it at the benefit.

August 12

Days Out Motel, Vancouver. Peggy at home with the kids and the dog.

No word yet from Jack before I left though there was a man's voice at the kitchen door at about three this afternoon. Hettie ran into the hall yelling, 'Daddy, Daddy, Daddo!' But it was the plumber. He said he knew it was a holiday but he was kind of busy next week and would I mind, he wouldn't charge extra. 'Too right,' I thought but could not stay mad for long. When he'd fixed the leaks he offered me a ride to the ferry. On the way he said he'd been doing a lot of *seen-kin* about the *trobbles*. Thought for a moment that I'd been less than discreet about the family's comings and goings until I realized he was referring to Northern Ireland.

'Oh, look,' I said. 'The ferry's in. 'I'm sure we'll be able to talk another time.'

Thinking about it, probability must be around 100 percent.

Had a disappointing dinner on the boat in the company of several marching bands from Seattle. Vegetarian menu possibly created by a beef lobbyist. Tofu spinach wrap released unappetizing green contents on first incision so went to the bookstore instead. Papers sold out but Marlene's book was there. Face out. Mine nowhere in sight.

Thought about Marlene on her flight to Toronto. She would be drinking rye and reading the Books pages, sharpening her mental faculties on the rough edges of lesser mortals. In Toronto she would take a taxi to her hotel, shower, anointing her head with perfumed conditioner, drop a few fluffy white towels around the place, maybe one for me, change, bring her expenses claim up-to-date, and start writing (on hotel stationery) the sparkling beginning of a new book before going down to the bar to meet her publicist. Publicist would arrive and whisk her off in a taxi to an exclusive interview. On the way back the conversation would turn to Marlene's estranged American family in Boston and the publicist would reveal—what a stroke of luck—that she too had connections there and would be happy to put Marlene in touch with an old and reputable publishing house that was looking to expand its list . . .

We docked. Fran, a volunteer from the Cod's Eye Fish Benefit, kindly came to meet me in a Honda Civic she said was called Sweetheart. She had a lot on her mind and did not notice at first that Sweetheart's engine had ceased to function in the middle lane of Highway 99. We lost speed rapidly. Closed my eyes and tried to remember a happy childhood moment. When I opened them we were safely on the hard shoulder. Fran was unruffled. 'Don't worry,' she said. 'We still have thirty-five minutes.' Arrived at the reading by tow truck. Driver a mature student in the English department at UBC. Quite smitten by Fran, who, it so happened, used to be a driving instructor. Wished I wasn't sitting between them like the original crash-test dummy. Could see at once how Fran and Stan were set on a course for true love and how the trip was for them so much more worthwhile than it was for me. Oh, yes, there were the fish to consider as well. The real benefisheries, as it were. But much as I love (to eat) them, I was not, when all was said and done, going to all this trouble just for my finny friends. The scales fell from my eyes. I could see the whole undertaking for what it was, an exercise in shallow self-promotion. Highway 99 was my Road to Damascus. No more flagrant lusting after fortune and especially not fame. No. It was time to stay home and weave a cocoon of care for my sorely neglected loved ones, a haven of comfort. Even if other people went off up the Amazon. So to speak.

Just this once more and I would give it all up.

Cultural Centre crowded by the time we arrived. Good news for the fish. Several well-known people had shown up unannounced to add weight to the proceedings. A smiling man in a Tilley hat, to signify, I suppose, the outdoors, was just pointing them out to me when I saw him, my Newfoundland poet in the soft shoes. Tom. Still wearing the long scarf—in August. I didn't hear anything else. He was over at the book table signing a book. He looked my way and suddenly it was fishing with dynamite, a depth charge. It was the emotional equivalent of when the natural gas line along the street blew up the hydro substation. It was the eye contact that did it. He looked up from his book. Just that. He looked up from his book and we were blown out of the water. Never known anything quite like it. Books and book table erupted in deafening silence as the friendly browsers flew asunder, blown backwards off their feet by the force, bit players in a disaster movie, and he and I slo-mo lovers taking long flying leaps through heat-heavy, sun-bronzed wheat fields, meeting in mid-air collision, spraying body fluid over the surprised, the still-falling browsers trying to gather their books, while the string section worked itself up to a lather. In the few seconds it took to reach the book table we did that scene several times, ordinary humans all around us felled, stunned by the shock of the impact, all the air a glass bubble with the sound vacuumed out. I was reeled in.

He was smiling. 'Finally,' he said. The most loaded word in all the language.

'You wrote to me,' I said. I thought I might suffocate if help didn't arrive. 'Nine one one,' would be my last words.

'Look,' he said, 'we can't talk here.'

'I'll see you afterwards,' I said. The man in the Tilley hat was telling me I was on. *Mouths of the Amazon* blindingly inappropriate but had nothing else with me. Suggested the environmentalists in the audience might like to listen out for places they had visited in their eco-war, and hoped it might divert their attention from the meaning. Or perhaps they wouldn't hear anyway since voice suddenly reduced to a breathy whisper.

Tangu/Love/Night/
Smoky/Woolgangle/
Vray/Grant/Cunupia/
Wetan/Gleason/Inga/Kississing/
Orla

Dear Lord. Supposing I had an orgasm onstage. And would it do the fish any good? But had to continue.

Kiso/
Kisu/
Kiskundorozma/
Kundelunga/
Slidre
Sleidinge/
Inn

And there was more. Pages of it. Wished I had limited myself to a single continent. Followed with a piece about a mad cow. It calmed me down. Decided that all the sexual salivating was a figment of my imagination. Nothing after all had been said. But no, as I went back to my table, I saw him looking over from where he sat doing a bit of semaphore. *Come on over here,* in capital letters.

I waved. Pretended to have misunderstood.

Did not hear the next reader at all. I was stepping onto a precarious suspension bridge, a flimsy thing of snapping lianas and frayed creepers strung high above the perilous abyss, the vertiginous fall. Was halfway across to a perfumed isle, the heady scent of night blooms already reaching me, when I looked back along the strained, the slowly tearing vines, and there on the grassy bank behind me, not perfumed but smelling of socks and wax crayons and toast and milk and nail polish and sleepy pillows was my whole family, all of them in all their baggy, scruffy, scrambled glory on the shore. And there was still time. There was Jack waving like crazy and there was Kate shaking her head beneath her shimmer, her goldrush of hair and saying quietly, without surprise, 'You're so *dumb*, Mother.' I looked at the poet. He was smiling. Bloody awful timing, I thought. Bloody awful. Waited till he wasn't looking, then slipped out.

There is always a taxi when you don't want one. I got in and said, 'Days Out Motel,' and it sped away, leaving behind forever the possibility of love and the certainty of heartbreak.

Twelve thirty, phone in my room rang. 'I hope you don't mind,' he said. 'I'm at the front desk.'

And so for the second time that night I was saved, and I'll always be grateful. Saved from the parched fate of the coward, doomed to live the rest of her life picking over the crumbs of what might have been. I told him what wretched timing it all was. He said he thought the timing was dead-on. And that's what did it: the overwhelming sense of destiny. That and the Irish accent. And the touch of his palm on the side of my neck. A cynic might point out that he had a bottle of Scotch in his other hand, but he reached behind him and stood it on the console and that's where it stayed for the duration of the night. I suppose, since I am almost married again (some would say never unmarried), you would have to call it adultery. But that wouldn't be the truth. It was more like a long renunciation.

August 14

Peggy was looking tired when I got back yesterday. She had been up half the night waiting for Felix, who had seized this new opportunity to break his curfew. Asked her if she'd like to stay and share my sandwich from the ferry. She has a particular facial expression she uses on occasion to question my good sense. She said sorry but she had to run. I didn't mind. I was still under the influence of last night's cosmic bounty. It was like waking up drunk. I said, 'I love you Peggy. Thank you,' and when she had gone I said yes to every request and demand that had been percolating in my absence. Offspring all taken unawares by this sudden onset of permissiveness. Treated me with the caution you might use around someone going mildly mad and offered to help get the place ready for the party. We swept the path, and cleared bikes off the drive (all the time expecting a taxi), and did a job on the house, removing the worst of the fetid family flotsam, leaving the rest washed up in unobtrusive corners. And for me it was all an Act of Love. I was a nun in a darned and dusty habit; no I was a Buddhist nun sweeping, sweeping the tailings of our existence, filled with benign acceptance of the rightness of all things.

Rain predicted for tomorrow. What to do with fifty-odd wet guests? Kate says don't worry. Only half your friends ever show up. But they will still get wet. Went ahead regardless and prepared food, working against the appetites of the ravening children and their friends who were eating it as fast as it was made. Picked up rented glasses and tableware. Kate's idea. Kate has style. Hope some more of it rubs off on me before she leaves home. Picked up the yield of an entire vineyard, stacked driftwood by the barbecue and covered it with a tarp.

Expected Jack all day but he hasn't shown up. He will. *I believe, I do believe, I do most firmly believe.* The only words I remember from the Act of Faith.

Can hear the rain starting now.

August 16

Ripped from sleep yesterday by the scream of a jet coming in for a practice run. And it was only seven thirty. No rain. Stiff, salty breeze had swept all the clouds away and left the sky a bright china blue. By ten o'clock had tables set up outside under the trees. Kate personally supervised their setting with starched white napery. Hettie followed with rocks to keep it on. Children most willing. Rewarded with an advance of funds for the purchase of several flats of pop and cartons of Popsicles for a business venture they have in mind; they left for the beach where they began to assemble everything they needed for the enterprise. Only the dog a teensie tiny problem. Had to be tied up when the food was carried out. Wished I could have sent him off on a bus to go to the movies or a mall.

First guests fall into one of two categories: those who do not really know you, and those who have another party to go to. In this case it was Keith and he fell into the second. He was with his partner T.J. so I curbed the urge to make hairdressing jokes and did not even say *Time for a quickie?* Settled them with drinks and the best seats on the deck. Rest of the guests arrived in a great clot and it took a while to recover from the initial confusion of the opening flypast happening simultaneously, but eventually the dust settled and it was the pleasantest time imaginable. Boats of all shapes and sizes had come in from miles around to take advantage of the clear view across to the airfield and so the bay had taken on a festive air, the white boats bobbing on the sparkling water. Were it not for the diesel fumes we might have been Edwardians at a regatta. 'Gay' is the only word to describe the scene and it is a pity we have lost it. From time to time jets ripped through the gaiety and performed ozone-depleting feats. They were treated to the same fickle attention one gives to fireworks, which seemed appropriate. By this time even the breeze had died down and the afternoon had grown very hot. Felix got the rowboat ready and Miles and Hettie loaded up with an ice chest full of potables. We watched them row out to the spectators and placed bets on the boats most likely to make a purchase. Soon became apparent that they were making a sale at every boat so we stopped that and went back to watching the planes. Felix and his crew continued profiteering for the better part of the afternoon. When the air show finished, several of the guests decided to swim, some left, others arrived, and from there the party took on something of the atmosphere of a cottage weekend. Time began to unwind in a very agreeable fashion. Or perhaps I should say time began to come unwound, for that is what it felt like. Annie was assessing psychic force fields under the apple tree as if the dome of her pregnant belly were some kind of astro-psychic power station. T.J. had found Miles's easel and started painting Keith. Guests at a sanatorium. I had just gone inside for more bread when Matt and his ex-wife appeared in the kitchen. I had invited them on the assumption that all things must surely one day return to normal. It does not do to harbour one's follies as if they are darling secrets to be cherished. It is better to put them in their place. We greeted one another with perfect cordiality. Was only later that my folly proved himself once and for all to be a total dick. We met in a quiet moment over the guacamole.

There was no one around to take any notice so I said, 'How are you, Matt? How have you been?' and looked him in the eye. There is a look you can exchange only with those whom you have known biblically and I gave it to him. And what did he say? With his mouth full of dip and holding the tub and the knife in the air with one hand and his glass of wine with the other, he said, 'Did you make this? It's really good.'

Things got busy after that. Hunger lent a sense of urgency to everything as it came close to dinnertime. Those who were not busy seeking food were hunkered down in random places having intense conversations over plates of it. I know there were important discoveries being made about the nature of the universe but I wasn't catching any of them. There wasn't enough beer and there were too many dirty plates. Began doing the hostess thing, picking up empty glasses, squeezing past clumps of people—excuse me, excuse me—smilingly, gallantly. This was loneliness. Saw myself falling into a spiral chute of activity that would end only at the washing up but was pulled to safety at the last minute by Mitzi. She said, 'Fuck the guests,' and took me out in the rowboat the kids had abandoned.

'The trouble is,' I said, when we were out on the water, 'it's the host I want and he isn't here.'

She said, 'Then think of the time elapsing as you would think of land that is fallow. Preparing itself for the fecund seed.'

'Mitzi,' I said, 'is Annie growing her own again?'

She said, 'Yes. Want to roll one?'

It was very pleasant sitting out there on the water. The sun was getting low and all the misty pinks and blues had arrived from Japan and were settling in layers. The other vessels had left and the bay was very quiet. Time was expanding. We could hear the voices and the music from the house. Shouts and murmurs. Kundera's laughter and forgetting. Slow time. Somehow it seemed right to ignore the one or two guests who were hailing us from the bank. It's the secret of living, stepping out of time. It's what nuns know and it's why they smile so enigmatically when asked how they can give up the world.

Understood what the semaphore had been about when we got back and tied up the boat. Someone had persuaded Felix and a couple of his friends to play some of their grunge. Live. Extraordinary idea. They had moved the chairs and plugged in on the deck. Some of the guests had taken to the water. Police were just arriving when I went up. They had turned off the siren but left the lights flashing. Had a strange sensation of strobe lights in the brain and hoped that my words weren't coming out double-spaced. It did not escape my attention that the team was led by Constable Trudy whose attention to duty has rocketed since *Fargo*. She said there'd been a complaint about noise and a report that someone was selling liquor out on the water. Danny said that was a funny idea and why wouldn't they drink it. Sometimes Danny needs a smack. Put on my best emollient manner and they were soon appeased, although Felix, I noticed, hid in the bathroom while they were here. Must look into that. They took a while to go. Constable Retchett had his trusty clipboard and somehow persuaded Kate to take part in a public relations survey. They sat on the front step together while she answered his questions. From the look on his face I gathered he was getting a favourable response.

Went back in and put on some quieter music. Things slowed down considerably and guests who were dancing began to do a lot of explicit leaning on each other. Was in danger of sinking into the quicksands of maudlin when, round about twelve, a taxi pulled up. It was quite a good entrance—one his daughter would have been proud of—arresting people in mid-sentence, mid-stride, like a video tape about to run backwards. Everyone seemed to decide at once to carry on as before.

I said, 'Some people get off on the solo moment.'

He smiled. He said, 'I feel as if I've just walked in on my own wake.'

Then Danny strolled over, looked Jack in the eye, and said, 'You're late. You nearly missed it, you asshole,' and they disappeared with a bottle of red.

'How much did that all cost?' Jack said this morning.

I said, 'If you lived here you'd know.'

He said, 'Good thing I'm moving back, then.'

That sort of remark could start a row in a less stable couple.

Spent the morning clearing up, restoring order, and generally putting the house to rights. I felt the pressure of what we were doing and said, 'Look, why don't we just give ourselves a break?'

Jack said, 'Your work ethic—' and stopped.

We spent an hour or two at the beach and then scrambled to get the rentals back on time.

This evening we sat on the deck and watched the sky begin to hint at its first wash of colour. The moment was mellow beyond words when out of nowhere—well, all right, out of my mouth—came a question as thin and spiteful as an electric drill. The mother of stupid questions: So did you love her? Can't think what came over me, everything settled, as nearly perfect as it could be. A dentist's drill. A question to set sparks flying, draw blood, inflame the whole evening with pain. So did you love her? Of course he did. Went on to all sorts of other stupid questions like, For how long? and more stupidity: So do you still love her? and retaliatory fire: Do you really want to know the answer? And on and on until we were both in a very dark part of the wood stumbling over loose rocks on the path and I was calling out to Jack in a thin high voice: 'Anyone else? Was there anyone else? Is there anyone else?'

And of course he said it: 'Yes.' And then there it was, the next thing, the next obstacle, the next impossible labour, right there in the middle of the path, the next question, the self-detonating device…'Who?'

'If you must know,' he said, 'it was Ryan's mum. But I got over it pretty quick.'

Went for a very, very long walk after that. Very long. Blackguard's tongue hanging out of the side of his mouth. He is not used to long walks. Sat down on a bank by the creek in the near dark so we could whimper together and it all started to come clear. There was a magnanimous stoicism in the way Jack had taken the hits and refused to embark on an independent enquiry of his own; the ground I was on suddenly seemed very swampy. Go after the truth like a bull terrier and you'll tear it to shreds. It was not very noble asking him to deny his feelings, betray his lovers. He had not asked a single question. Not one. He knew already as I did. Love is born and it dies. We are the midwives and the husbandmen. And sometimes love is reborn. But oh, the grassy bank is the precarious place, not the bridge, because the objects of our affection are unwary, are half asleep as we are and those soft shoes don't make a sound, can sneak right up on you anytime.

Ryan's mum. So recent and so regrettable. Nothing to envy there, nothing to imagine there that would not be cause for pain, especially for Jack. A furtive and unhappy coupling, soon erased from memory. And I love him for having the courage to admit it. I love that he relinquished his power, showed himself to be vulnerable and needy, hoping to just once at least catch the scent of someone who knew how to keep a clean house and change the sheets on time and practice some self-sacrifice and maybe even iron the odd shirt. And it had to have been only once, because she would have been guilt stricken, wouldn't she? And might, the poor soul, take that to her grave.

But who am I to dissect another's fall from grace, a moment's failing?

He was sitting in the dark playing music when I got back. I told him I had thought it all through and then I told him what had happened in Vancouver. He said, 'That's a funny way to show you still love me.' And then we did not talk at all. We danced long and slow to Diana Krall doing vivisection on her heart. Laughter and forgetting and tears. From both of us. And remembering.

And then we went to bed. And slept. Deeply.

August 17

A bill on the doorstep from the plumber. He must have

dispatched it by liveried footman. Six hundred and forty-two dollars. Rates surely comparable to what a tenured history professor might command if charging by the hour. No wonder he knew such a lot about Central Europe.

Marlene is back. She called. She asked if Jack was here. I said, 'There's no need to whisper. Anyway, no. He's at work.'

She said her son had seen him driving up the highway with a bed upside down on top of his car. She said didn't I think that was something? It had something of chivalry about it. Sort of like your lover meeting you at the airport wearing a suit of shining armour and bearing a dozen red roses.

I said, 'No. I thought it was a bit brazen, trumpeting one's sleeping arrangements to the world. It was like having a bumper sticker saying *I love sleeping around*. Besides we now have two box springs and two mattresses and there is nowhere to put them except on top of each other and it is like the princess and the pea and all my hopes of having a minimalist Japanese bedroom are dashed.' Asked her if Toronto went well. She said she couldn't tell me how well. 'Listen,' she said, 'I've got to go. I think my agent's on the other line.'

Kate has had a phone call from the young police officer. He wants to see her again. Felix has said he is moving out. He is not living with the enemy.

Jack at work all day. It seemed so long.

Keith called to say could I look for T.J.'s Ray-Bans. He said he and his partner had a great time. He was sorry they left so early but they had to rescue Biloxi from his auntie's. She lives out my way. Did I know? I said I didn't think so. Though this is a *very* small town.

He said anyway T.J. really enjoyed Felix's grunge band. But he was a bit deaf when he woke up this morning.

I said he should get his ears candled.

Keith said, 'Darling,' which I took to mean that he did not want to hear the details.

'By the way,' I said, 'I'm going to take your advice and get laser treatment for my vision.'

'Well I hope you pick the right doctor,' Keith said. He said he had this one client and her doctor—

It began to sound eerily familiar. I let him continue.

'I mean,' he said, 'how are you supposed to know you don't see as far as the next person? I mean, how would you?'

'Yes,' I said, 'how would you?' suddenly experiencing a new vision of my own, Keith in close-up. I didn't blink. 'It's like that thing with colours,' I said. 'How do you know red is red?'

'Wow,' said Keith. 'Do you think about that, too? You know I think about that all the time.'

And then, I don't know what came over me, but I suppose I had to know for sure, I said, 'It's probably the same with the sense of smell.'

'Well you know what I heard?' Keith said. I thought I probably did. 'A dog's nasal membrane, compared to ours...' But I wasn't really listening. I was creating a new Keith.

Had thought of him for so long as a kind of story-monger, a worker bee out there in the social clover, bringing back the honey. He wasn't supposed to regurgitate the queen's breakfast. It was curiously depressing and energizing at the same time. Then it came to me: Keith the sibyl of our community. We visit Bangs as we visit the sibyl's cave. To gather the gleanings of those who have gone before. For just as Biloxi tenderly sweeps the clippings at the end of the day, so Keith gathers in the stories and keeps them for the new dawn, when he can offer them, utterings from his own mouth, prognostications, warnings and heraldings, to chill us or hearten us as we desire.

Could not *wait* for Jack to come home.

After dinner we sat outside for a long while with Miles and Hettie and watched for shooting stars. Miles kept score. Hettie fell asleep and Jack carried her to bed.

When at last Miles too went to bed, we poured a glass of wine and went outside for a last look at the meteor shower.

'Stupid rats,' I said. It fell out of my mouth before I had time to think. I had heard scrabbling. Could have bitten my tongue.

Jack said, 'What?'

I said, 'Stupid rats. Out there. Stupid rats and gerbils, scrabbling about in their old nests. They see none of this'—gesturing to the stars. 'Cosmic fireworks. And all for us.'

Jack said, 'Good, isn't it?'

He was quiet for a while and then he gave a long, contented sigh. 'I heard this writer on the radio today,' he said. 'She was talking about archetypal myths and fables and she told this tale from the *One Thousand and One Nights* about a merchant. He has this stock of vinegar that he can't sell and he locks up his shop and he goes away on a voyage to bring back more merchandise. But on the way his ship is wrecked and he's captured by pirates and mishap after mishap befalls him, and eventually he escapes and after many perilous adventures he makes his way back, stripped of everything he owns, to where he started. He unlocks his shop and looks at the dusty bottles of vinegar. They are all he has in the world. He brushes the cobwebs off and uncorks one and to his surprise it's turned over the years into the finest and rarest of wines. So I've been thinking...'

He took a sip of his own wine. I felt ridiculously self-conscious, like waiting to be proposed to. Sneaked a look at him. He was still looking at the stars.

'I've been thinking,' he said, 'that's probably what's happening to those apples in the bags. Do you think you should do something with them? They're beginning to ferment.'

PAULINE HOLDSTOCK is an award winning novelist, short fiction writer and essayist. Her books have been published in the US, the UK, Australia, Germany, Brazil, and Portugal. In Canada, her work has been shortlisted for the Scotiabank Giller Prize, the Commonwealth Writers' Prize, and others, and has won the BC Book Prizes Award for Fiction and the City of Victoria Butler Book Prize. She lives on Vancouver Island.